CASH MONEY

Triple Crown Publications
2959 Stelzer Road Suite C
Columbus, Ohio 43219
www.TripleCrownPublications.com

Library of Congress Control Number: 2004115365
ISBN# 0-9762349-3-9
Cover Design/Graphics: www.MarionDesigns.com
Editor: Chloé A. Hilliard
Consulting: Vickie M. Stringer

First Trade Paperback Edition Printing January 2005

Printed in the United States of America

Dedication

This book is dedicated to my mom, because no one loves me more than you.

Acknowledgements

First of all, I would like to say that all praises are due to Allah. I am grateful he has given me the time to discover my talent. Second of all, I would like to thank my mom, Lori (Jamilah). You have given me your continued love and support despite all that I put you through. I love you, you are my best friend.

To my father, Harvey, sorry we are not closer. I would like to express my appreciation for my family: My stepfather, Umar, and my grandmother, Dorothy, thanks for being such positive role models. To my brother, Muhammad, stay focused, I'm not mad at you. Lemme find out you got editing skills. To my cousin, Danielle, I appreciate all long hours of conversation and advice exchanged. I know you always got my back (when you're not being judgmental).

Much love to Nafeesah, Saleenah, Madinah, Almirah Lailah, Umar and Haneef. Much love to my Auntie Karen, Uncle Glenn. Hurry up and make your way to the East Coast. Shout out to Uncle Hassan, Aunt Bonnie. Love and appreciation to Aunt Lillian and cousin Nita. To my cousin Jamaal, I see you doin' big things ova there. To my cousin Nafisa, thanx for helping a sister out. Much love, Ma. Special shout out to my cousins, Nia, Shanta, Meroe, Shug, Fat Face, Marcia.

To my better half, LaDrell, I love you, Boo.

To my girl Aminah, you next Ma. A special invitation to holla at me going out to a few of my niggas: Damont, Geezy, Jamal @ Jackmove, Scitzo, and Twoseat. Crazy thanks to all of my preliminary editors, Amanda Whaley, Lashuan James, Lisa Brown, Renee Foster, and Ebony Summers. Good lookin' out. Shouts to all my peoples from Brooklyn, Harlem, The Bronx, Queens, Highland Park, North East, South East, North West and anybody any place else who feels like I feel.

Special shout out to every body rockin' that Urban War Sport. And special, special shout out to everybody that got love for me over Southside.

Special thanks to Vickie Stringer for giving me a stage and being such a smart business woman. Keep up the very good work.

Special thanks to Shannon Holmes for plugging me back in and keeping it mad real. Good lookin' out.

Thanks to my editor, Chloé A. Hilliard, for helping me bring this joint to the next level. And shouts out to Tammy and the entire Triple Crown staff and authors.

Shouts going out to all the people who promised me the stars and then spun me around and tried to sell me dreams. It's super nuttin'. Do what you do best. To anybody that I forgot, please forgive me. I got you on the next go 'round.

"Bees are sometimes drowned (suffocated) in the honey they collect..."

-Nathaniel Hawthorne

Triple Crown Publications presents

Chapter 1

It was all Tanita's idea. While she and her best friend of eight years, Freeda, were stressing over what to wear to the upcoming 50 Cent concert, Tanita, who everyone calls Nita, came up with a plan.

"Look, the show is tomorrow. Girl, we should just call up Randy."

Randy, 29, was a local big-time drug dealer with an appetite for threesomes. Since Randy's potbelly constantly hung over his belt and his acne-riddled face was screaming for a shape up it was hard to believe he had slept with as many of the "fly girls" in town as he had. But Randy was a successful hustler who knew the number one rule: money makes things happen.

"You know he's fiendin' to get a piece of this and he pays outrageous," Nita continued in an attempt to convince a somewhat interested Freeda.

"Girl, you know I don't get down like that. Plus, that dude Randy is way ugly; nope, try again." *Sometimes she just goes too far*, Freeda thought. But her words went in one ear and out the other as Nita flipped open her Startec cell phone and scrolled down to Randy's number.

"I don't know about you," she said, "but I gotta get them pink suede Prada sneakers for tomorrow. My yellow ones are too

scruffy to be trying to pass for new." Before Freeda could think of a half-way decent substitute for the peach suede Prada sneakers she desired, but couldn't afford, Nita was speaking to Randy's voicemail. "Hey baby, this is Tanita. You told me to holla at you when I'm ready. Well...I'm ready. But, it gotta be today though, so call me back. *We'll* be waiting. One."

"We'll be waiting?" repeated Freeda, rolling her slanted, dark brown eyes that highlighted her lovely face.

After eight years, Nita knew her best friend well. If Freeda had her mind made up, there was no changing it. At the same time, she knew that her friend would not go to an event as significant as a 50 Cent concert wearing a pair of sneakers that weren't "fresh out the box." She would sell her ticket before doing that.

"What are you gonna do, sell your ticket?" Nita inquired. Before Freeda could answer, she continued. "Look, it won't be as bad as you think. I heard he cums faster than a speeding bullet and he's gonna pay us $1,000 apiece. We'll make him get two of those connecting rooms. That way we don't have to watch each other. Trust, it's well worth it and it'll be over before you know it."

"Girl! I don't know," was all Freeda could say. She was too busy thinking about how much of her grand she would have left after buying her sneakers and the white, peach and orange Roc-A-Wear short set she had her eyes on.

RRRRRING...

They were interrupted by Nita's cell phone. From her caller ID, she could see that it was Randy calling back. She shoved the phone in Freeda's face, so she could share her excitement. She waited until the third ring before answering and by the time she hung up she was grinning from ear to ear.

"Ohmigod! He wants us to meet him at the Holiday Inn downtown. He said he already got the room."

"So I guess you got it all figured out, huh?"

"Stop frontin', you know you wanna go to the show. Besides, you know them folks at Enterprise is gonna charge your mom's credit card whether we come up with the money or not."

Freeda hated to admit it, her girl was right. They bought the concert tickets from Ticketmaster a month ago and already reserved a 2003 Cadillac Escalade a week before. At the moment, they each had about $200 and had been depending on their current guy friends to provide each of them with an additional $300. It didn't surprise Freeda much when the twins, Marco and Marky, backed out. Both gave an obviously rehearsed reason as to why he couldn't come up with the promised funds.

"Something came up baby, but I got you next time," Marco told Nita.

"My tires is so old, the thread is showing and I got to take care of that this week," was the excuse Marky gave Freeda.

While Nita had been devastated by the twins fronting and was now desperate, 17 year old Freeda was no stranger to disappointment. Last year, she served 500 hours of community service in a nursing home and had spent the entire summer under house arrest. After finally being released from house arrest, she earned the nickname 'Free'.

Last March, she caught a possession of firearms charge while driving her boyfriend's platinum gray Infiniti Q45. As they drove through a well known section of a drug infested neighborhood they were pulled over by an unmarked police car. For reasons she didn't understand at the time, Roc, her boyfriend of three months, bolted from the car and into a nearby apartment complex, leaving a .380 semiautomatic weapon under his passenger seat. When the police officer that stopped them, as well as those that responded to the call for back up, couldn't find Roc, they had no choice but to charge Free with the .380. It didn't help her any when she told them she didn't know Roc's real name, or

where he lived. He knew the gun was under the seat, but when Roc jetted from the vehicle all he took with him was what was in his pockets, as well as Free's faith in men.

"So?" Nita asked, staring at herself in the mirror; admiring her 16-inch jet black wet-n-wavy micro braids, she had gotten a week earlier.

"Alright, already," Free gave in unable to think of any other alternatives. After all, it wasn't like she had a steady boyfriend to answer to. She had been anticipating the show for months. They were calling the Escalade and concert a high school graduation/pre-summer gift to themselves.

"He said he'll be there in thirty minutes, so if we leave now, we'll be good. Instead of sitting there looking stupid, you need to be thinking about how gangsta we're gonna look tomorrow. You know?"

"Whatever, Nita. Man, leave it to you to get something going."

They both laughed on the way out the door.

Chapter 2

Yeah, there was no doubt about it; 20 year old Barron Jennings was definitely doing his thing. With near flawless dark brown skin, his 6'1", 185 pound frame looked as if he'd been dipped in chocolate. His powerful physique intimidated, while his overly handsome face comforted. Still, one could never mistake Barron for a "pretty boy". A scar from the eight stitches over his left eyebrow (received during a junior high school brawl) accompanied by the Chinese symbol for "mother" tattooed on the right side of his neck, prevented folks from making that assumption. He was a sexy thug with deep, dark, brown eyes—full of intensity. His serious manner made people apprehensive, just as his natural humor put them at ease.

B.J, as he was called, had a soft, shiny layer of hair all over, arms, legs, chest, stomach, eyebrows and anywhere else you were lucky enough to explore. He wore a short well-kept mustache with sideburns that seemed to grow thicker each day. Even with a near perfect smile that seldom showed, gorgeous thick brows and long eyelashes; his best feature had to be the soft, healthy, black hair that sat in between perfect parts in five shoulder length cornrows.

RRRRRRING...

He awoke today the same as he did any other day—to the sound of his ringing cell phone. Some days he couldn't wait for

the calls to start coming in, while on other days, it was an annoyance. Today was one of those days. When he felt like sleeping late he wouldn't pick up the phone until at least three people called. It didn't make much sense to him to shower, get dressed and go all they way across town just to meet one or two people. So, he liked to wait until he had three or four customers waiting before he left the house. But today was Friday and since he always looked forward to the start of the weekend, he answered the phone

"Yo."

"You up yet?" asked Bug, one of his faithful customers from across town.

"Yeah, What's good, man?"

"Man you know how I do, ain't nuttin' changed over here."

"Dat's whassup. Let me get myself together and I'll hit you when I come out."

"How long before you think you'll be out?" asked Bug.

"Not long. You know what?" B.J. decided. "Just meet me at the mall in an hour." B.J. pulled the phone away from his ear to look at the time. It was 12:11 p.m. "You know what? Make it 1:30." While in the shower his phone rang again. He rinsed his hand, opened the shower curtain and grabbed the phone off the bathroom sink.

"Yo," he answered

"Yo," Taye answered back. Taye was one of B.J.'s good friends, or co-d's as he liked to call some of his boys. B.J. was smart enough to know that in the game there were no friends, just connects and customers.

"Whassup man?" asked an impatient B.J., ready to get back to his shower.

"You know whassup. I'm done."

"Took you long enough. Aight man, give me a minute and I'mma call you back."

"How long? Cuz I gotta-"

"About two."

"Damn man, why so long? Where you at? I'll come to you."

"Two o'clock, man," B.J. repeated, hung up, and returned to his shower. *Some people*, he thought. *They want you to drop everything when they call*. He finished his shower, dried off with one of his many Polo towels and brushed his teeth with a newly purchased electronic toothbrush. Next, came one of the two favorite parts of his day. No matter how many moves he had to make or how many folks, he had waiting, he always took his sweet time lotioning himself in the morning. He was sure to lotion every nook and cranny soothingly, simply because it relaxed him. He also used this special time to plan and ponder the day ahead. By the time he finished dressing, he had made arrangements to meet two other guys; one at a Bojangles Restaurant and the other at a car wash. Both destinations were less than two minutes from the mall.

Knock...Knock...Knock...

Securing the towel around his waist, he asked. "Who is it?"

"It's me!" answered T.J., his 12 year old brother.

"Come in." T.J. cracked the door and peeked in.

"You ready?" T.J. was fully dressed down to his sneakers.

"Nah man. We gonna have to do that first thing tomorrow. First thing, for sure."

"Aw man!" His little brother complained and turned to walk out the door, but not before calling out, "Don't forget!"

"You know I got you."

He had forgotten. Every other weekend he took his little brother shopping and let him pick out whatever he wanted. B.J. looked forward to these days just as much as T.J. If he knew T.J. had expected to go today he would have set up his appointments for later in the day. Nothing came before his little brother.

Now his older sister, Dana, was another story. The tall, slender, 27 year old beauty was a regular at all the happening clubs, restaurants, pool halls, and wherever else the popular people in town could be found. She was a part of the "in crowd" ever since B.J. was T.J.'s age and would probably be until T.J. turned B.J.'s age. Dana inherited her gorgeous face and long hair from their mother, Janice, and had no problem using them to get what she wanted. The only problem was Dana wanted it all. She had no job and any material desires she had could be fulfilled one way or another. When she heard that her younger brother was 'getting' money', she didn't waste a minute before asking for some. At first B.J. liked the idea of being able to provide for his only sister, but that feeling deteriorated rather swiftly. Before he knew it, the "can I have's" and "I need's" started coming more and more often. He had to put a stop to it.

Here I am throwing bricks at the penitentiary and instead of worrying about my safety and all she's worried about is making sure she doesn't wear the same outfit to the club twice. Women! B.J. was just the opposite. Even when he turns 21, he had no intention of being seen at the club every weekend and was far from a flashy dresser. Every month he bought 10 five-packs of white crew neck T-shirts, size 4x, so he'd never wear the same T-shirt twice. For less than $200, he had enough shirts to last an entire month. Dana would easily spend that on one shirt.

Today, B.J. chose a pair of blue Bo Jacksons Nikes. Finding a pair of clean blue jeans and brand new sneakers never took him long. His closet was packed full with them. Walking through the living room, he threw the keys to his 1994 Cadillac Deville on the sofa beside T.J., who was engrossed in one of his many video games. T.J. paused the game and went outside to start his broth-

er's car, while B.J. went around back and obtained one and three quarter kilograms of powder cocaine from his hoopty. That was enough to supply the three people who had called earlier.

"See ya later," B.J. said walking pass his brother with the coke stuffed awkwardly between his belt and stomach. He hopped in his Caddy, put on The Best of Lloyd Banks mix CD and headed in the direction of the mall. It was a little after one o'clock and with the two stops he had to make on the way he was running a little late. *But so what,* he thought. *Sometimes it wasn't bad to keep people waiting. That way they know your time is valuable.*

Less than an hour later, he had met with all of his people and got rid of all the drugs in his stash box, which was now full of money. He didn't like to go straight home, so he rode around talking on his cell phone, smoking blunt after blunt, and blasting his system. He stopped at the sportswear store downtown and bought himself a new Mitchell and Ness throwback basketball jersey. Although he already owned quite a few jerseys he hadn't even worn yet, he liked to reward himself after a day of what the hustlers called "hittin' switches"—switching drugs for money. Almost all of B.J.'s days were spent hittin' switches. Without a main girl, or any female in particular, that he trusted enough to ride around with, B.J. rode around alone. He used to ride around hittin' switches with his close friend Slim, but Slim made his baby's mother his wife and moved himself and the family to an Atlanta suburb. B.J. missed his boy Slim, who had been his day-to-day riding partner, but now rarely called or came to visit.

Slim had his own clientele and was nervous when it came to dealing with new people, so B.J. didn't have to worry about him trying to steal his customers. That was more than he could say about the guys he hung around now. He knew he could trust no one in the game, but he and Slim had grown up together. Though they dealt with different people, they both had started small and grew big together. B.J. trusted no one, but he respected Slim. These days, it was just the three B's cruising the streets: B.J., his baby blue Caddy, and his Beretta. That was enough.

After stopping at the weed spot, the barbershop, and the car wash, B.J. returned home to enjoy the second favorite part of his day. When the work part was over, he loved to sit in his room on his bed and count all the money he had made that day. It was a practice he began when he was working with less than $1,000 and continued now that he was on his way up to $100,000. Every night, he took his precious time counting and sorting the stacks of $20's, $50's and $100's—making sure all the bills were facing upright, in the same direction and separated by rubber bands into $1,000 stacks. *Cash Money. At the end of the day, that's all that really counts.*

Chapter 3

"We here, so what room is it?" Nita spoke into her cell phone as she circled the hotel parking lot in her 1996 black Honda Accord.

"It's room 123."

"Aight, cool." She hung up the phone then looked over at Free, who was nervously picking at the clear nail polish on her short nails.

"I don't believe you got me going out like this," she said to Nita, who was squinting her eyes trying to find the door that read 123.

"Oh don't act like I put a gun to your head. You need something to wear just as bad as I do." With that said she found the room and backed into a parking space directly in front of it, beside a white Ford Excursion.

They entered the room and were welcomed by the aroma of weed. Randy took a seat on the king size bed after answering the door and proceeded to smoke the blunt he had sitting in the ashtray.

"Whassup ladies? So glad you could make it."

"Yeah, Yeah," Free said dryly.

Nita scanned the room and noticed an unopened fifth of Hennessey and a liter of Hypnotic. "Ooh! I could get some of that?" she asked as she got herself a cupful of ice from the bucket that was also sitting on the dresser. Randy was busy lying on the bed, flipping through the channels with the remote control.

"Make yourself at home," he said. Reaching in the front pocket of his plaid Azzure shirt for a lighter Randy noticed Free, who had now taken a seat on the pullout couch, eyeing his blunt. He passed it to her and she accepted. Free loved to smoke weed, but cut back after constant complaints from her best friend.

"It's not ladylike," Nita would say. Today Free didn't care. She needed it and took one hard puff.

"What is this a Dutch?" Free asked after inhaling.

"Yeah Ma. Why?"

"I smoke Phillies. I don't really fool wit' Dutches." She inhaled four deep pulls before passing it back to Randy.

"You enjoy that?" He smiled revealing his two gold teeth. "I'll roll me another one." Four blunts were passed between the two of them, while Nita played bartender, making everyone Incredible Hulks—one part Hypnotic, one part Hennessey. After about a half an hour everyone was nicely buzzed and it was time to get down to business.

Randy got up off of the bed, and took his drink, blunt, and a small black book bag into the bathroom with him. Since he left the door cracked, even over Monica singing on BET, Nita and Free could tell that he was counting money. Five minutes and two music videos later, he had counted more than $2,000.

"You tryin' to hit this baby?" Randy yelled from the bathroom. Free's heart jumped as the sudden outburst interrupted their eavesdropping.

"Yeah sure," she said nervously walking over to the bath-

room where he passed her the blunt and made no attempt to hide the many g stacks that were sprawled out across the side of the tub. He just turned his back and continued to sit on the toilet top counting his cash. Free was impressed. She went back to join her friend on the bed, blunt in hand.

"Girl, he got g's all over the place in there. Let me find out he's giving us a bonus," whispered Free.

Nita turned the T.V. up a notch then spoke softly. "Naw, I doubt it. That's just all the money he has on him."

"He walk around like that on a everyday? Mmmh! Must be nice." Free was impressed; Nita had a sneaky look in her eyes.

"Man listen, forget a g? We should just take this dude for everything," she whispered.

"You crazy!" Free had to admit she could definitely put that kind of money to good use. Before either girl had a chance to further entertain the thought, a noticeably high and slightly drunk Randy emerged from the bathroom.

"Who's first?"

Neither girl wanted to be first, or was ready to go through with it, but it was Nita who spoke up first. "Me." Free was busy choking on weed smoke. Nita slipped off the yellow flowered flip-flops she was wearing and began to undress. It was now Free's turn to take her drink, blunt and go sit in the bathroom.

Before she closed the door she heard Randy say, "You ain't have to go nowhere, baby." *Yeah right*. She sat on the toilet top with her thoughts racing wild. *I can't believe this. What am I doing here? He got all that money on him. He should just buy us the Prada sneakers. Just my luck they won't even have my size in peach. Yeah well, I can always just get the baby blue ones. Please, wit' $1,000, I can afford to get the peach ones and the baby blue ones. He must be hustling real good if he can afford to pay a g per orgasm*. That's when it dawned on her. *It's only natural that he's gonna take longer with me cuz it's gonna be his*

second time around. The first one is quick; the second one always takes longer. Oh, what have I gotten myself into?

Meanwhile, a couple of feet away, Randy was near ejaculation. Nita was grateful because she was being smothered by his belly. Other that that, the sex wasn't *that* bad and that terrified her. Since she was being paid for it she expected to hate it, but made a mental note to relax and try to enjoy it. *This actually feels kinda good, and now it looks like he's almost finished,* she realized. When Randy was done with Nita, she quickly dressed and went to join her best friend in the bathroom.

"So?" Free asked, relieved to see her friend was still all in one piece; yet nervous because she knew it was now her turn.

"It wasn't too bad. He's actually workin' wit' suttin' down there."

"Did he pay you yet?"

"Nah, go head. He gonna pay us afterwards." Free went into the bedroom to join Randy and left Nita alone with her thoughts. *I wonder who he's gonna enjoy better. Well, I know my stuff is good so I don't have to worry about that. If he wasn't such a hoe, he would make a good boyfriend. He doesn't look like much, but damn he's paid. I could really get use to spending his money. Let me see, what am I gonna buy tomorrow. I know I want that D&G outfit. Umm, them sneakers. I guess I'll give my mom $50. Yeah, she could use it.*

In the bedroom, Free was under the covers with just a T-shirt on watching Randy put on a Magnum Trojan condom.

"Would you like to get on top?" he asked after the condom was secure.

"No, you go ahead." She just wanted the whole thing to be over with as soon as possible. Randy kneeled between Free's legs and lifted them towards his shoulders. She jerked with pain as he entered her then stared into his greasy face, fighting back tears. After about six minutes of pumping and sweating his

breath hastened, signaling the end of his sexcapade. He slid the condom off, and it joined the other in the small garbage can beside the dresser. Free grabbed her panties and blue jeans and practically ran into the bathroom.

When she opened the door and exchanged looks with her girlfriend, no words were needed. It was obvious what the other was thinking. *One of us needs to get out there before he tries to leave without paying us*. Without a word, Nita went back into the bedroom just as Randy was zipping his pants and fastening his belt.

"Let me get *ya'll* money together so ya'll can make moves."

"Yeah, that's about right."

When Free returned to the bedroom she was relieved to see Randy counting money. There was an awkward silence as he counted. He threw a large stack on the dresser, took a seat on the bed and shoved his little book bag slightly under the bed. Free rushed to the dresser. Nita watched where he put the book bag full of money then went over to the dresser to help Free count the money. Randy kept the corner of his eye on them.

When the girls finished counting, Free was the first to speak. "Okay, where's mine?" He nodded his head toward the stack of five dollar bills Nita was beginning to stuff in her yellow Coach bag.

"This is only a g," Nita said, taking the money towards him ready to recount it in his face

"Where's the other one?" Free asked, staring at Nita and then Randy. Either could barely tell who the question was directed towards.

"What other one?" Randy asked with a slick grin on his face.

"You said you was payin' us $1,000 each. Don't go gettin' amnesia," Free reminded him.

"I said I would pay ya'll a thousand dollars, ma. I never said anything about a grand a piece."

"What?!!" Nita yelled. "You know good and well when we was on the phone earlier you told me a grand for each of us. I don't know what the hell you smoking, but you need to come up off another g and stop playing." Randy got up, went to the sink in the back of the room and turned on the faucet.

"I ain't playin', ma." His voice was calm and direct. "I'm too old for games, but if I was, ya'll two is the only ones gettin' played." He reached for the small bar of soap and a washcloth off the rack while Free began to flip out.

"See, that's why we shoulda got paid first then we..." While she was busy cursing him out, Nita quietly reached under the bed for his book bag. Free caught on quick and kept talking, praying that Randy didn't turn around. "...Then we wouldn't have to worry about you trying to get over on us. See, that's the bullshit in your life coming straight to the surface!"

Nita secured the bag, opened the hotel door and threw the bag outside on the floor to the left—it took all of two seconds. He turned around when he heard the door open, but he was two seconds too late. Turning off the faucet, he dried his hands.

"I'm not tryin' to get over, I'm just tryin' to get by," he laughed sarcastically.

"Man, we outta here and you betta neva call me again!" Nita was already standing in the doorway.

"Oh don't worry about that," he answered. Free slammed the door on her way out and left Randy staring at himself in the mirror.

In less than fifteen seconds, they had grabbed his book bag from the side of the door and were pulling out of the parking lot, headed for the interstate. Because of their quick thinking Randy hadn't taken advantage of them. They got onto the interstate, laughing and pulling money out of the bag; unaware that their lives would never be the same again.

Chapter 4

Knock...Knock...Knock...

"Yo?"

"You ready B.J?"

"Yeah, give me five minutes."

B.J. was fully dressed this time—white T-shirt, blue Enyce jeans and a new pair of all white Air Force Ones. He rarely wore any jewelry, even though he owned several expensive pieces. Now, all he needed to do was grab his two-way pager and cell phone off the charger and he'd be ready to take his little brother to the mall. B.J. always looked forward to spending time with T.J. and had held off all his sales until later that evening. Although he kept over $50,000 at his mom's house and as many as three kilos of cocaine in the stash box of his hoopty, which was parked in the neighbors' backyard, he made an honest effort to keep his hustle away from his family.

Whenever he left his room he always did a once over, so when he returned he could easily spot if anything had been touched. He had more than enough money to move into his own place, but he felt his money would be safer at his mom's house. While he knew that people had plenty of nerve, he also knew that folks thought twice about breaking into a house that had an entire family living in it. His main concern was not mak-

ing sure that someone didn't break in, it was making sure that someone already in the house didn't steal anything from his room. That someone was his sister, Dana, who lived in her own apartment but still had a key or his drunken Uncle Leon, who came to visit often.

Once, B.J. made the mistake of leaving his money in a shoebox and stuffing it in the back of his closet. After his connect called him back to tell him that some of his g-stacks was exactly $100 short, it didn't take long for B.J. to find a new hiding place—under the tiles, behind the radiator in the corner of his room. That's where he went for the grand he would spend today in the mall. He rolled a Dutch Master cigar from the quarter ounce of weed he had purchased from one of his boys, the day prior, and was out the door. Mary J. Blige overwhelmed the Alpine speakers in his Cadillac as she sang beautifully about knockin' the hustle on Jay-Z's *Reasonable Doubt* CD. They barely pulled away from the curb good when T.J. started. "Can we stop at the store?"

"For what?"

"Some seeds."

"Nope. What I told you about eating them sunflower seeds in my car? Last time it took me about a week to get all them seeds from under the seat and stuff."

"I used a bag. All right, well can we at least stop and get some on the way home?"

"Yeah, we could do that." B.J. hopped on the exit ramp headed towards the mall, sparking his blunt and balancing the steering wheel with his knee. A few years ago, B.J. wouldn't have smoked weed in front of his little brother, but as T.J. got older his brother realized it didn't make much sense for him to go out of his way to hide his favorite pastime. Some of the boys at T.J.'s school had already started smoking weed, so he was familiar with the sight and smell. While B.J. was relieved that he could be himself around his brother, he warned T.J. that it was a bad habit to pick up.

After listening to about five songs on the classic CD, he pulled into the mall's parking lot. "Damn! What's going on out here?" B.J. asked noticing nearly all of the parking spaces were full.

"You know that 50 Cent concert is tonight," T.J. answered, surprised his brother didn't already know.

"Oh yeah! I forgot about that. You would think 50 was performing at the mall, with all these cars here." B.J. hesitantly pulled into a parking space that was about a mile from the main entrance. He hated crowds. Even though he had tickets to the show, he was seriously considering not going. Being seen by everybody in town just wasn't his thing. Actually, if he had remembered the concert was tonight, he might have waited until Sunday to go shopping. *But hey, he thought. Since I'm here I might as well get a outfit since I do have tickets.*

These brotherly, bi-monthly trips to the local mall never varied much. First stop, Foot Locker and Foot Action. This way they could buy their footwear and then find outfits to match. If they made the mistake of buying clothes first, there would be all kinds of limits and pressure when it came to finding matching shoes.

T.J. picked out a pair of all red suede 'beef and broccoli' Timberlands and B.J. liked them so much he asked for them in his size as well. Nevermind it was the middle of June. T.J. also got a pair of white and red Nike Air Force ones. He would always pick out two pair of shoes that were the same color. This week was red, last time they went shopping it was yellow, and the time before that it was royal blue. Before long, his collection of sneakers would be as extensive as his older brother's.

With their new footwear in hand they walked towards the Atrium for their clothes. B.J. noticed her as soon as he entered the store. She was taller than most girls he was use to running across, she had an athletic build. Her jet-black shoulder length hair sported honey blond highlights and hung freely over her gorgeous eyes as she looked down to find her size on a rack of

denim dresses in the women's section of the store. He noticed that she was in an obvious rush, as was everyone else in the store. More importantly he noticed her striking beauty—a perfect button nose and full glossy lips—she was the cutest girl he had seen in a while. Her clear complexion matched his exactly and as he walked closer he noticed she had an exotic type of look.

"You like these?" T.J. interrupted his brothers' gaze, nudging him in the side.

"Yeah man," he answered before even fully turning around to see the blue Azzure jeans with multicolored patches his brother was holding up.

"Yeah, just get a red T-shirt and you in there." As usual he was right. A red T-shirt would bring out the red stitching in the jeans and match both the sneakers and boots perfectly. B.J. was trying to concentrate on finding his size in a gray and red Roc-a-Wear sweatsuit but couldn't keep his eyes off the beauty, who was now on her way to the fitting room. He knew the triple XL sweatsuit he picked up was his size, but he still found himself grabbing it and walking behind her. *And she got a fat ass. A nice little walk. I see you, ma.*

As if she felt his eyes piercing into her back, she turned around just in time to see him choosing the fitting room to the right of hers. *Damn, he's cute as hell,* she thought. *I wonder what he's workin' wit'.* She tried to undress slow and sexy as if he could see her through the wall that separated them. Meanwhile, he sat on the small bench in the tiny fitting room and watched himself in the mirror thinking about what his best approach would be. He looked down just in time to see her bare foot slide out of the jeans she was wearing and hit the floor.

And she got pretty feet, too. B.J. never tried on the sweatsuit.

I'm glad I decided to go ahead and get that pedicure, she thought, admiring her toes.

"How does that fit, Miss?" asked an eager salesman speaking through the fitting room door.

"Yeah, it's cool. Thank you."

"Can I see?" B.J. asked stepping out of his dressing room after the sales guy, who he could tell had a crush on the girl, was out of listening range.

"Excuse me?" she asked, a hundred percent sure of who was asking, but not wanting to appear too anxious to engage him in conversation.

"You heard me. Come, step out and let me see you in dat dress." It sounded more like a command than a request. She slipped into her stiletto sandals and opened the fitting room door.

"What difference does it make how I look in my dress? You trying to pay for it?"

She had caught him off guard with that one, so he did what he always did when he was caught off guard. He looked her straight in the eye and intimidated her by answering a question with a question. Grabbing the price tag from the side of her hip, B.J. looked deeply into her light brown eyes.

"You mean to tell me you can't afford to pay for this dress?" He said with a clever grin. She didn't lose his stare and returned it with a smile.

"Baby, I can afford this dress, that sweatsuit and whatever else we might want to wear tonight. You got that?" She went into the fitting room to change back into her clothes.

"So, you going to the show tonight, huh?"

Yeah, he changed the subject pretty quick. He must be broke, Kenya thought. "Isn't everybody?" she answered, somewhat annoyed that he hadn't offered to pay for the dress. It wasn't that B.J. couldn't afford to pay for the dress; it was just that he had only bought a certain amount of money out of the house. Buying the $219 dress meant that either he or T.J. would have to sacrifice something they really wanted, or he would be spend-

ing down to the last penny in his pocket and she hadn't given him any reason to cut it that close. If he knew he was going to meet someone as cute as her, he would have brought an extra $250 out the house just for the occasion. But, he didn't stress it. There were two kinds of people in the game that B.J. had no love for—a snitch and a gold digger. And even though the girl was proving herself to be the latter, her attractive face and classy style intrigued him.

"So, what's your name? I'm tryna hook up after the show."

"Kenya," she answered in a sweet, somewhat shy voice, as she stepped out of the fitting room and headed towards the cash register.

Maybe I was wrong about her, he thought, trying to figure her out. "Kenya, that's a nice name. I'm B.J.," he stated confidently, noticing T.J. walking towards them.

Kenya dug in her Louis Vuitton saddlebag and pulled out an American Express card from her matching wallet. He watched, inconspicuously, as she passed the card to the saleslady and was able to read her name on it—Kenya Atkins. *She got her own hair and her own credit card. Yeah, I got to get her number.*

"All my stuff is already behind the register," T.J. said, pointing to the pile of clothes stacked on the back table of the cashiers' station. Kenya didn't waste a second before appraising the pile of clothes, the short sleeve Roc-a-Wear sweatsuit and the Foot Locker bags each of them were holding. *Maybe I was wrong about him,* she thought, trying to figure him out.

"Kenya, this is my little brother T.J.; T.J., this is my new girlfriend Kenya." He gave the introduction with a serious face as he watched her sign the credit card receipt.

"Are you guys ready?" asked the saleslady grabbing T.J.'s clothes, ready to ring them up. Kenya, who was flattered, but not surprised by her introduction, simply lingered around the register to see which of the brothers would handle the transaction and how he would go about doing so. B.J turned a little to the

side and dug in his jeans pocket, pulling out a stack of twenty-dollar bills. Usually, B.J. would have given the money to T.J. ahead of time and then let him pay because he didn't like handling or counting his money in front of people. He definitely didn't like the way Kenya lingered around the register, obviously eyeing the transaction. She wasn't doing a good job of pretending to be interested in the case of sunglasses that were connected to the register.

"That'll be $523.19." Counting out twenty-six twenties faster than an experienced bank teller, B.J. then dug in his other pocket and pulled out three singles and a quarter. He always tried to pay with exact change. Kenya didn't miss a thing.

"So boyfriend, how are we gonna hook up after the show?" She walked over as he and T.J. grabbed their things.

"I don't know," he answered sort of uninterested.

"I know." She quickly grabbed his two-way off of the clip on his hip and held it up to her's. While she was beaming their information between pagers, he took the opportunity to get a closer look at the girl, who would now have his pager number. *Her complexion is so pretty, so dark and her eyes are so light. I wonder if those are contacts. Her hair is so thick and so full and the highlights match her eyes perfectly. It can't be a weave. I can usually spot a weave. She's definitely a cutie. She needs to get rid of those fake nails, but other than that. Yeah, she could get my number.*

Kenya interrupted his stare. "I'll hit you up after the show," she said slipping his two-way back into the clip. She threw hers in her pocket book and was off without giving him a chance to respond. As she left, she waved good-bye to T.J., who was now standing next to the entrance.

"She's cute," T.J. said, as they walked towards the mall exit.

"Yeah, tell me about it."

Chapter 5

"Dat's it?" asked Nita in disbelief.

"Yup. If each one of these is a grand, then dats it," answered Free, disappointed as well.

Six thousand dollars was all that was in Randy's little black book bag. "It looked like so much more when I saw him counting it in the bathroom," Free continued.

"So, that's $3,000 a piece," Nita concluded as she got off at the interstate exit nearest her home.

"Plus the g worth of fives you already got in your pocketbook. That's $3,500 a piece," Free stated with a slight attitude. She already knew what Nita was thinking, but had no idea her girl would be bold enough to say it.

"You know the whole thing was my idea. I'm the one who called him and set the whole thing up. I'm the one who snuck the bag out of the room. Shoo! If it wasn't for me we wouldn't even have this money."

"So, what you tryna say Nita? If I didn't keep talkin' to him and distracting his ass, then what? Then he woulda turned around and, then what? But, you ain't think about that, huh?" Nita was silent for a moment.

"Yeah, you right. My bad." She spoke in a shameful tone. The damage was already done. Nita had tried to get over on her best friend. Although Free was soft spoken and not as rowdy as Nita, she was not the type to be gotten over on. Never the one to forget a fallout or a favor; Free didn't necessarily hold grudges.

They had decided to go to Nita's house to count and divide the money. Nita's 35 year old mom, Big Nita, never paid them much attention and being that Nita was an only child, there weren't any nosey siblings to worry about. Nita and Big Nita lived alone in a two-bedroom Section-8 apartment. Their complex was one of the better Section-8 developments the city's housing authority offered. Big Nita, who loved to bake, always complained that the kitchen was "too damn small," but still loved the idea of raising Tanita in a neighborhood that was cleaner and safer than the one she had grew up in. As an only child, Nita, named after her mother and her father Tariq, was not spoiled like one would imagine.

Once inside, the girls went straight into Nita's room where Free dumped all of the money out of the bag and onto the bed. Nita unzipped her pocketbook and took out the thousand dollars worth of five-dollar bills, as if she was doing Free a favor. While Nita was starting to unband and count each individual stack, Free searched the small compartment in the front of the book bag.

"And he got some weed in here, too." Free could hardly hide her excitement as she pulled out a little less than an ounce of some good green ganja. She untied the plastic sandwich bag, inhaled deep and realized it was probably the same kind of weed they had been smoking earlier.

"The money was one thing, Free. Now we taking drugs from that man. Damn, he's gonna come lookin' for us for sure now."

"What the hell you talkin' about? You think he's gonna come after us just for this little bit of weed. Like he's gonna be like 'I could live wit' dem gettin me for seven g's, but I'm not gonna let them get away wit' takin' that $200 worth of weed.' Come on,

you can't be serious! Trust, if and when he comes after us, it's gonna be for the money and not this little ass bit of weed."

"Yeah, I guess you're right. I'm just kinda nervy. But, it's not like he knows where I live or anything," Nita admitted.

"Right, and what's done is done. It's not like we can go and return it to him."

By the time they finished talking and separating the money it was almost 2:30 in the morning. Free had called home earlier and left a message with her 11 year old brother, Mathew, that she would be spending the night over Nita's house. Since it was officially the start of summer and she and Free had just graduated from high school a few weeks prior, she knew her mom wouldn't have a problem with it.

They pulled out Nita's day bed, took showers and talked late into the night. Free spent the night so often that she had her own drawer full of clothes. They talked about what they would buy the next morning, once they woke up early to go shopping. They talked in great detail about having sex with Randy, how it felt to do such a thing for money and what they would do if they ever saw Randy again. Since it seemed like everyone in town would be going to the concert, they realized the possibility of him spotting them there. Naively, they agreed that since he didn't actually see them take the bag, they would just deny it. It was his fault for trying to jip them in the first place. What sense did it make for them to miss the concert to avoid him, when the whole reason why they had hooked up with him was to get something to wear to the concert. They promised never to tell anyone how they got the money, not even Shamika and Nicole—their girls who had graduated with them and would be joining them at the show. They agreed to tell them that Marco and Marky had given them a little extra money. As for Randy, they weren't going to bust their brains worrying about him. His loss. "He'll just have to charge that to the game," said Free.

What surprised them most about the whole thing was the fact that Randy hadn't called Nita's cell phone. She planned on

not answering his call, but still, she anticipated it. Free was bothered as well. Maybe, there was a chance that Nita's number had been erased from his incoming calls log; however that wasn't likely. Either way, they were going to the Sprint store first thing Monday morning, right after they returned the rental car, to get Nita's number changed and buy Free her very first cell phone.

They awoke in a good mood, dressed, and hopped in Nita's car headed for the Ave. Normally, they would shop at the mall, but since this was a special occasion, they went to the Ave, where all the designer stores were.

The Gucci store was first. Nita bought a pocketbook for $580 and was so proud when she handed the money to the saleslady. It was her first Gucci bag ever and nothing could wipe the smile off her face. Free felt like she just had to buy something out of the store and settled for a $65 key chain and a pair of $250 sunglasses.

"Oooh! Let me see those?" Nita asked admiring the sunglasses Free had picked out. She tried them on then looked at herself in the mirror. "These are hot. Yeah, let me get a pair of these too," she told the saleslady.

"The same ones?" asked Free. She hated when Nita did that. She would go and buy the same exact thing that Free had, in the same color and everything. Free loved her best friend, but she loved her individuality too.

"Don't start trippin', Free. I ain't gonna wear them tonight."

"Yeah, whatever."

Nita spent a little under nine hundred dollars in the Gucci store while Free spent about three hundred and fifty dollars. Next, they went into the Prada store. Free bought two pair of sneakers—peach suede and baby blue leather. She had a thing for the All America Cup Prada sneaker. She and Nita already had eight pairs between them. Nita picked out three pairs—pink suede, royal blue leather and all gray. Her total came to $1,100 while Free's was about $750. After Prada, Free was ready to go back to the car and make their way to the mall.

"Why you in such a rush?" Nita asked, fiendin to cruise the Ave.

"What else you tryin' to get? You actin' like we got all day and you know the mall is gonna be packed."

"Oh, come on. I just wanna go in a few more stores."

It wasn't until after they browsed Fendi, Chanel and Louis Vutton before Nita was ready to go. Secretly, she relished the attention they were receiving from all the salespeople. Their huge shopping bags from Prada and Gucci had the salespeople following them around the store. In Fendi, Nita told the saleslady she would be back to buy the petite book bag she tried on.

She'll be back, Free thought. *With what?* On the way to the mall, Free decided to roll up some weed. As she split the Phillie she asked Nita for something to dump it in.

"Oh Boy! There you go."

"Whatever, give me a bag or napkin or something."

"Look in the glove box," Nita answered.

"Damn, this is some good weed," she said taking a pull. Nita had decided to let Free keep the whole bag. She didn't smoke so she had no need for it.

"What are you gonna do, smoke that whole bag?"

"Probably," Free said keeping her thoughts to herself. By the time the blunt was halfway finished, it was about two o'clock and they had arrived at the mall. It was so packed they could hardly find a parking space.

"I see everybody's getting last minute stuff to wear tonight."

"Yeah, I guess so."

They were right. The mall was packed full of teenagers, frantically searching for something to wear to the show later that night. Free already knew exactly what she needed to get and where to go. At the Atrium, they each bought a Roc-a-Wear velour short set. Free picked out the last peach, orange and cream-colored suit in a size medium. Nita chose the second to last pink, red, and white short set. All the racks in the store were more than half empty. Free also got a pair of Girbaud jeans and a few pairs of socks, bringing her total to a little over $200. Nita picked out a denim Dolce and Gabana shirt and pant set, plus a few matching bra and thong sets bringing her total to roughly $350.

There were so many guys in the mall, but neither girl paid them much attention. They felt there would be more than enough time to collect phone numbers at the show and the 18 and over after party they planned on attending. After leaving the mall, Free called her mom from Nita's cell phone and asked if she wouldn't mind meeting them at the car rental place. Mrs. Harrison was on her way to Bible study, but didn't have a problem with meeting them at Enterprise, which was five minutes away from her church. Reserving the Escalade on her credit card was something she promised to do a while ago as a graduation present for the girls. However, Mrs. Harrisson was not going to be able to list either of the girls as an additional driver on the rental contract because they weren't 21; nevertheless she trusted her daughter's driving and didn't want to break a promise.

After picking up the black Escalade the girls agreed to meet up at Free's house at 6:30 p.m. That gave them more than enough time to pick up Shamika and Nicole and make it to the coliseum by the start of the 7:30 p.m. show.

"Ma, where you at?" Nita called as she walked into the apartment with an armful of shopping bags.

"I'm in here, honey," Big Nita said from the kitchen. She was a young, hard working woman, who sometimes struggled to support her daughter and keep the bills paid.

"Look what I got, Ma." Nita set her many shopping bags down in the hallway and walked into the kitchen handing her mom two hundred dollar bills.

"Thanks, baby." Big Nita was not an affectionate woman. She never asked her daughter where she got the money she would often give her. She needed it too much to question it. Her secretarial job at a local accounting firm was just enough to pay the bills and didn't allow for many extras. So, whenever Nita got money from one of her many guy friends, no matter how small the amount, she would always come home and share with Big Nita. "Isn't that show tonight?" Big Nita asked looking up from the Essence magazine she was reading.

"It sure is!" Nita grabbed her bags from the hallway and hurried down the hall to her room to change. While in the shower, Nita intentionally wet her micro-braids so they would curl just right when she pulled them up into a high ponytail. Listening to the radio, she dressed then admired herself in the full-length mirror that hung on the back of her bedroom door. She looked good in the short set that exposed her curves and the sneakers matched perfectly. She even took the time to apply pink eye shadow and lipstick to her attractive, high yellow face. *Pink looks good on me*, she thought putting on her three gold rings and matching X and O necklace and bracelet set. Usually, she wore her diamond studs, but she decided on a pair of medium sized hoop earrings. All she needed to do was switch pocketbooks and she'd be ready to go to Free's house.

After retrieving her new Gucci bag, Nita stuffed her shopping bags into the back of her small cluttered closet. Her pocketbook was pastel pink, the same as her outfit and when she slipped it over her shoulder and looked in the mirror, she felt like a million dollar bill. Switching all of the items from her old Coach bag into her new Gucci bag, she saw the knot of five-dollar bills she had split with Free earlier. Confident it was $500, she put it in her top drawer. Reaching in her Coach bag for the rest of her money, she pulled out two fifties, seven twenties, and a couple of wrinkled five and one dollar bills. She looked deeper, but there wasn't any more money there. *How did I spend almost $3,000 in one day?* She sat on her bed and counted out all of her money to be sure. Nita only had $753 left. *Oh well, she thought. It's free money. But damn, it's almost gone already.*

She stuffed $250 in her new bag, looked herself over in the mirror once more and left for the concert.

Chapter 6

The show was a blast! Everybody, who was anybody, was seen at the sold out success. There were four different "official" after parties and B.J. was in the mood to drink and chill. He was riding with Taye in his 2000 midnight blue Yukon Denali on 23" rims. The fellas looked good in the truck, passing blunts and cruising in the traffic jam/car show that usually followed major events in Greenveiw. Taye lived for this kind of thing—driving his big truck and showing off. Every five minutes he'd roll down his window to holler at all the passing girls. B.J., who was rather low key, just enjoyed playing the passenger seat, listening to music and rolling his weed behind the deep tints.

Most people were planning on going to the after party at The Drop and that's where Taye wanted to be seen, but he knew B.J. wasn't going for it, so they decided on Club Macho's. Taye, 23, didn't have a problem getting into any club, but B.J. had to rely on a bouncer he could bribe. He slipped the ID guy $100 and that didn't include the $40 admission fee, or the $50 VIP pass. Once inside the VIP section, he felt his beeper vibrating and realized it was Kenya, the girl he had met in the mall earlier. Her message read: WSUP? Where you at? I'm trying to see you. He responded: I'm at Macho's. Come thru. Taye was on his way back from the bar carrying two bottles of Cristal. That's the type of guy Taye was. Someone on the outside looking in would assume Taye had more money than B.J., but it was just the opposite. After the down payment on his truck, Taye had about

$25,000 to $30,000 left compared to B.J.'s $70,000. Still, Taye made his way through the crowd as if he was the richest guy in the place.

As it turned out, this was the most happening jump off. All the popular people in town were there. The deejay was breaking a sweat, spinning all the latest hits. Taye popped the corks on both of the bottles and he and B.J. unconsciously established their own section within the VIP section. Before they knew it, girls were crowded around them looking thirsty and dancing. They had their own audience. Through the crowd, he spotted Dana and her little crew talking their way into the VIP. He sent Taye, who wanted to be on display anyway, to go and get them. He brought them back to the VIP section, but not before taking them to the bar and buying them all drinks.

On their way back, Taye was throwing game at Dana's best friend, Mi-Mi, who was catching every line and throwing it right back. Dana looked flawless, as usual, in a black mini dress, black leather strappy sandals and her white gold matching jewelry set. Her jet-black weave was parted, slicked, and hung to the middle of her back. She looked good and she knew it.

"Whassup, lil' brother?"

"Hey baby. You lookin' good."

"Yeah, I know...I know. But I'd look even better if me and my girls was poppin' bottles."

"Yeah, I'm sure you would," B.J. replied, knowing exactly what she was implying. Dana didn't budge. She knew she could get her way with her little brother.

"Come on B.J., we want a bottle," she whined, grabbed his arm and pulled him through the crowd in the direction of the bar. Rather than spending $350 on one bottle of Cristal, like Dana suggested, he bought each of the girls a bottle of Moet. At $80 a piece he hoped the girls would be grateful. They were. Dana, Mi-Mi, and the other two girls, who never introduced themselves, gulped down the drinks Taye bought them then

danced their way to the other side of the club, where they would sip their Moet, collect phone numbers and look cute for the reminder of the night.

Taye was busy being the life of the party. He was posted up at the picture booth with a gang of guys from his side of town. He had taken off his white T-shirt and just had on a wife-beater, blue jean shorts and a pair of Timberlands. He was posing in over a dozen pictures, showing off his nonexistent muscles and many tattoos—the most noticeable being the detailed portrait of his baby girl Alexis, on his right forearm.

B.J. was busy making serious eye contact with a red headed Hispanic girl who was seated with one of her girls at the bar in VIP. He glanced over and spotted Kenya looking even more gorgeous than she had at the mall earlier in the day. She noticed him looking at her but tried to pretend she was interested in the conversation she was having with a former lover. He was screaming something in her ear about hooking up later. Kenya wasn't trying to do that. She had plans to be with B.J. later. Ending the conversation with a "call me later," Kenya made her way over to where B.J. was seated.

"Oh, you didn't have to hit me back when I paged you earlier," she said in his ear in a voice filled with sarcasm.

"What are talkin' about, Baby? I hit you back." When she scrunched her lips at the corners in an expression of disbelief, he reached for his two-way to show her the page he had sent earlier. He flipped open his pager only to find that the page was still in the process of being sent.

"Oh, it didn't go through. The service must not be picking up in here," he said showing her his pager.

"Oh, okay," she said, with a near perfect smile. She slipped his pager back in the clip on his hip, creating a deja vu moment for the both of them.

"So, you didn't even get my page? You just came on your own, huh?"

"When I rode pass, I could just feel your presence in the building," she joked. Actually she had hoped he went to Macho's and was disappointed when he hadn't returned her page.

"Is that right?" *Maybe I could use somebody like her around. She could tell me when she feels the police presence,* B.J. laughed to himself. She eased a little closer after being nudged in the back for the fourth time by a couple dancing nearby and spoke into his ear.

"So, your girlfriend just lets you hang out all hours of the night?" she asked in a flirty, nosey kind of way.

Now, why she didn't just come straight out and ask me if I have a girlfriend, he thought but answered, "I don't know, you tell me. I thought you was my girlfriend."

"Good answer. But the right answer is no, I don't let you stay out all hours of the night. So, be ready to leave in about an hour." Once again, she walked away without giving him a chance to respond and all he could do was smile. He had to admit, he definitely liked her style. Not to mention, she looked so put together in the denim dress she bought just hours ago and a pair of bright red Manolo Blahnik stiletto construction boots. He didn't even care if they were the cheaper Steve Madden version.

B.J. couldn't think about anything but Kenya for the rest of the night. He wondered how old she was. If she was seeing anyone seriously. She didn't necessarily come across sleazy, so most of all he wondered what she had planned when they left the club. The night progressed smoothly; the city's "who's who" were dressed in their best drinking, dancing, and mingling. The packed club was a sea of basketball jerseys, baseball caps, stilettos, and weaves. People were actually breaking a sweat as the hottest D.J. in the city spun all the mainstream and even the latest underground hits. As the speakers blasted and the drinks settled, it was one of those nights nobody wanted to end.

When Dana came by to say good-bye to the guys, Taye and Mi-Mi exchanged numbers and promised to call each other the following morning. Around three a.m., when it was obvious the night was winding down, Kenya made herself visible to B.J. She felt she had been too forward earlier, so she didn't walk over. Instead she positioned herself up against a wall opposite him, so he would have no problem finding her when people began to leave. He didn't hesitate either.

"Whassup girlfriend? You ready? Who you came wit'?"

"I came by myself. Yeah, I'm ready when you are."

"Alright, let me go find my boy," he said, then thought for a minute. "So ain't nobody ridin' wit' you?"

"No, I just told you I came her by myself," she said, confident of what he was getting at.

"So I should ride wit' you then, huh?"

"If you want to," she said in her shy voice, not wanting to sound too eager.

"All right. Let me go holler at my boy. Stay right here, I'll be right back."

B.J. walked back through the thinning crowd and found Taye talking to the same red headed girl that was seated at the bar eyeing him earlier. The girl, who Taye introduced as Jisella, gave B.J. a bad vibe instantly. He wasn't feeling the way she was hanging all over Taye after she had just finished giving him "come sex me" eyes less than thirty minutes ago.

"What's good?" B.J. greeted her.

Taye didn't even give her a chance to answer. "You ready?" he said to the both of them then turned to B.J. "Jisella's riding wit' us."

"Oh is she?" B.J. asked not feeling the idea at all, but he had

other plans on his mind. He didn't like how Taye invited the girl to ride with them without running it passed him first. He also had a problem with the way Jisella dumped her girlfriend she rode to the club with to leave with Taye. It bothered him, but it wasn't that serious. "Look, I'm out. I got me a ride. Holla back."

"No doubt." Taye didn't think twice about it. He didn't want B.J. to ride in the car with him and Jisella anyway. The sooner they could be alone, the better.

As B.J. walked back through the club to find Kenya he thought, *What kind of girl leaves her friend to ride with a dude she just met? Or better yet what kind of girl goes to the club by herself?* Kenya had come to the club by herself and he couldn't decide if that turned him off or on. Either way, when he found Kenya, he picked up his cell phone and called Taye. "Yo don't leave the parking lot. I'll be at the truck in a minute."

Kenya gave him a strange look, but didn't dare say anything. She was feeling a nice buzz from three Belvedere and Cranberries. She followed him out of the club and directed the way to her 1999 burgandy Dodge Durango. She was proud of her vehicle as she pressed the button on her remote control key-pad to unlock the doors and start the car. Once inside B.J. instructed her to drive over to Taye's Denali. See, B.J. was kind of drunk, too. He was a liquor drinker so the champagne was starting to get the best of him. However, he wasn't drunk enough to forget that he had left his phone charger and his "baby", in Taye's truck: He retrieved them and the two couples set off in separate directions; Taye and Jisella were going to the Marriott, B.J. and Kenya headed to the Waffle House. On the way to breakfast the conversation was light, but informative.

"Whose truck is this?" was the first thing B.J. asked. He was not about to be caught up in some guy's truck. He should have asked as soon as she pointed her remote control, but the champagne was taking its toll. Besides everything about Kenya felt so right to him.

"It's mine," she answered fidgeting with the remote control

radio. He found out she was 22, with no kids, no boyfriend and her own one bedroom apartment. She discovered he was 20, with no kids, no girlfriend, and still lived with his mother; a fact that didn't impress her in the least. The conversation continued over breakfast with B.J. asking most of the questions. He wanted to find out as much as he could about her because so far, other than her fake acrylic nails, he hadn't found anything he didn't like. As it turns out she didn't have a lot of girlfriends and the one girl she was close with was out of town visiting her boyfriend, who was doing a five-year federal bid. B.J. was enjoying her company and the feeling was mutual. They laughed at each other's jokes and everything just felt right about them being together. B.J. paid the bill and they were grateful to leave the overcrowded restaurant. They walked back to the truck in awkward silence. *What are we going to do now?*, they both thought.

The truth was, B.J. was now a little in his feelings about Kenya. She just got her first strike: not thanking him for breakfast. Being the playa he was, B.J. gave girls three strikes before they were out. That's not to say that they couldn't return to the game after riding the bench for a while; it was just his way of doing things. If he paid for someone's meal, he liked to hear a simple, "thanks for breakfast," or "thanks for dinner," whatever the case may be. Kenya neglected to do so, but that didn't mean she didn't have any manners. It just meant that maybe she had forgotten. If he didn't pay for the meal she would have never forgotten that.

Kenya broke the silence. "So where to from here?"

"Stop at the store for some blunts. Dats if I can smoke in here."

"Yeah, you can smoke in here." He had discovered earlier that she was a non-smoker, he wasn't sure if she was on of those people who didn't allow smoking in their vehicle. He wanted to smoke a blunt to balance all the champagne in his system, but he needed to get some condoms. He wasn't sure if she was the type to give it up on the first night; if she was, he was going to be prepared. When he got back in the truck, this time it was B.J. who broke the silence.

"Where to from here?" Who were they fooling? It was going on five o'clock in the morning and neither had to tell the other that there was no place to go, but home or to a hotel. B.J. looked up from rolling his blunt to answer his own question. "You tryin' to go to the Ramada or the Marriott?" Kenya was ecstatic. She liked the way he made it seem like they were automatically staying together and the only choice in the matter was where. She was so excited, thinking about how she couldn't wait to be alone in a hotel room with him, that she didn't answer him right away. He respected her hesitation and almost thought she was getting ready to say something about her going home rather than spending the night with him so soon.

"It doesn't matter. It's up to you."

He decided on the Marriott, partly because that's where Taye was. It was also closer to their current location. On the way, they exchanged thoughts on the concert and their chance meeting in the mall. They rode and he couldn't help but notice the truck's well-kept interior and high quality sound system as he relaxed in the passenger seat.

"So, where you work at?" he asked.

"I do hair at this shop downtown. What about you?"

"Me? Well, I'm in between jobs," he answered. It was the truth. When he was sixteen he once worked as a counselor at a local YMCA. He hadn't had a job since then, so technically he was in between jobs. It all depends on how you looked at it. He liked a woman with a decent job and her own money. He also liked the fact that beauticians were known to have flexible schedules. But still, he needed to know more.

"You must be doing your thing over there," he concluded. "You dressed clean, ridin' big. Maybe I need to start doing hair."

Kenya knew it was coming sooner or later. It seemed like whenever she met a new guy he couldn't rest until he found out how she paid for her truck. It wasn't that the truck was so expensive as much as it was the way she had it hooked up on the

inside. Whenever someone found out she was only 22, he or she always assumed that someone else had paid for the truck or was still paying for it. She gave B.J. the same answer she gave everybody else who asked, the truth.

"My ex-boyfriend bought me this truck before he got locked up," she said full of pride.

"Oh alright."

He had figured her out. He knew there had to be more to her story, but he was no longer interested in hearing it. Kenya was a high maintenance broad who was accustomed to having the guys she dated spend large amounts of money on her. That was his opinion of her and he had heard enough. They pulled up at the Marriott, Kenya found a parking space and they entered the lobby. He gave her $150 then took a seat on a sofa in the lounge, while she went over to the front desk to get them checked in. He just laughed silently and shook his head when the clerk asked, "Would this be cash or charge?" Kenya slipped his money into her wallet and pulled out the same credit card she had used in the mall earlier.

"Charge."

What?!, he thought. *Strike 2*!

They entered the smoking king size room and relaxed. Kenya kicked of her red suede boots and B.J. secured a damp towel at the foot of the door. He began to roll another blunt while she made preparations to take a shower. He took this opportunity to peek inside of her boots. He was just curious as to whether or not they were official. They were. He immediately began to wonder why a girl as pretty and as well off as Kenya would be ready to spend the night in a hotel with a guy she had just met less than 24 hours ago. She emerged from the bathroom wearing only a white towel and asked him for the wife-beater he was wearing under his sweat suit. He unzipped his jacket, took off his gray and red top and slid off the undershirt.

"Don't say I never gave you nothin'. Here, I am giving you the shirt off my back." She grabbed the scented wife-beater.

"Don't front. You know it'll look better on me," she said as she walked into the bathroom.

"I know, so hurry up and get back out here. I'm tryna see you in that."

Kenya came out of the bathroom this time wearing nothing except B.J.'s under shirt. B.J. took his sweatpants off and laid them on a recliner chair, closest to the side of the bed he planned to sleep on. It felt like the temperature in the room had increased by twenty degrees. Kenya was pleased to discover his boxer shorts were Roc-a-Wear, the same as his sweat suit. Unfortunately B.J. didn't get a chance to enjoy that same pleasure. He never saw what kind of underwear Kenya had on. He loved to see girls in a matching panty and bra set and she had taken that enjoyable experience away from him. It was just, Boom! Now, she lay on the bed completely naked under his thin wife beater.

B.J., sensing no real challenge on Kenya's part, was struck with a sudden wave of boredom. He was still interested, but he had learned long ago that when things came easy they weren't usually worth having; things of great value didn't usually come easy. She rested her head on his chest as he continued to smoke his Dutch Master and flip through the cable channels. It was the wee hours of the morning and Kenya closed her eyes. B.J. began to think and his erection grew. *Now she lying up against me in the bed with no panties on. If she don't give me none, she's a tease. If she does give me some, she's a hoe. Strike 3.*

Before he turned the T.V. off, he two-wayed Taye and told him to page him as soon as he woke up. He knew his boy was probably asleep and would get the page later in the morning. Just in case he didn't feel like riding with Kenya, he would now have the option of riding with Taye.

Neither of them were asleep, they laid in silence minutes

before sunrise. B.J. eased up and kissed Kenya on the forehead. She opened her eyes and stretched out flat on her back. The sight of his wife-beater clinging to her hips bought his erection to its full capacity. He began to kiss her ear, gently blowing small breaths of air. This caused Kenya's spine to tingle and her body jerked lightly from the sensation. B.J. moved down to her neck where he soaked up her scent and used his fingers to move her hanging hair. After lingering there for a minute he continued on his downward path. He moved with tiny, tender kisses from her neck, to her shoulders, and ended up with his face in her breasts. She arched her back in an attempt to make her 36 B's appear larger than they actually were. B.J. really preferred a handful, but her's were only a mouthful and he treated them as such. He took one of her nipples in his mouth and massaged it with his tongue. Her breath hastened. He then reached for the other nipple he had neglected up until that point, and gave it the same treatment. She wanted him and her hands began to think for her. She reached between his legs and found eight and a half inches of thick, solid manhood. He was ready to enter her and she was more than ready to be entered.

He reached his hand over to the chair, dug in his pants pocket and pulled out a Magnum Trojan condom then stood up, stepped out of his boxers, and slid it on. Kenya laid back on the king size bed and waited patiently. B.J. climbed back on the bed, spread her legs, and pushed himself inside of her without further delay. As he began to stroke she responded by arching her back upward and pushing her pelvis towards him. B.J. didn't hold back his ejaculation and the whole act lasted no longer than ten minutes. He came, took off the condom, washed himself off, and then returned to smoking the remainder of his blunt. Kenya didn't wash up, instead she laid there basking in the after glow. It didn't take long before B.J. was asleep.

He woke only a few hours later to a strange feeling. It was Kenya under the covers with her lips on him. Like a pro, she fingered and licked all of the right places, gaining his full attention. He was shocked and a voice inside of his head told him he should stop her. B.J. listened to the voice in his head more often

than not, but this time he found himself completely overwhelmed. He gyrated his hips towards her face as he whispered, "Don't stop."

At B.J.'s command Kenya continued until he couldn't take anymore and was near ejaculation. B.J. simply wasn't used to this type of treatment. The last girl he had dated despised morning sex, so waking up to a blowjob was something he had never experienced. "I'm cummin', I'm cummin'," he warned her. She removed her lips from his penis and replaced them with her other pair of lips. "Whoa! Whoa! Wait!" he began, but that was as far as he got. He exploded inside of her as she played her position, riding him until he was weak and limp again.

Chapter 7

"We should get an apartment together, Free."

"You think so?"

The girls were riding to the car rental place to return the Escalade and relishing their final moments of riding in the luxurious SUV.

"Whose name could we get it in?" asked Nita.

"I'll ask my mom tonight. I mean it's not like we're not old enough."

"Yeah, you're right."

And she was. The girls were about to become college freshman. Nita had applied and was accepted at several historically black colleges, but decided on a less prestigious community college. Free, on the other hand had no intentions of traveling out of the state and had only applied to one community college. As it turns out they would be attending the same school in the fall.

They spent the remainder of the ride quiet, but their thoughts were similar. They were imagining what it would be like to have their own apartment. They weren't sure if they would be able to afford it. The $3,500 they had came up on fueled their desire to do better. They had stepped it up a notch. It was apparent in the

way their girlfriends, Shamika and Nicole, had treated them Saturday night and it was also apparent in the response they received from the concertgoers. They had caught the attention of folks, both male and female, who normally wouldn't have given them a second glance. Nita and Free were outstanding females, but for the first time in their lives they actually stood out. They were always well kept and dressed stylish, but Saturday night was different. They took extra care with their make-up, had actually popped the tags on everything they had on, and they had a newfound confidence. Saturday night, Nita and Free felt like they were on top of the world and neither girl wanted to come down.

They pulled into the car rental place and found Marco and Marky already waiting for them. The twins had noticed how good the girls looked even without their money and couldn't wait to see them again. They had joked with each other that the girls would probably show up at the concert looking cheap and "last minute." Neither girl wanted to deal with her guy since they had backed out on their promise, but the fact was they needed a ride from the rental place, so lunch with the twins didn't sound like a bad idea.

While the bread sticks with marinara sauce were being served at the Olive Garden, Marco inquired about the money the girls obviously come across. "Must be nice to ride in a big Escalade and wear new Pradas and you ain't got no job," he joked. Marco could be real nosey sometimes. Free and Nita gave each other a quick glance. They both knew exactly where he was trying to take the conversation. Before they could come up with a clever response, Marky chimed in.

"I know right? Seems like ya'll did just fine without our little money."

"Little money," Nita replied. "I can't tell it was little the way ya'll was holding on to it."

"And I guess you got it to give now," Free joined in, "since your car still got the same tires," she said to Marky. Even though she had about $1750 left, she was still trying to get the $300 out of Marky.

"You know I got you," he said.

Lunch was served and the subject was changed. Their relationships had disintegrated overnight. It wasn't just because the girls slept with someone else. It had more to do with the fact that every time Free looked at Marky, or Nita looked at Marco they were instantly reminded of the act they were trying so hard to forget. If the guys hadn't backed out on them, they would have never slept with Randy, or robbed him. In a way, they felt if Randy sought revenge it would be partially the twins fault. No matter how much they wanted to go back to normalcy they could never forget the other night, or forgive the twins for abandoning them.

There were other reasons for the girls no longer being satisfied in their current relationships. The twins were small time weed hustlers, who dropped out of high school during the girls' junior year. At the time, they were too thrilled to be dating drug dealer dropouts, who could afford to keep their hair and nails done. But now that they had slept with a major hustler and had gotten a little bit of money of their own, the thrill was gone. Nita and Free were thrill-seekers, if nothing else.

Back at Nita's house they were excitedly discussing plans for their new apartment. They were already deciding who would get the master bedroom and who would do most of the cooking. The conversation was almost phony because they both were having doubts about whether they could actually afford their own place. For Free, who still had over $1,500, it was more of a reality. Nita had a little over $300 left after paying Free's mom for the Escalade. Mrs. Harrison had told her daughter she did not have to pay for her half of the Escalade. She called it a graduation present. Free was grateful.

Free took out her new cell phone and began storing numbers in it. She dug in the black Coach bag she had worn Saturday night and started taking out small crumbled up pieces of paper.

These were all the phone numbers she had collected over the weekend. Instantly, Nita grabbed her Gucci bag and they both went through their collection.

"What about that guy in the Benz?" Free asked.

"Yeah, I got his number right here. Didn't he look good?," She held up a small blue piece of paper.

"If you don't do nothing else, make sure you call him."

They continued to sort through phone numbers.

"IIIIII!" Free screamed, holding up a small receipt. "I think this is that one guy's number."

"What guy?"

"You know who, looked like he been chewing rocks all his life." Nita grabbed the receipt right out of Free's hand and tossed it in the wastepaper basket. They were laughing so hard remembering the guy with the ruined teeth, they didn't even notice that she had missed and the paper had landed on the floor beside the garbage. Free was having a hard time putting a face to some of the numbers she found in her pocketbook. Nita, on the other hand, didn't have that problem. Whenever she received a guy's phone number, she always put a small note beside his name. Whether it was the guy's car, his shoes, or his hairstyle, she always jotted down a memorable detail, so when she went back through all of her phone numbers looking for a date, she would never make the mistake of calling the wrong guy. Needless to say, she didn't always use this method. She adopted it after sitting through a dinner date with an 'undesirable' all because she had mistaken his number for a guy who drove a Beamer.

"I wonder whose number this is," Free held up a Big Red gum wrapper. The paper simply read 'Ed'.

"Well, call him. That's the only way you're gonna find out," Nita suggested.

Free picked up her new phone and anxiously dialed the number. She could have easily used the house phone, but she wanted to use her new cell. "Hello, Can I speak to Ed?"

"Who's this?"

"This is Free. You met me Saturday night."

"Free, why didn't you call me sooner?" Ed asked in a deep West Indian accent. Instantly, Free remembered him as being the short, brown skinned, West Indian guy with the long dreadlocks. While he was semi-attractive, she had never dealt with a foreigner before and was sort of reluctant to continue the conversation.

"Well," she said. "I had a copula things to do yesterday."

"Oh, okay. I can't be mad at that. What time are you going to be free today. I want to take you to Red Lobster or something."

"Umm, what time can you come and pick me up?" She was not one to turn down free seafood.

"Is this your cell?"

"Yeah."

"Alright. Let me make a few runs and I'll call you as soon as the sun goes down for directions."

"That's cool," Free agreed. "I'll store your number in."

"I'll store yours too, baby. Talk to you later."

"What did he say? Who was it?" Nita was all in her face before she even had a chance to press the end button on her cell.

"It was that guy I met with the dreads," Free told her.

"Oh, but I thought you didn't like him."

"I don't, but I'm tryin' to go to Red Lobster tonight."

Nita picked up the small blue piece of paper that held the number of Mr. Benz. Suddenly, she wanted a dinner date. She called him to set up a dinner date for later that evening. He told her that he had a lot of running around to do, but he would get back to her as soon as he finished and was "definitely trying to see her".

The girls spent the rest of the day sitting around in Nita's room watching music videos. They talked about how Shamika and Nicole had hated on them saying, they thought they were cute in their Roc-a-Wear hookups.

"Be clear," Nita told them. "We don't think we cute, we *know* we cute. Don't be J." Shamika and Nicole were feeling a certain kind of way because they were wearing the same Mitchell and Ness throwback jersey dresses they had worn to the Great Adventure senior trip.

"Let me find out that's their fly uniform," Free joked. They both laughed hard. It felt good to be able to outshine Nicole and Shamika, if only for one night.

Shamika and Nicole were hands down the flyest of the fly girls at Woodrow Wilson High School. All their gear was official and they never missed an appointment to get their acrylic nails refilled. Shamika kept her thin, black hair in a short Caesar type cut and Nicole was known for her ever changing weaves. Actually, they were especially jealous of Free, who had her own hair that hung past her shoulders. Nita, who was desperately trying to grow her hair out after cutting it, usually kept it in some type of braids. All of the girls were physically above average. Shamika and Nicole just seemed to run across more guys, who were willing to spend money on them.

"So, how much money you got left?" Nita was fiddling with her braids in her dresser mirror. She knew Free had more cash than her, but she had no idea how much more.

"Girl, I got like $1,700 left. What about you?"

"What?!" Nita couldn't believe it. "How you got so much money left?"

"Dat's cause I haven't been spendin' all crazy. Why? How much you got left?"

Nita hesitated and exaggerated the truth a little. "Girl, I got like $500 left."

"What?" Now Free couldn't believe it. She was at a loss for words. Nita had spent $3,000 in three days. Instantly, Free became proud of herself and cracked a little smile; however her best friend quickly rained on her parade.

"I don't know what you holdin' on to it for. You betta spend that free money, Free." Free thought for a minute then realized she shouldn't have told Nita how much money she had. She promised herself she would never make that mistake twice.

"Right now, my life could be in danger and I had sex with a complete stranger for this money," Free raised her voice a notch. "I ain't in no hurry to spend it all."

"You don't have to get loud. All I'm sayin' is after all you had to do for it, you should at least enjoy it."

"Oh, don't worry. I will," Free replied.

They spent the rest of the early evening discussing plans for their new apartment. They popped popcorn and just hung out like they usually did. Sure enough, when the sun went down at about eight o'clock, Ed called Free. She gave him the directions to Nita's house and he was on his way. Free made preparations for her date by putting on a light coat of make-up. She was wearing her usual white T-shirt and a pair of blue denim Capri pants. She had on white ankle socks, a pair of black Jordan's and her everyday black leather Coach bag. She felt a little under dressed, but she didn't think it was serious enough to borrow something from Nita to wear. They wore the same exact size in clothes and shoes, but Free didn't like borrowing other people's clothes. When she got dressed that morning she had no idea she would

be going to Red Lobster later that night. *If he can't accept me for my everyday self then he doesn't deserve me. We just going to get something to eat anyway. He's gonna be alright.*

"That's what you wearing?"

"Yes, Nita. Why you not feelin' it?" Free asked, spinning around modeling her casual wear.

"It's okay, but if you want to be more dressed up, you know you can always borrow something of mine."

"No, I'm good. I'm tired of girls thinkin' they have to be all dressed up and guys just show up wearin' whatever they want."

"I guess you right," Nita agreed. "Do you."

Nita was a little disappointed that Mr. Benz hadn't called her for directions yet. "Have fun," she told her friend after Ed called about fifteen minutes later and announced his arrival.

"I will. You have fun on your date, too. I'll call you in the morning or just call my cell." Free smiled.

"Alright, Baby. Don't do nuttin' I wouldn't," Nita said smiling back.

"For sure." She was out the door and walking towards a navy blue 2002 Acura Legend. As soon as Free took a seat in the Ac, she was welcomed by the familiar smell of weed smoke. She broke the ice by asking if she could roll up.

"Sure," he said. "Go right ahead."

Ed was an easygoing, mild-mannered Jamaican, who had been living in the United States for the last eight of his 24 years. Free found him attractive, but she didn't like his dreads. If she had been following Nita's system and wrote 'dreads' on the piece of paper containing his number, she may have never called him. As they smoked and chatted she decided that she would just be cool with him. Besides, he was seven years older

than her. They took the streets rather than the highway to Red Lobster, so they would have ample time to smoke the blunt Free had rolled from her own weed and get to know each other.

"This is some good weed, baby. You tryna sell some of it?" Ed had already eyed her bag while she was rolling up. Free got nervous. Since it was Randy's weed, she became paranoid. *Ohmigod! What if he knows Randy. I don't even know this guy. I should have never pulled out the weed in front of him.* For the first time Free realized she didn't know how to sell weed. Whenever she bought some it was just a dime or two and now she had a whole ounce. For the most part, she had been getting weed from Marky free of charge. She could try to sell him a dime or two but his demeanor painted the image of someone who had more than $10 or $20 dollars to spend with her. She pulled the sandwich bag out of her purse.

"That depends. What you tryna spend?"

"What you want for that whole bag? What's that about an ounce?" She knew she had smoked at least four blunts out of it since yesterday and she figured it was probably an ounce when she got her hands on it.

"It's a little less than an ounce, but you know this ain't no regular weed." She said this hoping he would give her some type of price range.

"Baby, I deal in weed everyday. I know it ain't no regular weed. I got good regular weed for days, weeks even. I want some of that for my personal. That's some crucial. What you want for it?"

Her heart was racing 55 miles per minute. Two hundred and fifty dollars popped into her head. She didn't know where it came from, but she learned to always trust her instincts. *But what if that is too much? What if it's not enough? And if he does buy it, what will I have left to smoke on?* "Just give me two-fifty," she said naturally and handed him the bag. Ed took one hand off the steering wheel, grabbed the bag from her and untied the knot

with his teeth. He didn't speak for a few seconds, examining the contents of the bag closely and had even turned on the light for a better view.

"I'll give you two-twenty."

He went for it! I did it. "Dat's cool, but for two-twenty you gotta let me take a dime out."

"You ain't easy, you know," Ed said with a laugh. He liked her. "You hungry?" he asked. They were at Red Lobster and had smoked up a decent appetite. Once they were seated, it was time to get to know each other a little better. Free talked about being anxious to start college and Ed conversed about his two sons he adored and lived for. They had a good camaraderie building. He ordered himself a double shot of Hennessy and when the waitress asked for his identification, Free's hopes of ordering a Pina Colada were crushed. The waitress checked his ID, placed a basket of piping hot, buttery garlic and cheese biscuits on their table and left. Free had an announcement to make.

"I want a Pina."

From their conversation in the car, Ed knew she was nowhere near old enough but he said, "anything for my Free." She just smiled. The extra friendly waitress returned to the table with the lobster fondue and buffalo wings they had ordered for appetizers.

"Let me get a Pina Colada with an extra shot of Vodka," he told the waitress then winked at Free.

"And anything else for you, ma'am?" she turned to Free.

"Yes. Can I have some blue cheese please?"

"Sure," she replied then walked briskly towards the kitchen area.

"You know if she catches me drinkin' that Pina, we goin' down like the Titanic," Free joked.

"Don't worry, I got your back." For some reason, Free could tell there was nothing but truth in his statement. She didn't get caught either. She gulped down the Pina Colada whenever their waitress was out of sight. They enjoyed sneaking around all through dinner like little kids. Ed gave the waitress a generous tip, Free thanked him for the meal, and they were back in his Acura. Ed had her roll up some of the skunk he had just purchased from her. While doing so, she took her dime out and he paid her. By the time they got in front of her house, she was high, tipsy, and didn't want to go straight inside. They just sat in front of her house joking and enjoying each other's conversation.

RRRING...RRRING...RRRING...

Free wondered why he didn't answer his phone. *That must be his baby momma calling,* she thought.

RRRING...RRRING...

"That must be your nigga callin' since you actin' like you don't hear your phone ringin'"

"Huh? Oh!" Free had forgot she had a cell phone. She reached in her bag. "Hello."

"Whassup girl? You still out wit' ya boy? I seen his Ac. Where ya'll at, or did he drop you off?" Once again, Nita had 21 questions.

"Yeah, I'm still chillin'. I'm getting' ready to go in the house. Whassup wit' you? Where you at?"

"I'm waitin' for the dude wit' the Benz," Nita said, looking out her bedroom window.

"He ain't got there yet?"

"No, but he been on his way for about an hour."

"Oh. Well, don't do nuttin' I wouldn't. I'll call you from the house in a little while to check on you."

"Dat's whassup."

Nita hung up and continued to peek out of the blinds of her bedroom window. It was well after ten o'clock. If a guy picks a girl up for a date after ten o'clock, he usually has one thing on his mind. If his vehicle wasn't so elaborate, Nita would have seriously considered giving Mr. Benz a rain check. But she had never been out with a guy with a Benz before and didn't want to miss the opportunity. She didn't want to call him back again either. The last time she had spoke to him, he had called at about nine o'clock to get directions to her house. He said he had two stops to make and he planned to be there in thirty minutes. That was almost two hours ago. Big Nita was in her bed watching the ten o'clock news. She had her bedroom door closed and Nita knew she would not give her a hard time about what time she was leaving out. *Still, what time does Mr. Benz think he's gonna show up?*

Twenty minutes later, just as she was getting fed up and ready to take a Noxzema pad to her made up face, she saw bluish lights outside her window. She rushed to the window, saw a big Mercedes parked outside, and then her cell started ringing.

"Come outside," was all Mr. Benz said when she answered.

She looked in the mirror once more and approved of her grey Levi's baby Tee, black denim Levi's mini skirt, grey ankle socks and new grey Prada sneakers. Nita put her cell in her gray leather Coach bag and left for her hot date. *A late date is better than no date.*

Chapter 8

"Alright. Holla at me a little later. I should be finished wit' everything tonight," Taye yelled out his truck window.

"Fo' sho'," B.J. responded, opening his Caddy door.

Taye pulled off, as did B.J. shortly afterwards. On the way to his house B.J. dug in his pocket and discovered he had only $200 left. He had left the house with a grand. *See, that's why I don't go out,* he thought.

When Taye paged him this morning, he was happy to hear it. He liked Kenya, but after the episode she pulled he wanted to get from around her as fast as he could. Taye had sent Jisella home in a cab and met B.J. in the lobby. On the ride to B.J.'s car, they exchanged stories about their night in the Marriott. As it turned out, Jisella hadn't gone all the way with Taye. She told him she liked him, but didn't want to do the deed until she got to know him better. He accepted her "no" and they made plans to see each other the very next day. B.J. told Taye how easy Kenya was and he had a hard time believing it judging by her looks. By the time he got to the part about her going down on him they were pulling up behind B.J.'s car.

B.J. didn't allow anyone to know the location of his house. That included his close boy Taye. Whenever B.J. rode with him, or anybody, else he would always have him, or her, meet him at his car, not his house. He would keep his Caddy parked on ran-

dom streets in a totally different side of town from where his house really was. This way he could sleep a little easier at night knowing that no one he dealt with knew where he was resting his head.

As soon as B.J. turned onto his block, his heart skipped a beat at the sight of two local police cars. One car was directly in front of his house and the other was in front of his next door neighbor's house. Out of a force of habit he grabbed his seatbelt and held it in front of him so it appeared buckled. He continued to drive down his block extremely slow, but didn't stop. Lowering the music, he stared at his mother's front door as if he was looking at it for the last time. He saw a uniformed police officer in the doorway of his neighbor's house. For the first time since B.J. turned the corner, he breathed. He was relieved to see the officers weren't at his house, but became instantly concerned about his hoopty parked in the neighbor's backyard. It held half a kilo under the passenger seat.

B.J. nervously circled the block and parked at the beginning of it, where he had a clear view of his neighbor's front door. He managed to see that his hoopty was still parked in the backyard. It appeared to be untouched, so he relaxed, reclined his seat back even further and watched the scene unfold.

Apparently, Barbara and her boyfriend, Lucky, had gotten into yet another physical brawl and the boys in blue were answering yet another domestic violence complaint. Barbara had called the cops on Lucky after he threatened her with a beer bottle. He had threw the empty Heineken bottle at her and when he missed he reached for another. All of this because Barbara had caught Lucky cheating, once again. Their arguing was a routine occurrence and the continuous abuse was not enough to drive Barbara away from him. Barbara was an attractive woman, but deep down she didn't believed she deserved better, so she put up with Lucky and received all that he had to give.

This was the third time officers had been called to the residence and B.J. was fed up. He had agreed to pay Barbara's cable bill in exchange for her allowing him to leave his old Buick in

her backyard. He had once paid a lady's $500 rent per month for this same service. Over time, the lady began asking questions as to why he was willing to pay so much just to park his car. He learned from that experience and when he approached Barbara he did no more than offer to pay her cable bill after she told him it was about to be cut off. As a result, she didn't have a problem with letting him park his Buick in her backyard, no questions asked.

Now, B.J. sat back in his Caddy and realized that he had to find another parking space for his hoopty. He came to the conclusion that he had exhausted almost all of his safe parking spaces. After brainstorming he would find the perfect place to park his stash car, but he needed to move it tonight. He didn't feel safe with Barbara and her boyfriend's erratic and unpredictable behavior and his nerves couldn't take arriving home to the sight of police cars again. Yeah, he was only twenty, but he almost had a heart attack just now.

After about ten minutes, the police finally pulled off and the coast was clear. B.J. made up his mind—take the Buick to his boy's auto shop to have it tuned up and painted. He figured no one would suspect it was a stash spot if he began to fix it up as if he was going to drive it. In the meantime, he would keep his coke inside of his house somewhere in his room. It wasn't the best idea he had ever come up with, but he couldn't take the chance of making himself vulnerable to thieving watchful eyes. B.J. made the decision against his better judgment, but he knew that no one knew where he lived and he felt his product would be safe inside for a week or two. Pulling out of his inconspicuous parking space at the corner, he drove further down the block, parked in front of his house and went inside. As soon as he went inside, he heard the sounds of his mom's favorite Oldies but Goodies radio station and smelled the unmistakable aroma of bacon frying. He went straight into the kitchen where he found Miss Janice cooking Sunday morning breakfast—french toast, scrambled cheese eggs, sautéed potatoes and onions, and beef bacon. Miss Janice didn't always cook dinner for the boys on the weekdays, but without fail, every Sunday she would wake

up and make a mouth-watering breakfast. It was something B.J. always looked forward to, no matter how he spent Saturday night.

"Hey beautiful," he grinned, kissing his mom on the cheek. He always called his mom beautiful and who could blame him, she was. Even after suffering from a crack addiction that lasted nearly seven years, the streets didn't steal her beauty. She was now in full recovery and had been clean for almost five years.

"Hey baby," Mrs. Janice looked up from her frying pan to greet her eldest son.

"What's up wit' Barbara?" B.J. wasted no time asking what he needed to know.

"Oh, you know, baby. More of the same and ain't nuttin' changed. Her and that ole knucklehead at it again. I guess he was really 'bout to take it to her this morning. She done up and called police again." Miss Janice didn't know for a fact her son was a drug dealer. She'd been around long enough to know that since he didn't have a job in years and never want for much of anything, he had to be selling something. The fact that he paid all of the bills around the house and had just bought her a new Dodge Intrepid didn't bother her in the least. While she worried about his safety, she knew he was a man of his own decisions.

"She ain't gonna be satisfied 'til they callin' a ambulance ova here." B.J. gossiped with his mom even though he didn't care much for other folks business. He never missed an opportunity to chat with his mother.

"Oh, don't worry," Miss Janice assured him. "She'll be over here in a day or two to tell me all about it."

"I know it and I can't wait to hear what it was this time. I'll be right back," B.J. said on the way to his bedroom.

"Tell your brother to come eat," she yelled before he was out of earshot. As usual, T.J. was in the living room with a Play Station 2 controller in his hand.

"Hey Lil' Man, food is ready so get from in front of that video and get you some before I eat it all."

"Here I come, let me just get off this board, so I can use my memory card," T.J. answered but B.J. had already left the room. T.J. had Nintendo, Sega, Super Nintendo, and Play Station, the only one he played nowadays was his Play Station 2. Every cartridge or accessory he even thought he wanted, he owned, all thanks to his older brother.

B.J. opened his bedroom door and walked over to the window. Since his room was positioned in the back of the house he had a perfect view of Barbara's backyard and his Buick. Just as he thought, the car didn't appear to be touched. Still, with the police making routine stops at Barbara's house, he knew he had to go along with his plan to move the coke. His mind was made up. He left the window, put both his two-way and cell phone on their chargers and went downstairs to devour his mom's breakfast.

"I saw Dana last night," B.J. announced as the three family members enjoyed their meal.

"Where?" T.J. asked before Miss Janice could get the same exact word out.

"At this party I went to."

"Really?" Miss Janice asked. "I wonder when she's gonna settle down and stay outta the clubs with you carefree teenagers."

"You know Dana, Ma. Not a care in the world," B.J said.

"And she ain't getting no younger. I mean, can I get a grandbaby?"

T.J. laughed and almost choked on his pineapple orange juice. "You got me, Mom!" T.J. smiled.

"Boy, you ain't no baby, you act like one sometimes." Miss

Janice waved her hand at T.J. and turned to B.J. "I got you making me a grandma before she does," she said.

"Don't hold your breath, Ma. I can't even find a decent girl to call my own."

"That's cuz-" T.J. started.

"Oh, what do you know? You ain't even in high school yet," B.J. teased, taking advantage of the fact that his little brother was nervous and at the same time excited about starting high school in the Fall.

"But, I will be in two months," T.J. bragged.

"That's right," Miss Janice supported him. "My baby's starting high school in September."

"But Ma, you just said I wasn't a baby."

"Boy, don't you question your mama." They all laughed.

After they finished eating, Miss Janice cleared the table, T.J. went back to his game and B.J. jumped in the shower. Washing her scent off of his body, he thought of Kenya for the first time since he left her in the hotel bed. He spent extra time scrubbing his groin area, finished his shower and stepped out of the bathroom to start his day. After he dressed he had a few calls to return and sales to set up. He was really waiting for Taye's call, so that he could collect his money and go to see his connect. He only had half of brick left and people were already waiting for that.

B.J. went outside the front door and around back to his hoopty. He grabbed up his package from a hidden compartment behind one of the speakers and went back inside the house. Since he only had such a small amount left, he broke it into eighths. This way he could charge an extra $250 for each eighth and make an extra thousand dollars. That grand would replace the one he had spent frivolously the night before. It was the last of his supply, so his customers would pay whatever price he

threw at them. He put his scale back in the hall bathroom under the sink, wiped the powder residue off of his dresser, and hid his package in the front of his pants. He looked himself over to be sure his bulge wasn't obvious and rushed back towards the front door. His mom spoke to him when he breezed pass the kitchen.

"B.J., you know I wouldn't be surprised if the cops come back before the week is out, just to check on Barbara. You know this is the third time they done come out here."

"I know, Ma. Tell me about it." B.J. appeared as if the information didn't affect him in the least. He was curious as to why his mom felt the need to bring it to his attention. *Mothers don't miss nuttin'*, he thought as he kissed her on the cheek and prepared to leave.

"Just something to think about, is all. Have a good day," she called out to him.

"You too," he answered on his way out the door.

B.J. had four different people to meet, two of whom were already waiting. Although he was busy hittin' switches, his mind was focused elsewhere. For one, he was thinking about why his mom felt it so important to call him back into the kitchen to tell him about the chance of a police return visit. He began to worry that maybe it was obvious to everyone where he was keeping his stash, further fueling his decision to move the Buick as soon as he returned home.

B.J. was also pondering the meeting with his connect, which was scheduled for later that day. He was meeting Papi as soon as he caught the rest of his sales and collected the rest of his money from Taye. He planned to purchase three keys. His last few purchases had only been for two and a half keys and he was proud of himself for stepping his game up. At $22,000 a piece, Papi was looking out for him, but since B.J. had been steadily increasing the quantities of his purchases, he felt Papi could give him a better price. He would bring it up later. B.J. rode without music all day, gathering his thoughts. As the day turned to night, he called Papi and put his order in.

"Whassup, Baby! I'll be thru there in about a hour."

"Alright, my friend. Just call me when you're on the way," Papi answered, happy to hear from one of his favorite customers.

"Alright, but listen. Remember last time when I told you the pictures wouldn't be ready for about two and a half weeks?" B.J. was speaking in their usual code.

"Yes, my friend. Mi remembre." Papi had a thick Spanish accent.

"Well, I just spoke to the girl and she said it's gonna be about three weeks instead of two and a half."

"Three weeks, huh. Okay no problem, my friend. I can handle that."

"So, I'm gonna get myself together and call you when I'm on the way," said B.J.

"Okay, my friend."

Now all B.J. had to do was wait for Taye, who owed him $13,500. "Yo, my man. I'm fresh outta cash and I'm tryna get a haircut. I need that change. Where you at?" B.J. got right to the point.

"I don't got no money on me. All my change is at the crib," Taye explained.

"I'll meet you at your crib in thirty minutes."

"Nah, I got a shorty wit' me. You know what I'm sayin'?" Taye was busy chilling with a girl he didn't trust enough to bring to his apartment, instead of handling business. B.J. didn't understand him sometimes.

"No, I don't know what you're sayin'," said an aggravated B.J. "All I know is I'm flat broke. I need to get that up off you."

"Man, meet me at my joint in thirty minutes."

"Cool."

B.J. already knew what Taye was going to do. He was going to bring the girl to his apartment anyway, rather than drop her off and take care of his business. This probably meant Taye had already sold the rest of his work and he decided to hang out with some random chick, before calling B.J. back. This from a guy who had 'M.O.B.' tattooed in huge letters down his spine.

Since B.J. had a little time to kill before heading to Taye's apartment, he drove to his house to get his money together for Papi. He got 43 g's out from his hiding place, behind the radiator in the corner of his room, and sat it on his bed. He already had $15,000 in the stash box of his car and he was to collect another $13,500 from Taye. He counted out 5 g's from his 43 and put it back in his hiding place, leaving 38 g's on his bed. In total, he'd be bringing Papi 66 g's for the three keys. He put the 38 g's in a plastic Foot Locker bag and stuffed the bag in his temporary stash spot—down the front of his pants.

When B.J. pulled up in Taye's apartment complex he was disappointed to see Taye in his Yukon with Jisella. Beautiful women were always Taye's vice. He had parked in one of the guest parking spaces rather than in his usual space that displayed his apartment number. B.J. took notice that he was smart enough to do that, but still he knew that before long Taye would have her in his apartment. Taye hopped out of his Denali and jumped in B.J.'s Caddy.

"What's good, playboy?" B.J. greeted him.

"Ain't nuttin'," Taye lifted his T-shirt revealing a medium sized Ziploc bag containing B.J.'s money. He handed the bag to B.J.

"This is twelve," he informed him. "I'll hit you wit' dat otha fifteen huned first thing tomorrow."

"What? Oh no. I'mma need dat fifteen cent tonight. This ain't even mine and dude been pagin' me all day about dat." That was the game; it was always somebody else's money or drugs, never yours. Taye was famous for trying to pay somebody in pieces and

B.J. knew that Taye had almost 50,000 upstairs in his apartment, so why was he trying to run B.J. around over fifteen hundred? B.J. had brought exactly enough money out of the house to pay Papi. He wasn't going to run all the way across town to his house for fifteen hundred with over $60,000 in his car. Sure, the money was secure in his built-in stash box, but still it was the principle.

"Aw come on, man," Taye pleaded. "You gonna make me go all the way upstairs again. I'm not tryna be doin' all that in and out. Plus, I got shawty in the truck. Next thing you know she gonna be wonderin' what I got up dere dat got me runnin' in and out."

"Man, listen. I ain't tryna hear no sob story. You shoulda grabbed it all one time. When you holla'd at me, I ain't say 'Here's 17 ounces and I'mma call you later and run you all the way across town to pick up one more.' No, you got all of yours at one time. Stop playin' wit' me, man."

"Man, you makin' me hot. Aight wait here."

He can't be serious. B.J. sat alone in his Caddy. *Here I am frontin' him quarters and halves for cheaper den I sell 'em and he goes and buys a big truck, then tells me I'm making him hot.* He looked over into Taye's truck and saw Jisella chatting on her cell phone. *All he's worried about is impressin' these chicks. He needs to be worried about impressin' me. I'm da one who's lookin' out for him.*

"Here you go, man," Taye said getting back in the Caddy and pulling a wad of money out of his jeans pocket with his right hand, holding two Coronas in the other. "So, when you gonna be straight again?" he asked, all in the same breath.

"The day after tomorrow," B.J. lied. "Holla at me." Taye got out of B.J.'s car grabbing the two Coronas he had bought with him and jumped back in his truck. He didn't even offer B.J. one. Not that B.J. would have accepted, but it was just the principle. B.J. pulled off to call Papi and tell him he would be arriving shortly. Taye handed Jisella one of the Coronas and pulled two Ecstasy pills out of his pocket, ready to enjoy the rest of his night.

Chapter 9

"How you gonna do it wit' him after you just did it wit' Randy less than a week ago. Dat's sad, you just met him. I don't care if he do got a Benz. What about the three week rule?" Nita and Free had concocted a three week rule after they lost their virginity back in their freshman year of high school. The rule stated that the girls would have to know a guy a minimum of three weeks before sleeping with him and after they did have sex with a guy, they had to wait at least three weeks before they were able to have sex with another guy. When Nita had sex with the guy with the Benz on their first date, she violated both principles of the rule. Her only justification was that he had sent her home with $300 in her pocket.

"I ain't tryin' to hear that," Nita retorted. "You just mad because your dude picked you up in a Ac and my dude picked me up in a Benz. Don't be J."

"What the hell I got to be jealous for?" Free asked.

"Just forget it," Nita responded, not wanting to argue.

It was forgotten. The girls were headed to the mall to do a little shopping. Free was tired of having to depend on Nita to go places and she was seriously considering trying to put enough money together to purchase her first vehicle. She figured she would have to do some serious saving because she had no intentions of riding around town in a beat up hoopty. The girls made

some light purchases, collected a few phone numbers and made their way back to Nita's house. Free's cell phone was filling up with new guys, as was Nita's. Once they were back at Nita's house, Free began to feel claustrophobic. She didn't necessarily feel like going home, but she didn't feel like spending the beautiful summer evening in Nita's bedroom. Just as she was deciding who wouldn't have a problem picking her up right away, her cell rang. It was Ed.

"Wassup Free? Are you at your girl's house?"

"Yeah, I am. Why? Where you at?" Free asked anxious to leave the house.

"I'm right up the street. Come outside in ten minutes."

"Okay." Free agreed not knowing where he was planning on taking her. All she knew is that they would be going somewhere, anywhere, it didn't really matter.

"Who was that?" Nita asked.

"That's my Ac coming to pick me up. What you got planned for the rest of the day?"

"I don't know. I'll probably just get in my car and ride somewhere. I might call that one dude I met at the mall earlier."

"Yeah, he was cute," Free told her.

"So, I see you're starting to change your mind about ya boy?" Nita asked, talking about Ed.

"I think he's cool. I mean it's not like that or anything. We just kick it."

"Oh, is that right? Well, you betta tell him to kick some money. Your time is valuable."

"Whatever, Nita." Free got off the bed, went over to the mirror and applied a thin coat of "Ooh Baby" MAC lip-gloss. She didn't wear a lot of heavy make-up, but she always made sure

her lips were well moisturized. Ed gave her his "I'm outside" call and she was on her way.

"See you later," she told Nita.

"Don't do nuttin' I wouldn't," Nita replied.

Free just looked at her. *Why does she always say 'don't do nuttin' I wouldn't', but when it comes to money, there doesn't seem to be very much she wouldn't do?* "Whatever," Free smirked then went outside. Ed was happy to see Free. Aside from the fact she was beautiful, he could honestly say that he genuinely enjoyed her company, even if they had only been out one time.

"Roll up," he commanded as soon as she shut the passenger door. That was exactly what Free wanted to hear. She pulled a honey flavored Phillie blunt out of her pocketbook and began to split it. "I want you to take a ride wit' me. You got a license, right?"

Free's guard went up immediately. Nine times out of ten when a guy asks a girl if she has a license, it's because he's dirty and wants her to drive. Even though Free had a perfectly legit license, she wasn't eager to hop in the driver's seat. It didn't matter, wherever Ed was trying to go, she had been down that road before. The last time a guy had asked her if she had a license she had ended up spending three months under house arrest and serving five hundred hours of community service. Still she found herself answering.

"Yeah, I got a license, where you tryna go?"

"Not far, not far at all. About an hour away. I just gotta go pick up a little suttin' suttin' from one of my boys," he said in an attempt to simplify things. She thought for a minute as she held out her hand for him to give her some weed to put in the blunt she was rolling. "You don't got no more of that fire?" he asked referring to the good weed she had sold him the night before. When she shook her head "no", he told her to call up whomever she had got it from. "We need some more of this," he stated

pulling the remainder of his bag from out of the console in between the two front seats.

"He don't got no more," she told him then grabbed the bag hoping he would not inquire further. "I bought the last bit," she added convincingly.

"Damn, that's too bad. So, let me know. Are we gettin' on the highway, or not?" They were approaching the Interstate entrance ramp and he had put her on the spot. She stopped sealing the blunt with her tongue and teeth.

"What's in it for me?" Free was no fool. She had dated and been around enough hustlers in her 18 years to know that they were willing to pay for anything they wanted or needed.

"You ain't easy now, you know. What's in it for me?" he mocked her. Ed never did answer Free, he just pulled into a nearby gas station to fill his tank. Free sat in the car waiting to spark the blunt once they pulled off. Free didn't want to be greedy, but driving back and forth an hours distance while dirty was worth at least $500 to her. When Ed got back in the car she decided that's what she would ask for. He came out of the store carrying a plastic bag containing two sodas and a box of blunts. Rather than walk to the driver's side, he came around to the passenger side. This threw her off guard. He opened her door and Free took that as her cue to get out and walk around to the driver's side. She adjusted the seat and all of her mirrors and they got on the entrance ramp, which was less than half a mile away. Ed sparked the blunt and reclined his seat all the way back.

"You comfortable?" he asked.

"Yeah, but I'd be even more comfortable wit' $500 in my pocket."

"Five hundred dollars?!" Ed asked in disbelief, wondering if she would back down.

"Yes, $500." Free looked him in the eye and held her ground.

"Alright, you got that," Ed agreed then passed her the blunt. He liked how thorough she was. "As a matter of fact, I'll do you one better," he told her.

"That's whassup," she said smoking and driving. She was relieved he went for the $500 and couldn't believe that not only was he going to pay it, he was talking about doing one better. *This is my day*, she thought.

They smoked two more blunts, talked about weed and rap music and by the time they looked up, Ed was telling her to get off at the next exit, Harristown Parkway. Free would always remember the exit because it sounded like her last name, Harrison. After a few "make a left's" and one or two "make a right", he was telling her to pull over on a residential street and park behind a white Ford Excursion. Free began to panic. Randy drove a white Excursion. She started to think she was being set up. *Oh my goodness! He knew where I got that weed from the whole time. That's why he kept asking me so many questions about it. I don't even know where I am right now. Nobody even knows I'm out here. I'm goin' down.* Her thoughts were racing and the weed she'd been smoking had her super paranoid. That's when her survival instincts kicked in. She began to look around at her surroundings and think of a way out of her present situation.

"Ma?" Ed called for the third time, breaking Free's state of panicked concentration.

"Huh?" Free returned to Earth and looked at him pleadingly.

"Pop the trunk," he demanded. She reached down on the side of her seat and lifted the lever to pop the trunk. "Gimmie 'bout ten minutes and I'll be right back." He got out the car, went around back to the trunk and retrieved a brown paper bag and then went into the house in front of where Free had parked. It was the longest ten minutes of Free's life. Nervous and impatient, she picked up the phone to call her best friend.

"Girl listen. Why I'm out wit' dude and he got me in the mid-

dle of nowhere. Girl, tell me why I'm outside this house he just went inside and guess what car is parked outside?"

"What car?"

"A white Excursion, girl. I am so scared right now and I don't even know where I am for real," Free confided.

"Oh my goodness. Why did you go wit' him? You don't think…"

"You don't want to know what I think. It's like the same exact Excursion, but I don't really know. Alright, get a pen and write down the address just in case anything crazy happens."

"Okay, but I'm drivin'. Just tell me what it is and I'll memorize it. I promise," Nita assured. For the first time since Ed went into the house, Free looked over at the small duplex in search of the exact address. She didn't see any numbers anywhere on the house.

"Wait a minute," she told Nita. She looked over at the house to the left and read the numbers 3220 and looked over at the house to the right and it read 3216. Then she squinted her eyes until she was able to read the corner street signs. "Okay it's 3218 Towson Parkway. I'm in the country somewhere. I'm not sure where," she admitted frantically.

"Alright, alright. Calm down. I got your back. What the hell are you doin' way out in the country?"

"Well…he…" Just as Free was about to explain everything to Nita, she felt a presence behind her and turned around. She had purposely positioned herself in the car with her back facing the house, so that if someone were inside looking out of the window, they wouldn't be able to get a clear view of her face.

"He's comin' out of the house. Call me back in five minutes and check on me."

"Okay, Baby. Be careful." *3218 Towson Parkway, 3218 Towson Parkway*, Nita thought. *Okay, I got it.*

"Everything alright?" asked Stephen. Nita had met the handsome, somewhat muscular second year college student a few days earlier and this was their first date. After Free left her house, Nita called him even though when she met him she vowed she wouldn't. Stephen was just a regular guy in Nita's eyes. He had no jewelry, no job, he lived on campus and Nita later found out that he didn't own a vehicle. She didn't discover he was carless until the end of their first phone conversation and by then she had already agreed to hook up with him. Rather than decline an offer she had already accepted, she agreed to pick him up from campus. They were on their way to Nita's favorite Mexican restaurant and Stephen kept asking Nita questions about herself in an attempt to get to know her better. After dinner they had plans to go to the movies and after the movies Nita was going to drop Stephen off and had no intentions of ever seeing him again. She was even entertaining the thought of calling Mr. Benz after she dropped Stephen off on campus.

"Yeah, everything is fine," she said without breaking the pattern of short answers she had been giving him. By the time they reached the restaurant five minutes had passed and she was calling Free back. *I'm so glad she finally got herself a cell phone*, she thought as she waited for Free to answer.

"Is everything cool?" Nita asked without wasting a second.

"Whassup, girl? I'm cool." Ed was back in the car and she did not want to let on that she had called her friend out of fear and desperation.

"Are you sure you straight?" Nita asked again.

"Yeah, girl. Call me later."

"So, that wasn't his truck?"

"No. Thank God. At least I don't think it was. I'll call you when I get home." Free pressed end, slipped her phone in her purse and looked over at Ed, who was rolling yet another blunt. "Do you think it's smart for us to be smokin' like this?" she asked.

"Free, baby, if we get pulled over the little bit of weed in this blunt is the least of our worries."

That was one way to look at it and he did have a point. Still, Free did not feel comfortable smoking especially when she did not know the contents of the bags in the trunk. As it turns out, Ed's 'lil' suttin' suttin'' was eighty pounds of mid-grade marijuana he had bought to the car in two oversized duffle bags and stuffed in the trunk.

"Well, what's in dem bags? Let me know what I'm ridin' wit'. It looks like you got two bodies back there."

He laughed hard. "Nah, it ain't no bodies in the trunk, Baby. What kind of guys you accustomed to dealin' wit'? It's just a little weed back there. Nothing more."

"Oh." Free was nervous, but confident. She would rather be driving than in the passenger seat. Although she didn't own her own vehicle, her driving game was up to par and after suffering so many consequences from being pulled over last summer, she told herself she would never be pulled over again. If she was stopped by the police right now she would be looking at some serious jail time, but the five hundred plus she was expecting to be paid kept her focused. It took every bit of her will power to not ask him how much he was going to pay her. She learned that you get more when you appear to want it less and something is always better than nothing. She didn't believe in counting money before it actually reached her hand, so she just relaxed a little and smoked the blunt when he passed it.

They made it back to the city safely and Ed told Free to drive to her house. When they arrived, Ed thought for a second, grabbed a striped long sleeved shirt from the backseat, told her to pop the trunk and jumped out of the car. After about a minute, Free heard the trunk slam and Ed returned. He passed her the striped shirt, which was now being used to conceal a pound of weed.

"Here you go, Baby. For your troubles."

Free was skeptical. She took the shirt from him, unwrapped it and when she discovered a large Ziploc bag full of bright weed, her eyes nearly popped out of her head. *Now, what am I supposed to do with all of this. Is he tryna be funny? I like to smoke, but it'll take me all summer to smoke all of this.* "Thank you," she managed to utter in the midst of her contemplation.

"It's nuttin'. Call me later." He signaling for her to get out of the car, so he could take care of his business.

Free hopped out carrying the shirt in one hand and reaching for her house keys with the other. *Now just my luck, Mom will be right at the door waiting for me.* But luck was on Free's side and Mrs. Harrison was stretched out on the sofa watching Law and Order. Her little brother, Mathew, was in his room with the door open chatting on the telephone. She rushed passed his room and into her's to put the shirt somewhere safe before coming back out into the living room to greet her mother and Mathew.

Back in her room, she sat at the foot of her bed, eyeing her new possession. Half of her wanted to call Ed and tell him that she didn't want it and she'd rather have the $500 she was promised. The other half of her knew what she had before her eyes was worth more than that. She began to wonder exactly how much it was worth. She figured it was one whole pound and she knew that Ed hadn't given it to her for her to smoke it all. He wanted her to sell it. At that very moment Free knew where she was going to get the money for her first car.

Hustlers are born, not made. Anybody could get his or her hands on a little piece of something, but not everybody could hold onto that little piece and turn it into something worth talking about. It's like a talent. Either you got it or you don't. Free had it in her all along, she just needed to get her hands on something that was worth something. Had Ed not put that first pound in her hand she would have gotten her first score elsewhere, sooner or later. It was just a matter of time. Now that she had something to start with, there was no turning back.

"Hey, whassup? What are you doin'," Free spoke into her cell phone.

"Me and my brother just chillin' around the way. What's up wit' you?"

"I want to talk to you about somethin'. I got some good news. Come thru."

"Good news?" Marky asked. "Alright, give me a minute and I'll be thru there. Where you at, Nita's house?"

"No, I'm at home."

"Okay, I'll call you when I get outside."

Free didn't really have a definite plan for the pound. The only scale she had was the one she weighed herself with and so she called someone she knew would be able to help her in that department. Since Free had been throwing him shade, Marky dropped everything and rushed over to her house. They hadn't had sex in almost three weeks and he thought maybe the good news was that she would be willing to give him some if he paid her the $300 he was supposed to give her last week. After all, that was the offer Nita had called Marco with. Marco quickly accepted and paid Nita. Still on the drive over, Marky told himself that he would only give Free two-fifty since she waited so long before calling him.

When Free got into the car carrying some type of striped cloth, he began to think his assumption was wrong.

"Can you take me around the way, so I can use your scale?" Free got straight to the point and was dead serious.

"What do you need a box for?" He said referring to his small digital unit.

"I got to break this down." She unfolded the shirt, revealing a compressed block of weed.

Marky was instantly impressed. It just so happens, his connect had been experiencing some kind of drought and neither he nor his brother had been able to get their hands on any decent looking pounds for weeks. That was the real reason they hadn't given the girls the concert money like they had promised.

"How much you want for this?" he asked with his face stuck in the bag.

It hadn't dawned on Free that she could sell the whole thing at one time. She was prepared to measure some into ounces and then bag some into dimes. Now that Marky was talking about buying the whole thing, she was beginning to realize how long something like that might take. In less than an hour she discovered a fact known to all hustlers. The break down is worth the wait, but you see your money faster when you sell weight.

"You could give me nine hundred," she concluded.

Marky took his nose out of the bag and looked over at Free. He felt a certain kind of way about spending his money with her, but there was no way he was leaving without the light green, near seedless brick on his lap. It was too good a thing for too cheap a price. He had to have it and much more of it, if possible.

"I'll give you eight, right now," he bargained, reaching into his sweatpants pocket.

If he'll pay eight, he'll pay nine. And technically he still owes me three hundred dollars. I shoulda told him a g. Free was a natural and it didn't take her very long to realize the only reason he was giving her a hard time was because they had a personal relationship. If he was dealing with his regular connect he would pay the price instead of sitting there trying to talk her down. She spotted his game and switched her approach accordingly.

"Look, this ain't even mine. The guy said he wants nine for it. If I sell it to you I'm not even makin' nuttin', but I'll do that as a favor to you. If you don't want it just let me use your scale so I can try to make somethin' off of it."

"Yeah, aight," he agreed then dug in his pocket. When he finished counting out her money he looked at her with one thing on his mind. Now that it wasn't hers and she wasn't makin' anything off of it, it was much easier for him to cop from her. He would rather pimp her than help her make a little money, even if he did need the weed.

"Listen," he continued. "You gotta call your boy cuz I'mma need more of dese."

"You are?" Free asked. She couldn't believe her luck. Not only had she sold the whole pound in less than an hour, she now had the potential to sell more. "How many more?" she asked in a calm voice, regaining her composure.

"About five. My brother might want five, too. So dats ten. But ain't no way we gonna pay nine hundred a piece. Call ya boy and see what he can do and den call me and let me know what he says. Okay?" he asked, now that he was finished giving orders.

"Okay," responded Free, letting it all soak in.

"And Free." By now she was out the car and standing on the sidewalk in front of her house. "It gotta look just like this," he warned.

"Dats whassup," Free confirmed. Slamming his car door, she walked towards the front steps of her house with Ed's empty shirt draped over her shoulder and Marky's $900 stuffed in her back pocket.

Chapter 10

"So you really not gonna do that for me?" Dana was having a hard time dealing with what she was being told. She had asked her older brother to buy her a pair of Giuseppe Zanotti boots and not only did he tell her "no", he didn't even offer to give her half of the money.

"Dana, *I* don't have $500 boots, so what makes you think I'm tryna buy you $500 boots. I just got your hair done for you and bought you a two-way. I love you, baby, but I don't got it like dat." She looked at him, speechless. B.J. had made his point. She grabbed her truck keys off of the kitchen counter and stomped out of the house. *Her leaving like that makes me think the only reason she came over here was to ask me for money. If she hadn't left with such a bad attitude, I would have offered to give her half the money in a few days. She need to be asking Mike for it,* B.J. thought as he fixed himself a turkey and cheese sandwich.

Dana reminded you of Ginger from the movie 'Casino'. She was well-liked by a lot of major moneymakers in town and she was a pro when it came to draining their pockets. Her walk-in closet was full of expensive shoes, clothes, purses, and more. She took pride in training her gold digging girlfriends with less experience than herself. Yet, with all of her winning assets, she couldn't loosen the grip Mike had on her, no matter how hard she tried. Mike was the sexy con artist with a big dick she had been with since her teens. Instead of using him, like she did

everyone else, she allowed him to run things with the remarkable power he possessed over her. Dana would meet a guy, milk him and then turn around and give it all to Mike. And Mike, he always had a story. Either he was waiting on a front, or waiting to re-up. He never had big money, but he had big dreams and to hear him tell it, the money was right around the corner.

"All I need is a g and I got this guy who's gonna look out for me," or "If I can just get my hands on a ounce 'cause we got dis spot around the way dats jumpin'. Give me a week and I'm gonna buy you suttin' real nice." Every time it was the same thing and every time Dana believed him. She stuck by her man through thin and real thin. One day, luck would come his way and when it did she would be right by his side, she thought. Dana paid the rent and all the bills in their one-bedroom apartment, which was where she went after leaving her mom's house.

B.J. sat eating his turkey and cheese sandwich, thinking about women and their ways. After growing up watching his older sister have her way with many different men, he vowed at an early age never to give his money to the women he dated. He wanted a girl he did not have to spend his money on. He wanted a girl that would love him for him and not the paper in his pockets. If he ever found a girl like that, well there was no limit to what he would spend on her. As he day dreamed about an honest, independent girl his two-way went off. Once again it was Kenya. She had been paging him nonstop for about a week.

When B.J. first spoke to Kenya after they spent the night together, she had invited him over to her house for dinner. For lack of anything better to do, he had agreed and asked for directions. After realizing she lived in one of the worst hoods, the only reason he showed up was because he wanted her to stop paging him. Kenya lived in the projects and B.J. didn't have a problem with that, what he did have a problem with was the fact that she answered the door dressed flawlessly, while her apartment was a complete mess. Magazines, clothing, CDs, and roaches were scattered across the living room. The carpet had so many stains he could barely decipher its original color. Her coffee table was cluttered and crowded, as was her sofa, and that

was just her living room. Her kitchen was filthy as well. Granted, she had just finished cooking for him, but some of the dishes in the sink looked and smelled as if they had been sitting there for days. He counted three roaches in the sink alone.

Needless to say, B.J. didn't enjoy the meal. He ate a portion of the soggy fried chicken, box macaroni and cheese, corn on the cob and biscuits and left shortly afterwards. That was the last time he had seen or spoken to Kenya and she had been paging him ever since. He decided to call her back this time, or else she wouldn't stop calling him all day.

"Hey, what's up?"

"Nothing," she answered. "I haven't spoken to you in a while."

Nothing? She pages me all week and when I finally take the time to call her back and ask her what's up, she tells me nothing. If nothing is up, then what the hell have you been paging me all week for? "I know. I've been kind of busy. Listen, let me call you right back."

"Make sure you do cause I gotta ask you somethin'," she informed him.

"Oh yeah? What you gotta ask me?" *What could she possibly have to ask me?*

"Well, if you busy, it could wait." She wanted to make sure the moment was right.

"Go 'head and ask me now."

"Well," she began. "Two of my clients canceled on me this week and my rent is due and I'm kinda short. You think you could help me?"

"Umm. I don't really got it like that. I'll see what I can do. Let me call you back."

"Okay, baby."

Money. I knew it was coming sooner or later. Now she need rent money. She betta figure somethin' out. She shorter than a midget on his knees cuz I ain't got it.

He had it. He had gotten rid of almost all of his last purchase from Papi and in a couple of days B.J. would be ready to see him again. All the money he collected over the past few days and the remainder of his coke was stashed away in his room. He had several sales to make that day and a few set up for tomorrow. By then he would have made eight thousand off each key, totaling the profit of his recent re-up to $24,000. Not bad for a few days work.

Although he was making money, B.J. didn't feel the need to shower people with expensive gifts, as did some hustlers. He didn't consider himself to be a baller, he considered himself a survivor. He had more money than the average 20 year old, but he didn't spend outrageously. Showing off the money he earned illegally would only draw attention, so B.J. refrained from making expensive material purchases. Yes, he wanted to enjoy the cash he risked his life everyday for, but he planned to enjoy a little over a long period of time rather than a lot of enjoyment over a shorter time period. It was longevity he sought.

If Dana had told him the money she wanted was for rent or some other necessity, she would have had a better chance at getting it. As for Kenya, who claimed she needed rent money, well he didn't feel as if he knew her well enough to be paying her rent. Especially after turning down his own sister. *One day I will find a girl who's smart enough to know that I could never give her more than she can give herself.*

Chapter 11

The "in" circle opened and allowed Free and Nita an entrance. They jumped in with both feet and didn't look back once. Within weeks, they began to gain popularity amongst the many hustlers in town and both of their cell's phonebooks were filling up fast. Nita was spending less nights at home and more nights out with the many different men she was meeting. The girls were coming up in the world.

Nita had made up for not hearing from Mr. Benz by dating other guys with vehicles just as luxurious as his, if not better. She never had a hard time spotting a flashy hustler but she now began to appraise the guys that she met more closely. With her good looks backing her, she weaved her way through the players in the game in search of the real big dogs. As of yet, she wasn't a jackpot winner, but she was sleeping with a few worthwhile mentionables.

Technically, Nita didn't formally charge these guys for sex, but then again she never came home empty-handed either. Sleeping with different guys and then asking them for money actually came quite natural for Nita. Ever since she had asked Free how much money she had left, she had been playing a game of catch up. After the episode with Randy, she told herself that the next time she gave up her goods for free, she would have a ring on her finger. In her mind, only the man that married her deserved to make love to her for free; everyone else had a price

to pay. She often reflected on how great it felt to shop with someone else's money. According to the new Nita, sex equaled shopping. She enjoyed having sex and viewed her recent activities as simply a way of making her ends justify her means. Nita didn't realize the depths of the vicious cycle she was now trapped in: using her physical body to gain materialistic rewards, which only attracted more men, who were interested in one thing—her body.

Meanwhile, Free was making a few connections of her own. Thanks to Ed and the twins she made almost $5,000 in less than two weeks. Ed had been giving her pounds of weed on consignment for $600 apiece. That was about a $150 cheaper than he normally sold it, but he figured that Free's pretty face would bring him more money from guys he would never have met otherwise. He saw hidden potential in her. Besides, Ed had taken a liking to Free and as it turned out, she hadn't fallen short of his expectations. He had been back and forth to her apartment in the past two weeks, dropping off a total of eight pounds.

Four of those pounds of good green she sold to Marky and the other four she sold to his brother, Marco. She had held her ground and made them pay $900 for each of them. They had pressed her to lower her price and when she didn't they continued to call. She profited $2,400 off of the twins plus, she still had $1,200 left from that night with Randy. That was not including the $900 she collected from the free pound Ed had given her. She was definitely feeling herself. She had access to something the twins wanted and needed. They begged to be introduced to her connect and promised to look out for her if she did. She knew that wasn't the smartest move, but still she told them that she would talk to him about it.

"Nita's here!" Mathew yelled upstairs to Free then sat right back in front of the television. It was the summer before he began eighth grade and lately, he wasn't doing much of anything until summer camp started.

"Come upstairs!" screamed Free. When Marco told Free about Nita sleeping with him for $300, she was shocked her best

friend had kept it from her. She planned on picking Nita to pieces once she arrived. It was Nita's idea to go out for lunch and she had even offered to treat. Nita rushed up the stairs leading to Free's bedroom, eager to surprise her best friend.

"Hey girl," she smiled, entering the room and giving Free a customary kiss on the cheek. They hadn't seen each other in four days.

"Ooh! Look at you," Free exclaimed. Nita was wearing a knee length white, cotton sundress and a dark gray leather Coach bag, but that wasn't Free's focus. Her eyes were on Nita's black and white G print Gucci wedge sandals and matching visor. The outfit looked fantastic on her and Free couldn't wait to ask. "Look at you," she repeated. "Where did you get those?"

"What?" Nita knew good and well that Free was talking about the hat and sandal set she couldn't wait to show off.

"Them sandals and that visor. What you thought I was talking about?"

"Oh, this?" She acted nonchalant. "I got these at the Gucci store. You like?" She pointed her foot and turned it to the side, admiring them as well.

"Yeah, those are hot. And you got the little visor. Okay, I see you." Free teased. She figured that was what Nita had done with the money Marco had given her, but she decided to bring that up over lunch. What she didn't know was that Nita had been busy sleeping with different guys and collecting money for the past two weeks.

Nita collected $300 from Mr. Benz, a couple of hundred from some random dude who called himself Sincere, along with the $300 from Marco. She had spent the rest of Randy's money on her new ensemble. Although proud about the little thousand dollars she had saved up, Nita couldn't help but be ashamed about the way in which she earned it. But hey, she felt like there was nothing wrong with doing a lil' something for something.

Nita's new outfit lit the fire that burnt a whole in Free's pockets. Free was saving up for a car, but she now had a sudden urge to shop. The only thing that stopped her from telling Nita to skip lunch and drive to the mall was the fact that she knew Nita was unaware of the amount of cash she was collecting. The twins had revealed Nita's secret, however Free felt confident that they hadn't done the same with hers. She was their new connect and they'd do anything to keep that secret. For the first time in eight years, the girls were keeping something from each other. One of Nita's secrets had been exposed, but not Free's, which gave her the upper hand.

Free began to feel underdressed. Her brand new all white Air Force ones, blue jeans and plain white T-shirt had her feeling inferior next to Nita's Italian designs. But what she had at home, sitting in her panty drawer, gave her a built in confidence. *Nita can afford to dress that way, she reasoned. She already has a car. I'm tryna get where she's at,* she thought on the way to the restaurant and fought back the urge to tell Nita to stop by The Avenue.

Once they were seated at Ruby Tuesday's, Free couldn't hold her tongue any longer. She looked passed Nita's innocent face and into her mischievous eyes.

"So, what's up wit' you and Marco?"

"Huh? Oh, we alright. Why you ask?" Nita was surprised by the question.

"Oh, no reason. I just thought we wasn't messin' wit' dem like dat no more."

"Girl, please. You know Marco is my baby," Nita smiled, looking at the menu and trying hard not to make eye contact with Free.

"Oh, okay." Free was holding back what she really wanted to say.

The rest of lunch was spent making plans for the weekend.

A few comedians were coming to town and the girls were thinking about attending the show. Like the 50 Cent concert, you had to dress up and Free wasn't sure she had a suitable outfit.

"Girl, you can just go and get something," Nita told her.

"Yeah, maybe." The waiters came with the check and Free reached for her back pocket.

"I told you it was my treat," Nita stopped her, reached in her bag and pulled out every dime she owned. Free couldn't help but notice and respond.

"Mmh! Must be nice," said Free.

"You know how I do," Nita beamed, placing the money plus tip on the table.

"No, I don't. Won't you tell me how you do, Nita."

On their way back to the car, Nita looked at her friend and wondered how much she knew. If Free knew she had been sleeping around and had basically thrown the three week rule out the window, she would have said something. Once inside of Nita's car they continued their conversation.

"I get down for mines."

"Do you?" Free loved Nita and didn't want her acting like a hoe. "But, do you get down for yours or go down for yours, 'cause there's a big difference, you know." Nita almost choked on her slurpee. She put it back in the cup holder then looked over at her best friend.

"What you mean by that?" Nita knew, but she wanted to hear Free say it.

"I mean, what the hell you been up to that you ain't been tellin' me about?"

"What!?" Nita played defensive. Free had a way of asking questions she already knew the answers to.

"You *know* what? Why you ain't tell me that you made Marco pay you $300 before you let him get some?"

"Why you keep bringin' up Marco? Just because his brother ain't givin' you no money, don't be J. I make moves like a shoe. Trust, I gets mines." Nita pulled down her sun visor and checked herself out in the mirror.

Free sat in the passenger seat with a silent smirk on her face. What could she say? That Marco and Marky was giving her all their paper and she hadn't taken her clothes off once. Already, she had five times the money Nita had and the potential to make more. She wouldn't tell her best friend that, or that she was acting like a two-hundred-dollar-hoe. "Whatever. Which one are we going to first?" Free pulled out the apartment listings. The girls were still talking about living together. They had already submitted one application at a complex ten minutes from their new school, but were still shopping around, just in case the two-bedroom townhouse they wanted wasn't available.

"We gonna try that one spot with the fire place and the balcony."

"Oh, alright." Free's mind was elsewhere. The twins were supposed to be calling her for two pounds later that night. She had already counted that $600 and now she was just waiting for her phone to ring. She was also thinking about how she could help out her best friend. Being the unselfish person she was, Free felt a little guilty about all the money she was making off of the twins. She wanted to include Nita, but that didn't seem like a reasonable option. Her guilty feelings were quickly replaced with the realization that Nita had been keeping secrets from her. Up to this point, the girls had never hesitated when it came to sharing the details of their sexual experiences. Nita's keeping the incident with Marco away from her only made Free assume the worst when it came to what other secrets Nita would keep from her.

RRRRING...

Nita answered her cell and after a very brief conversation, she immediately put on her signal and swerved into the far right lane.

"Where we goin'?" Free demanded. They were still three exits from their original destination. Nita exited the Interstate made a series of left turns and got back on the highway, going in the opposite direction.

"We gonna go check on the apartment tomorrow. I gotta go back home."

"Why? What happened?"

"Nothing serious. Just that my dude called and said that he wants me to meet him."

"I can't tell it's nuttin' serious. For a second there I thought we was in a car chase. He must be some kinda cute. What's his name?" Free asked. She knew the guy didn't have to be that cute for Nita to stop and drop everything.

"He's so cute. I met him at the Exxon last night when I was on my way home. He got this big blue Yukon. And the rims? Girl, the rims is crazy."

"So crazy that you couldn't tell him to come in a hour because you was takin' care of suttin'."

"Stop trippin'. Them apartments will be there tomorrow. So, what are you doing tonight? Stayin' in the house?" Nita quickly changed the subject before Free could get upset.

"Yeah probably," Free huffed.

They were quiet the rest of the way to Free's house. Nita had went out and bought the Gucci sandals and visor two days ago and she put it on this morning for her date tonight. She was beginning to take notice of the way certain guys were starting to give her more credit and attention than she was used to. High priced clothes made her a high priced broad and Nita took on

her new role with pride. When it came to the opposite sex she only had one question. 'How much can I get outta him?' Free broke the silence as they approached her block.

"So, where you and dude going?" She didn't really care she just wanted to see what her girl would say.

"Oh, I don't know. He just said he wanted me to meet him. I didn't think he was gonna be ready 'til later. I'll probably park and ride wit' him."

"Okay sweetie." Before getting out of the car, Free turned and looked Nita straight in the eyes. "Don't do nuttin' I wouldn't." She got out and slammed the door.

Before Nita even got off the block, the phone was at her ear. "Hey, where you at?"

"You ready?" asked Mr. Yukon.

"Yeah, where you wanna meet me at?"

"Uhh, come to the gas station I saw you at last night. How long are you gonna be?"

"About fifteen minutes."

"Alright, Boo."

Nita hung up and applied a coat of lip gloss and looked herself over in the sun visor's mirror. In no time at all she had parked her Honda on a residential street around the corner from the Exxon and was riding with her date.

"What's up, ma? Where you tryna go?" he asked.

"It don't matter. It's up to you."

"You smoke," he asked.

"No."

"You drink?"

"Yeah."

"Alright, we'll go to the liquor store."

"Dats cool."

"But listen, ma. I really ain't tryna ride around drinkin' so I'll just get us a room or suttin'."

"Okay."

And just like that they were headed to the hotel.

"So, what you drinkin', ma?"

"I like Alize, Bailey's, Hypnotic. Whatever, it's all good."

"Oh, alright."

When they arrived at the Super 8 Motel, he sent Nita in with $70 to rent the room. She paid then hopped back in the truck and handed him the key, receipt, and his change. They rode around to where the room was located and he handed the key back to her.

"Look ma, I'm gonna run ova to the liquor store and I'll be right back. You make yourself comfortable," he said with a smile that conveyed his hidden message.

He returned an hour later with a fifth of Hennessy, two liters of Vanilla Coke, a box of Corona Deluxe Dutch Masters and a box of Trojan condoms. He told Nita he'd only be able to chill for an hour or two and then he had to go. Actually, his new girlfriend had cooked for him and the food was ready and waiting at home.

"I thought I told you to get comfortable," he said placing some bags on the dresser.

"I am comfortable." Nita had only slipped out of her sandals and visor. She stretched back on the bed with the remote in hand, while her date fixed two strong Hennessy and Cokes. They drank and talked about themselves and what they wanted to do with their lives.

"I don't do much," he said. "I'm just tryna make money."

"Dats whassup. I'm just tryna make money, too."

"And how you tryna do that, ma," he looked over at her and asked.

"I don't discriminate, baby. Anyway I can."

He gulped down the rest of his drink. "Is that right?" He knew exactly what she was saying. He wasn't the type that had to pay for sex, but at the same time he didn't mind looking out for the girls that gave him some. He thought she was pretty and her white spaghetti strapped sundress turned him on like a light switch. By the time he finished his second drink, he would find out just how much she cost.

"You want another drink, ma?" He walked over to the dresser.

"Let me find out you tryna get me drunk," Nita laughed.

"Neva dat. I wouldn't want you to do anything drunk that you wouldn't do sober."

"Anything like what?" She kneeled on the bed looking at herself in the mirror across the room.

"Anything at all, ma. Anything at all." He slipped out of his Timb's and T-shirt, made them both a second drink, and lounged on the bed beside her.

"So whassup, ma?"

"You tell me." Nita said, taking a sip of her drink.

"You know what I'm tryna do." He stared at the box of condoms on the dresser making sure his point was clear.

"Well, I already told you what I'm about."

"And what's that?"

Nita held her hand up and rubbed her thumb across her fingertips.

"How much, ma?"

"My car note is due and I need $300," she said in her sweetest, sexiest voice.

For the first time he thought about her car and how he would have to drive her back to it when they were finished. *She chargin' me three hundred. I should just leave her ass here and make her take a cab.* "Aight." He reached in his jean pocket and counted out twelve twenties and one ten. "I got two-fifty, ma. Whassup?"

"That could work," she said taking the money out of his hand, indicating a done deal. They had sex and he left promising to return after he took care of some business. When he didn't, she spent the night alone in the hotel room and called herself a cab in the morning.

Chapter 12

"So, what you tellin' me for?"

"What you mean what I'm tellin' you for?"

"Look, ma, I'm kinda busy right now. I don't got time for no games."

"This ain't a game, B.J. If you come over here I'll take a test right in front of your face."

"I'll be thru in a hour."

B.J. was heated. First, this chick jumps on his dick raw dog. Now, she's calling talking about she's pregnant. *She can't be,* he thought. *And if she is, it ain't mine.* He figured her for the type who would fake a pregnancy just to come up on some 'abortion' money. Before, it was rent money and this time it's abortion money. *This chick got all the sense.* He had a few stops to make then he would go pick her up for lunch. That's after he went inside and watched her pee on a stick, right in front of his face.

B.J.'s first stop was meeting Taye at the car wash. Not only did Taye owe him $2,500, but he also said that he had to holler at him about something. By the time he finished dwelling on Kenya's phone call, he had pulled up at the car wash, parked and was now riding with Taye.

"WDUP, Dawg?" Taye greeted him once he was seated in the passenger seat.

"What's good, Baby?"

"Roll up." Taye lifted the door on the arm-rest compartment, B.J reached in and grabbed a box of Corona Deluxe. He split the blunt and started to roll up some hydro he brought with him.

"This is some fire," he said passing a rather large bud over to Taye for closer examination.

"Yeah, that is some killa. Call ya boy. I need some of dat in my life," Taye said.

B.J. made a call and put the order in. He told Taye they would have to ride across town to pick it up, but neither of them had a problem with that. It gave them ample time to smoke and talk.

"I got that money for you," Taye said reaching for his pocket, but not going in it. "I'm just tryna get my money together for this power move I'm about to make." He looked over at B.J. to be sure his words sunk in. As usual, B.J. was expressionless. He never let his emotions show, especially not on his face. You never knew what B.J. was thinking, even when he did open his mouth. "I got a thing about to hop off. I'll let you get down if you want. You know it's all love."

"Get down? Get down wit' what?" B.J. passed the blunt.

"I got a good thing hoppin' off wit' my peoples. Shorty said I could get dem things for like eighteen. Eighteen, Dawg. That's so gravy. You could get down if you want."

"Who is this shorty? Is it official?" B.J. was immediately skeptical. Anyone who could offer a kilo for just $18,000 deserved questioning. Especially, if they were right here in town. Eighteen thousand was cheaper than Papi's price and B.J. had been dealing with Papi for five years. Who could offer such a price?

"This shorty I been dealin' wit'. Her peoples is official. Straight like dat. And we ain't got to go nowhere."

"Word?"

"Word. I'm getting' two, but she said if I get three they'll drop it like it's hot. Seventeen. Now dats gangsta."

"Yeah, dat is gangsta," B.J. had to admit. "Who is shawty? Anybody I know?"

"Remember that Spanish mami I met at Macho's last month. Shorty got the connect."

"Oh, alright. That sounds good, but I'm cool. I really ain't tryna deal wit nobody new. But take your time though. Eighteen, damn that sound real decent." B.J. knew exactly who Taye was talking about—Jisella. He remembered that he didn't trust her that night either.

"I know, right," Taye gleamed then passed the blunt, proud of his new connect. Up until now, Taye's connect was B.J. That was the origin of their relationship. Now with Taye finding his own connect, things would change. All B.J. could think about was 18g's, 18g's and 18g's. If he didn't know better he would have told Taye to order him four of those things. But he wasn't about to jump out there like that. He would let Taye test the waters first and if all was well, he might consider joining him. All B.J. could hear was a voice saying, "If it ain't broke don't fix it." When a person already has a hold of something and they try to grab more, half of the time they are going to drop what they already had a hold of. Don't be greedy, he told himself. The $4,000 difference was not worth the risk and stress that came along with dealing with a new connect.

"That's why I'm tryna get my scratch together. I'm scrungin' my pennies. Her people supposed to be here the day after tomorrow." Taye eyed B.J. hoping he was catching his drift.

B.J. passed the blunt. "Just take your time." By this time they were arriving at the weed spot. Taye gave B.J. $125 and B.J.

returned with a quarter ounce of fresh dro. He rolled up another blunt, this time out of Taye's bag and they were on their way back across town.

"Remember that pretty brown-skinned chick I left Macho's wit' that same night you met shorty?" B.J. asked.

"Yeah, wit' da Manolo's. What was her name again?"

"Kenya."

"Yeah, that's right. The one who woke up hungry." They both laughed. B.J. abruptly put an end to the laughter.

"Well, why the chick called me today talkin' about some she's pregnant?"

"What?" Taye was halfway serious.

"Did I stutter? The chick called me earlier talkin' about some she need to talk to me and it's important. Then she hits me wit' dat joint. Man, listen."

"I got her frontin', tryna come up on three-fifty. Damn, pregnant? I thought she woulda hit you wit' da rent money joint before the abortion joint."

B.J. looked over at his boy. "Man, she did hit me wit' da rent money joint. I told her I ain't have it."

"Have you seen her since that night?" Taye was finding B.J.'s situation humorous.

"Yeah, yo, I went over her crib one night, but I ain't stay though. That joint looked like it ain't been cleaned since the seventies. That hoe is gonna be alright by her damn self cuz I ain't foolin' wit' her."

Taye couldn't help but chuckle. It was hard for him to be serious. He was feeling himself so much lately, it would take a lot to alter his mood.

"So what you gonna do?" he asked.

B.J. had it all figured out. "I'm gonna stop and get one of those pregnancy test. I'm gonna ride over there and make her take it right in front of me. I mean, I'm gonna go in the bathroom with her and everything. When it turns out negative, just for lyin' to me, I'mma tell her ass don't call me no more. I was gonna take her to get something to eat, but I might don't even do dat."

"And what if it doesn't come out negative?" Taye passed B.J. the blunt and looked at him. B.J. sat with the idea for a few seconds, taking a pull on the near perfectly rolled cigar.

"Dawg, what part of she's lyin' you don't understand? She's just out for money and that's exactly why she can't get none. If she woulda been straight up instead of comin' at me sideways den..."

"Speakin' of straight up. I had this cute, fly little chick the other night. You wanna talk about straight up? Shorty straight up charged me like I'm some trick. That's alright cuz when I hit then split, she figured out she was dealin' wit' a pimp. Too bad, cuz she was real pretty, too."

"We don't love dese hoes." B.J. did his best Snoop Dog imitation.

Back at the car wash, B.J.'s baby blue Caddy was sparkling and waiting for him. Taye started in with his sob story about how he was gonna pay B.J. the last $2,500 after he made his power move in two days. He claimed he needed every dollar because he barely had enough money for the two keys he had ordered. B.J. told him that that was his thing and he wanted nothing to do with that.

"I got you," Taye pleaded.

"Don't got me. Get me." B.J. warned. Taye knew he was serious, so he dug in his pocket for the rest of the money he owed, which was already wrapped in a single rubber band.

"About that thing wit mami-" B.J. said getting out of the truck.

"What?" Taye interrupted before B.J. even had a chance to finish his sentence. He just knew B.J. was about to ask to be put down.

"Take ya time, Dawg."

"Always."

B.J. over tipped the two workers who had shined his Cadillac and hopped in headed for the drug store. He had a sale waiting, but his coke was all the way at his house and he was eager to handle his business with Kenya first. She wasn't getting any money out of him and he was going over there to tell her just that. If she wanted to charge him she should have thought about that before she slept with him. Now, it was too late and she couldn't get a dollar out of him.

"I'm on the way." He phoned Kenya and pulled up to her place minutes later. Grabbing his freshly rolled blunt and CVS bag, he and bopped his way over to her door.

"Hey, whassup, baby?" She opened the door wearing only a red DKNY T-shirt.

"Hey, ma. You mind if I smoke dis?" he asked removing the blunt from behind his ear as he walked in.

"Sure, go right ahead." She was thrilled, thinking he planned to stay longer than the time it would take to view the pregnancy test. "Do you want something to drink?" She was trying to be a good host. He looked around and noticed her apartment was still in shambles. He found himself a seat on a recliner with nappy upholstery and reached in his sweatpants pocket for his lighter.

"No, I'm good. Do you need something to drink?" he looked over at her. She had taken a seat on the sofa opposite him. Her hair was pulled up in a loose, last minute ponytail and her face

was natural. As mad as he was, he had to notice her beauty. And all she had was a T-shirt and panties on.

"Huh?" she asked in a cute, ditsy kind of way.

"Huh?" he mocked her. "Do you need anything to drink before you take the test, ma?"

"I told you I already took the test. Let me go get it." Kenya rose off the couch and walked over to the bathroom. He took a pull on his blunt and just watched her walk away. She came back with a pregnancy test that had two pink lines in the result window. She handed him the test and then the box it came in and pointed to where the two pink lines declared a positive result. B.J. was not convinced. He had heard stories of conniving girls using their pregnant girlfriend's urine to fool a guy into believing she was pregnant. Something about the test she handed him didn't look right. He asked again. "Do you need anything to drink, or do you already got to pee?"

"So you want me to take another one and you got the one I just took right in your face? What you think, I used somebody else's pee?"

Here we go, he thought. "You said it, not me."

"Well, I only bought one test, so..."

B.J. nodded in the direction of the kitchen counter where he had placed the CVS bag. She walked over to the counter and snatched the test out of the bag.

"Oh! So you went and bought another test after I told you I already took one. Well, I don't even know if I have to pee now."

Here we go, he thought again. "Back to my original question, do you need somethin' to drink?" B.J. asked calmly.

Kenya didn't answer. She just stood there staring at him. When she realized he wasn't going to crack a smile or speak, she poured herself a glass of faucet water. She drank the entire

eight ounce glass in two gulps, with an attitude, then looked over at the handsome fellow, who had been giving her a hard time. Looking at him she wanted nothing more than to be his girl and wondered why he wouldn't want to be with someone as pretty as herself. Kenya wanted desperately to get to know B.J. and become an important part of his life.

"So, what you got planned for the rest of the day?" is all she could think of in an attempt to engage him in conversation while they both waited on her bodily fluids.

"Nuttin' really. Why? You hungry?"

Lookin' at her exposed legs and pretty face, he was having a hard time remembering the purpose of his visit. His dick was getting hard and his weakening willpower was trying to stop him from lifting her T-shirt to find out what kind of panties she had on, or if she had on any at all. He leaned back further and continued to smoke.

"Yeah, I am kinda hungry. You wanna get something to eat?" She had eaten at KFC less than two hours ago, but how could she not take him up on his semi-offer? As pissed as he was at her for making him come over there, B.J. could not deny his attraction to her. She was so sexy in a high saditty kind of way.

"Yeah, we could do that." They both knew these were the last minutes of neutral time they would share. Once Kenya went in the bathroom to take the test, everything would be different. If she came back out with a negative result, he could no longer respect her. How could she stoop so low for a couple of hundred dollars. It was highly unlikely she could take one test and it come back positive and then take a second test a few minutes later and that one come back negative. If she came out the bathroom with a positive test result and tried to say it was his, B.J. felt that was highly unlikely, too. Either way it went, after Kenya took the pregnancy test, B.J. was not trying to hear anything she had to say.

"Well, go 'head and handle that, ma. I'm kinda hungry, too."

B.J. told himself he would take Kenya to lunch and then let her down easy. She would have to stop beating his phone down and he decided being truthful with her was the best way to handle this. She walked her fine ass into the bathroom, test in hand. B.J. smoked and relaxed. He decided against going in the bathroom with her. While she might have used someone else's urine for the first test, he doubted she would go through the trouble of saving the urine in anticipation of a second test. If she did have another positive result, he would make her take a third test and that's when he would stand watch over her. For now, he just smoked and listened to her pee trickling onto the absorbent stick. *Now what kinda crap is she gonna come out the bathroom wit'?*

Inside the messy bathroom, Kenya was aiming her urine and making speculations as to what kind of guy she had gotten herself involved with. *I can't believe he got me takin anotha test like he ain't buss all up in me that morning.* She wiped herself, flushed the toilet and hurried out of the bathroom with the test. She placed it on the kitchen counter and sat back down directly across from him. She didn't speak. He inhaled and looked at her with an indescribable look on his face. He felt cheated as if she was somehow trying to get over on him. B.J. broke the awkward silence. It was evident Kenya wasn't going to.

"Whassup?"

She didn't answer. She only nodded in the direction of the test, just as he had moments earlier. He did not get up and rush over to the counter as she expected. Instead he leaned forward on the chair to pluck ashes from his blunt in an ashtray on the coffee table. There he found at least half a dozen cigarette butts. He eyed them, then her.

"I see somebody was ova here smoking like a chimney."

One of Kenya's many male friends had spent the night and Kenya, who was usually on point about those type of things, had neglected to empty the ashtray. *Why is he tryna change the subject?* she thought. "Oh, my cousin came ova last night. He smokes a lot, doesn't he?"

"Yup, your cousin sure does."

"Yeah, let me dump this."

B.J. watched as she walked over to the garbage in the kitchen and dumped the ashtray. Not once did she even look in the direction of the counter. Inside he began to panic. Her failure to glance over at the test, reflected her confidence in the result. B.J. was taking a mental note of his pocket money. He calculated that he had enough to take her to lunch and give her $350 without touching the money Taye had given him.

"You ready?" he asked, finally rising off of the chair and placing the end of his blunt in the now empty ashtray.

So, he's not even gonna look at the test?, she thought. "Yeah, let me just slip on some jeans and grab my pocketbook."

So, she's not even gonna tell me to look at the test. B.J. couldn't believe this chick.

Kenya stood right in front of him and slipped into a pair of jeans that she had laying on the couch, some flip flops and grabbed her pocketbook from a hook in the hallway. B.J. made his way over to the door. Before he reached the door he stopped at the counter and picked up the test. He placed the test back down on the counter, gazed his deep brown eyes over at her and walked out of the door with Kenya following closely behind. Once they were in his Caddy, he dug in is pocket, counted out $350 and then passed it over to her.

"Take care of that," he instructed, pulling out of the parking lot. Kenya was dumbfounded. She counted the money, slipped it in her bag, and turned to him.

"Thank you," she told him sweetly.

"So, you gonna take care of that, right?" he asked seriously.

"Take care of what?"

"You know what, ma. You gonna get rid of that problem, right?"

"Huh? No, honey. I am not murdering my baby."

Here we go. Without saying a word he blasted Ja Rule's 'Venni Vetti Vicci' CD and they rode.

"You like Chinese food?" he asked. Regardless of whether or not she liked his favorite kind of food, they were already around the corner from the restaurant.

"Yeah, dats cool."

They sat, ate, and didn't talk much. B.J. was feeling a certain kind of way based on Kenya taking his money and not planning on using it for its intended purpose. At the end of the day she had still gotten him for three-fifty. He was upset about that and pissed about the fact that Kenya was pregnant and claiming that he was the father. There wasn't much he could say in the way of denial. He remembered vividly the morning he had let loose inside of her, some kind of crazy. He had a bad feeling as soon as he woke up with his dick in her mouth.

After leaving the restaurant, B.J. wasted no time dropping Kenya off. She had an attitude because B.J. hadn't spoken two words in her direction since they left the apartment.

"So, you don't have anything to say to me?" she asked before getting out of his car.

"Take care of yourself, ma." B.J. didn't even look at her.

"Take care of myself? What you mean by that?" she said raising her voice.

"Use that little money to take care of yourself."

"Yeah, aight."

What did she want him to say? What did she want him to do? She insisted on making him a father against his wishes, so what

did she really expect from him? He would be there for baby and love the baby, but Kenya? She had nothing coming. He was mad at her for jumping on top of him that morning. He was mad because he had always dreamed about marrying the mother of his kids and he did not consider her to be marriage material. He was mad because his mother's prophecy was coming true. He would be making his mom a grandmother before his sister, Dana.

B.J. was on his way home to pick up four and a half ounces for a sale he had waiting. Once he got there he went straight to his room, as usual. He didn't break the news to his mom just yet. He didn't want to acknowledge it with hopes that it would disappear. However, that was not to be the case.

First, B.J. put up the money he had collected from Taye. Then he dug in an Adidas shoebox he had in the far left corner of his closet and retrieved the remainder of his busted down brick. He was enjoying the convenience of keeping his product right there in his room, but at the same time it was making it a little harder for him to sleep at night. The hoopty was repainted and had been parked in front of the house for weeks now. He had just been too busy to get around to relocating his stash from the back of his closet to the Buick. He opened the Adidas box and retrieved a medium sized Ziploc bag. He folded the top of the bag and was about to stuff it in the front of his pants, when he noticed something. The powder had begun to leak out of the bag. He was positive that he had sealed the bag before he put it up, so he was having a hell of a time figuring out why it was now open. His instincts told him to reweigh the bag before bringing it to his customer. He went for the scale under the bathroom sink, only to find that he now had his hands on four ounces rather that four and a half. *Here we go.* His customer was expecting four and a half ounces and four ounces would not do. He would either have to take a short on the $3,500 he was expecting to collect or crack open one of the bricks he had taped to the back wall of his closet.

While he was busting down the brick, the wheels in his mind were burning. How did the sack go from four and a half ounces

to four ounces? He went over his calculations to be sure he had subtracted the right amount of weight for the Ziploc bag. He did. He reweighed the sack for the fifth time just to be sure he was reading the scale correctly. He was. He broke half an ounce out of the fresh key then rewrapped it, stuffing it in the back of his closet. He reweighed the original bag, which was now the correct weight his boy was expecting. B.J. secured his belongings and made his way back out to the car. All that was on his mind was, *how does an half an ounce just disappear?* He could have lived with a few grams coming up missing, but a whole half an ounce? That was too great and too precise an amount. It was not so much the $400 loss that troubled him as it was the unexplainable disappearance. Now he felt like he had given Kenya seven-fifty instead of three-fifty. In the game there were no coincidences and more often than not, things that were lost were actually stolen. A whole fourteen grams missing. There was only one explanation and it hurt B.J.'s heart to think that someone in his family would steal from him.

What is done in the dark…

Chapter 13

Things were going well for the girls. They were basking in the glory of the come up. Their apartment was lovely and they were working on getting it fully furnished. Each bought their bedroom set from home and were now waiting on their living room furniture. They had ordered a 52-inch screen T.V. and a two piece leather sofa set from Rent-A-Center. Their bill was an accommodating $37 per week, which left them with plenty of money for other expenses. Their $640 rent included utilities and their only other expenses would be the telephone and cable bills. That seemed easy enough for them to handle.

Nita had been giving Big Nita $100 every week or so and promised to continue even after she moved out. Both Big Nita and Mrs. Harrison wished their girls the best with their new apartment. As it turned out, they were able to get the apartment in Nita's name. Being a college freshman and 18, Nita was easily approved by the flexible apartment complex resident manager. As a housewarming gift, Mrs. Harrison purchased an 8-piece pot set and 24-piece dish set for the girls. Big Nita took the girls to Wal-mart and spent over $200 on groceries, kitchen and bathroom accessories. Everything was falling into place and all they were waiting for now was the furniture delivery. One of Nita's guy friends, Stephen, had even promised to use his credit card to buy her a DVD player.

Stephen was the college sophomore Nita had been playing

to the left. Every time he called for a date, she either didn't answer or was too busy to oblige him. Stephen persisted to no avail. He saw through the expensive attire and genuinely wanted to be with her. He was attracted to her natural beauty, assertiveness and intelligence. He couldn't wait for the semester to start so he would have the chance to spend more time with Nita. And Nita? She couldn't wait for the semester to start so she could have an inside scoop on all of the college parties. However, it wasn't the college guys she was after. No, Nita wanted hustlers, plain and simple. Guys with lots of money turned her on and she had become a gold digger overnight.

Never mind the fact that Stephen was majoring in Pre-Med and was prepared to offer her anything she would need. Never mind the fact that Stephen saw in Nita a girl he could grow with and be loyal to. He wasn't interested in what kind of jeans she had on or whether or not he could get in them. He wasn't interested in what kind of car she drove and whether or not she could chauffer him around all day. Without desperation, Stephen wanted Nita and he felt that no female he'd met as of yet could compete. He appreciated her light brown, almond-shaped eyes, high cheekbones and creamy complexion. He thought that the freckles on her upper cheeks were cute, in a little girl kind of way. Her urban edge complemented his old fashioned demeanor. While Stephen couldn't necessarily buy her all that she may have wanted, there was nothing she needed he could not provide. He saw in her beautiful face a girl his mother would be proud to claim as her daughter-in-law. All Nita saw was a free DVD player.

Dozens of guys were lined up at Nita's door, but like Free, when it came to true male companionship, she was lonely. Free had made two new male acquaintances, but she considered them to be nothing more than customers. They were purchasing several pounds of good green from her every week. Every time one of their names appeared on her caller ID, she counted $300. Ed had even let her borrow his 1992 Sonata from time to time, which she was in the habit of using to make deliveries. They had even talked about him selling her the car, but were still negoti-

ating the price. To be honest, Ed wasn't sure if he wanted to get rid of his little hoopty.

Ed called Free and needed to meet with her immediately. She had a good idea what he wanted. It had been a little over a week since she drove him to re-up for a second time and according to her calculations it was about that time again. He had paid for her time and troubles with another pound of weed and Free was looking forward to her payment for their third trip out of town. She already had someone waiting to buy the pound of good green and mentally added that $900 to her growing stash. All that was left to do was take the trip. Ed knew the location of her new apartment and would be arriving shortly. Free told Nita she would be back a little later and went outside to meet her boy.

"Whassup, Free?"

"What's good, Baby?"

"You know where I'm tryin' to go," said Ed, sure she knew what he wanted.

Yes! "Huh?" she asked, not wanting to sound too eager.

"You know exactly where I'm tryin' to go," he repeated then looked at her and hopped out of the car. He walked over to the passenger's side and opened the door for her. What could she do? Instead of getting out, she climbed over the arm rest and into the driver's seat. Ed got in, impressed by her gangsta, pulled a blunt out of the ashtray and reached for his lighter.

"Why you still sittin' here, Free? You know where the highway is."

They were off. Once they were on the Interstate, Ed dropped the bomb on her.

"You know this trip is on the house."

"What?" she asked even though she had heard him loud and clear.

"What?" he mocked her. "I said this one is on the house. You scratch my back, I'll scratch yours." He passed her the blunt. What could she say? He had been looking out for her a great deal by giving her the weed for so cheap and allowing her to drive his car to get rid of it. She was grateful, but still the little voice in her head was telling her she should not be taking the trip for free. *There goes my $900,* she thought. Now she was counting what she planned to make off of the pounds they were on the way to retrieve.

This time, Ed didn't have to tell Free which exit to get off. Not only did she remember the exit, she had a pretty good idea of which turns to make. When they arrived she saw the same white Excursion parked in the same place it was on their previous visits. This time it didn't bother her as much and she was even able to relax while Ed went inside to handle his business. Within minutes he returned to the car with two large garbage bags and Free had the trunk open waiting for him. He jumped in and they were on their way back to town. They hadn't even been there for ten minutes.

On the way back they smoked and talked. Business blossomed their relationship and their pockets at the same time. Ed was gaining a liking for Free. He respected her work ethic. No matter the time of day or night, whenever she had a sale, she didn't hesitate to pick up the phone and tell Ed that she needed to meet with him. Ed was all business and his heart went out to anyone who was coming up off an honest hustle. Not to mention, that she was getting rid of his work and now driving him to re-up, free of charge. Of course, he wanted to see her succeed.

"I hope you not spendin' up your money only shoppin', shoppin' about," he inquired. The statement sort of threw her off guard. On the one hand her hustler instincts kicked in and caused her to question his motives. *Why is he worried about what I'm spendin' my money on? It's none of his business.* On the other hand her girlishness challenged those thoughts. *Aww! Let me find out he's concerned about how I'm spending my money and doesn't want me to spend it foolishly. He cares enough to not want me broke and desperate.*

"No, I'm not goin' shoppin' wit' my little money," she replied humbly. "I'm actually tryin' to save up to buy me a car since I see you ain't tryna sell me yours. You know I start school in a few weeks."

"Dat's good, Baby. What you mean little money? You getting...I mean you should be doin' alright."

She knew exactly what he was getting at. He wanted to know what her pockets was looking like and she wasn't about to tell him. Flipping the script, she put him on the spot.

"Yeah, I'm doin' alright, but I'd be doin' even betta if you dropped that price and gave me a betta number to work wit'."

He laughed. Free was learning fast. Actually she just repeated a line one of her customers had thrown at her. She had run across two new customers while going on an occasional date here and there. She had pulled out her personal smoke sack and boasted about its potency. On both occasions, after a close examination of the product, the guy agreed and before the night was over, they were asking where they could get some of their own. Now, she had a total of four customers who called her at least twice a week to cop a pound, or two, or three. With the price she was getting them for, she was doing alright. She had more than enough money to cop a decent used car and still keep her side of the bills around the house paid. She now had her hands on more cash money than she had ever possessed in her entire life.

Ed never addressed the subject of lowering his price. However, he did send Free in the house with four pounds and told her to call him when she was finished with them. She was satisfied with the advance and appreciated the trust he had in her. Actually, he was actually tired of having to drive all the way to meet her every time she called. This way things worked out better for him and he didn't see her as the type that would try to steal from him. Free was grateful and counting the $1,200 profit she planned to make.

"Okay, Ed. I'll call you tonight so I can meet you and bring you dat."

"No doubt."

Free grabbed the blue Wal-Mart bag containing the four pounds and made her way to the front door. It wasn't until she put her key in the lock that her mind started to ponder places to keep the weed. Up until that point, she had only had one or maybe two pounds in her possession at one time. Now that she had twice that amount it wouldn't be as easy to hide the weed or the noticeable scent it produced in her room.

Free opened the front door to find Nita entertaining three rough looking young men, who were sitting on the living room floor watching videos. Nita had dragged the 32" inch television out of her bedroom and into the living room for the occasion. Not, expecting company, Free was thrown off when she entered her apartment. She felt like her thin Wal-Mart bag was completely see-thru and everyone in the room knew what she was carrying. She was annoyed, didn't feel like talking, and headed straight for her room. Nita stopped her in her tracks.

"What's wrong wit' your cell? I called you like ten times."

"Huh?" Now Free had to stop and talk. If she rushed off to her room, she would raise suspicion. So she sat her bag on the floor in the kitchen and went into the living room to chat briefly. "Oh, I don't know. I didn't get any calls. My battery is probably dead." Sure enough, she reached inside her purse for her cell and it was turned off. "Yup, my battery went dead. Let me go put this on the charger."

She grabbed her bag off the kitchen floor and all eyes were glued to her as she made her way down the hall to her room. Nita was so worried about what Free was carrying and why she didn't answer her phone that she hadn't even introduced her to the three guys sitting in the living room. Free slid her package under her bed, put her pocketbook on the bed, her phone on the charger and went into the hall bathroom. She didn't need to use

the toilet, but she didn't want to go straight into the living room either. She looked in the mirror, flushed the toilet, wet her hands then finally returned to the front room. All eyes were on her.

"This is Dee, Los, and this is Black," Nita announced, giving Free a formal introduction. Judging from the introduction and the look of things, Nita appeared to be paired off with the dude named Black, the best dressed and most handsome of the three, which didn't say much because all of them looked as if they hadn't showered in days.

"Hey," Free replied, disinterested. She went into the kitchen to get herself a glass of red Kool-Aid.

"So?!" Nita came into the kitchen on her heels.

"So, what?" Free asked praying she wouldn't inquire about where she had been or what she had in the bag.

"So, which one do you like? Black is my dude, but the other two are free and they both want to talk to you. They want you to pick one. I think the one with the Yankees cap is the cutest but it's not up to me."

"I don't know, girl. I really didn't get a good look at them but I think I'm good. Where did you meet them?"

"Well," Nita thought back. "Black was with some guys that was with Shamika and Nicole. When I first met him I wasn't feeling what he had on, but now I think he's kinda cute."

Free decided to indulge her in conversation rather than share her genuine thoughts about the visitors. "What did he have on?"

"Not much of anything and his sneakers had the gangsta lean. They were so run over I thought me eyes were playing tricks on me."

"Really?" They both snickered.

"Come on let's go see which one you want?" Nita suggested.

They walked into the living room and Free examined the two available guys closely and decided she wanted neither. She just wasn't feeling either of them and she saw no reason to pretend. The one with the Yankees fitted cap was the cuter of the two, but under his cap was a gray looking durag that was once white. In fact, everything about him and his crew looked dingy.

"What's up, Free?" Los, the guy with the dirty durag, greeted her. She didn't want to sit and talk with him and luckily the ringing of her cell phone saved her. Up until that moment she had forgot about the package waiting under her bed to be sold and paid for.

"I'll be right back. Once in her room, she picked the phone up from the charger and was able to recognize from the caller ID that it was, Juwan, one of her new customers. "Whassup, Baby?" Free smiled.

"What's goin' on? You straight yet?" He had been waiting for her call all day.

"Yeah, where you at?"

"Why you ain't call me? I been callin' you all day."

"My bad. I had to go take care of that for you. Where you at?"

"Umm. I'm around my mom's house. Can you come through here?"

"Yeah, I could do dat. How many T-shirts you want me to bring?" she asked.

"Well, I need two and my boy needs one. And I might need another one cuz my other boy around here talkin' about he might want one, but he got to see it first. If it's the same like last time then he's probably gonna get it. This dude got the scratch, but he's real picky, na'mean? But I definitely know I need three."

"Alright, I'll see what I can do. Give me like fifteen minutes and I'mma call you when I'm on my way."

"Okay. One."

That worked out well. She had exactly four and if they didn't buy but three she would just call one of the twins while she was out and tell him that she had something for him. She knew that since they hadn't hollered at her in a few days, they would buy it with no problem. Now she had fifteen minutes to sit around before leaving the house to meet Juwan. She would have liked to count out the thousands of dollars in her drawer, examine the new batch of weed and maybe smoke a blunt out of it. If it wasn't for the strangers in her living room, she would have done just that. Instead she pulled out the four Ziploc bags to get a closer look. She noticed that they were even lighter in color than the last batch. She was pleasantly satisfied and she knew her customers would be too. She grabbed a small bud out of one the bags and a cigar out of her pocketbook and went back into the kitchen. She split the blunt over the kitchen garbage and Nita came to join her.

"Illl! Why you bein' anti?"

"I'm not bein' anti. I'm about to come out there now." Free picked her bud up from the counter and went into the living room to roll her blunt. Black, Los, and Dee were drinking E&J out of plastic cups and engrossed in a heated discussion about a gambling session that had taken place the night before. Free took a seat on the carpeted floor, up against the wall.

"What's that shorty?" Los asked as he stared all in her hand.

It's a pipe. What does it look like? "Just a blunt. Why, you smoke?" she asked. He looked over at his boys and they all found her question funny.

"Do I smoke? Shorty, that's all I do is smoke."

Yeah, it looks like that's all you do. "Well, you can hit this," she offered kindly. By the time they finished smoking she would be ready to leave to meet Juwan. She barely got a chance to hit the blunt. From the way the guys were steaming it, she couldn't tell they smoked often. They smoked her little blunt like a bunch

of junkies with a free fix and when it finally got around to her, it was a roach. *So much for that,* she thought and was ready to leave their presence. She dropped the roach in the ashtray and went back into her bedroom to gather her belongings. Had she thought about it, she would have sat the weed in the Sonata and come in the house empty handed. How could she have known she would be walking into a house full of people? Now she had to lug the bag right back outside. She decided to put the four Ziploc bags full of weed into one of her Tommy Hilfiger book bags. That way, when she walked out she didn't have to worry about anybody trying to peek and see through her bag. Judging, from the way they smoked her blunt, there was no doubt in her mind that Nita's visitors were thirsty for weed. Nita came skipping into her room just as Free threw the book bag on her back.

"Where you off to?" Nita asked, nosily looking around Free's room for the blue Wal-mart bag she had seen her bring in the house.

"Nowhere special. I just gotta go take care of something. When are they leaving?" Free said, referring to the dusty crew, who had made themselves comfortable on the living room floor.

"That's what I came to talk to you about, but I see you getting ready to leave. Where you going?" Nita was showing her nosey side again.

Free had her 'mind your business' face on. "I just told you where I'm going."

"Excuse me. Well what time will you be finished taking care of suttin'?"

"I won't be long. Why?"

Nita's first thought was that she should drop it, but she went ahead and gave it a shot. "Well," she started, "Black is gonna spend the night and Los wants to know if he can spend the night, too."

"No, he can't. Why you lettin' Black spend the night? I thought you didn't even know him like dat."

"Oh, he's mad cool." Nita tried to convince her friend even though she wasn't even convinced herself.

"Well don't do nuttin' I wouldn't." She was beginning to think that she should just start telling her 'don't do nuttin'.' Just then Free's cell rang and it was Juwan.

"I'm on the way," she informed him before he even had a chance to say a word.

"I'll see you later," she told Nita as they left out of her bedroom.

"Ooh! Let me find out you got a booty bag," Nita teased once she noticed the Hilfiger bag on Free's back.

"See, there you go worried about the wrong things. You need to be worried about why you lettin' dat dude spend da night. He looks like he just stepped out of a mop bucket. What's really good?" Nita didn't get a chance to respond. Free walked out of her room. "It was nice meetin' ya'll." Free said, as she passed through the living room and out the door.

Perhaps, she should have been a little worried about collecting $3,600 from a guy she hadn't known for very long. Perhaps, she should have traveled with someone, or took some kind of safety precautions. People were getting killed everyday for that amount of money, as a matter of fact they were getting killed for way less than that. Free was aware of this, but still she took the chance and went to make the delivery. The drug game is full of everyday risks and in Free's mind the $1,200 profit she stood to gain was well worth the risk. On the way to Juwan's house, Free recognized the possible threat of danger. If she was to get pulled over, she feared a trip to the city jail. If she did make it safely there was no guarantee that Juwan wasn't the type who would rob her or even kill her for four pounds of weed. Still, she went anyway and thought about her $1,200 profit the whole way there. About half an hour later she was speaking into her cell phone.

"Where you at? I need to see you."

Ed was happy to hear it. It wasn't even ten o'clock and she was calling already.

"I'm not far. I'll be around your joint in ten minutes," said Ed.

"Make it fifteen." Free pulled into her parking lot like a soldier returning from war. She had ventured onto new ground and came home victorious. She had $3,600 in her purse to prove it. One thousand two hundred of which she would get to keep. She had sold all four pounds in one stop and was about to tell Ed she needed three more. Job well done. Before she got out of the Sonata and into Ed's waiting Ac she separated her money from his. No sense in him seeing how much she was making. He had once questioned her and told her she'd better be charging $800 for each pound and not a penny less. She just smiled. He would have never guessed that she was getting nine every time.

Once inside the apartment, she went straight to her room with an empty book bag on her back. She walked past the living room and was happy to see the unwanted threesome was no longer there. She didn't see Nita's car in the parking lot so she assumed she was home alone and started to settle down in her bedroom without closing the door. When she was in the midst of counting her money, she heard the noise. It was a rhythmic, squeaking sound. She used her comforter to cover all of her cash and tiptoed into the hall. There she heard moans of pleasure escaping from her roommate's room. *It can't be*. Sure enough, Nita was on the other side of the door with her feet in the air, getting her back blown out by Black.

Free turned around, went back in her room and slammed the door. She continued to sit on her bed and count out all of her cash. She should have been content, being that she counted out over $8,000. She should have been ecstatic, but she wasn't. More than anything she was lonely. She laid on her bed with all of her money tucked under her pillow and wondered why she slept alone every night.

Chapter 14

If something happens once it can be considered an acceptable mistake. It could've been a glitch in the thought process, or a slip of the fingers. Something like that could happen to even the most careful person. But twice? No, there was no mistaking it. There had to be more to the story.

For the second time in two weeks, B.J. went into his coke stash only to weigh it out and find that there were grams missing. Not two or three grams either. Two or three grams could be forgotten and forgiven. But a whole 28 grams? The first time he had suffered a 14 gram loss and today, his stash was missing a whole ounce. A whole ounce. There was no mistaking it. He had put nine ounces in a medium size Ziploc bag. He would never bag up eight ounces. Why would he do that? Why did he reweigh the bag on the way out of the door only to find that it was an ounce short? Exactly an ounce. How could that be? B.J. thought he had the answer.

"Ma?" He left his room on a mission.

"Yes, honey." Miss Janice was sitting in the living room braiding T.J.'s hair into short cornrows.

"Did Dana come over here last night?"

"Yes. As a matter of fact she did. Why?" she eyed him suspiciously.

"No reason."

B.J. knew better than to let his mother know that he was keeping anything in his room that would interest Dana. He decided the gig was up and he would have to stop being so lazy and start keeping his work outside again. The fact was he had gotten too comfortable. Still, he believed he should be able to keep his own work in his own room without it being tampered with. He assumed Dana was stealing for her broke ass boyfriend, Mike. The fact that exact amounts of coke were missing both times led him to this belief. His second thought was that maybe his Uncle Leon was sneaking into his room and stealing from him, but he doubted that. He did not think Uncle Leon was sophisticated enough to find the scale under the bathroom sink and then take the time to weigh out exact amounts. Uncle Leon would have just grabbed a handful of powder and went about his business. No, whoever was stealing from B.J. knew something about drugs and their intentions were to sell it. B.J. didn't want to believe his older sister would go as far as to steal from her own brother. As if she was the devil, Dana came to visit right after B.J. had just finished asking about her.

"Hey," she greeted her mom and youngest brother, who were still seated in the living room. B.J. did not leave his room, but he did overhear her and was prepared to confront her. He changed his initial thoughts quickly, figuring a confrontation would do him no good. It would not get his coke returned nor would it force a confession out of Dana. If he wanted to catch her he would have to go about it another way. He had a sadness about him when he left his room to join the rest of his family. The last thing he wanted was problems in his household.

"Hey, lil' brother." Dana gave B.J. her usual greeting accompanied by a kiss on the cheek.

"Hey." His response was noticeably dry. "Nice boots," he commented, noticing the Giuseppe Zanotti boots she wore with a faded blue denim mini skirt. The boots looked as if they were being worn for the first time.

"They hot, aren't they?" she grinned.

"Lord knows you don't need another pair of shoes," Miss Janice chimed in.

B.J. stopped examining the brown suede stiletto boots long enough to ask. "How much did they run you? Let me guess, $500?"

"Oh, something like that." Dana obviously was uncomfortable talking about her new boots. "Mike bought them for me," she said looking over at B.J.

Yeah, I bet he did, he thought. It was mighty funny that Dana had asked B.J. to buy the very boots she had on her feet. When he told her he didn't have the money, she must've been forced to use other resources. All B.J. wanted to know was whether or not her resources were sitting in the back of his closet.

"What's Mike up to these days?" B.J. kept the heat on his sister.

"I'm so glad you asked because he told me to tell you that he wants to holla at you," she told him and then looked over at Miss Janice, indicating that this was not the type of conversation that she wanted to have in her presence.

"Tell him to give me a call." B.J. had a good idea what Mike wanted. In the streets when someone wanted to holler at you, nine times out of ten, it's about money. Either they wanted to spend money with you or they wanted you to spend money with them. *Let me find out broke ass Mike got money to spend.*

Dana had come by to pick up a piece of her Louis Vutton luggage set. Although she hadn't lived there in three years, she still kept quite a few items there. She and a few of her girlfriends were going to Miami for Labor Day weekend. Last year they went to the Source Awards in Los Angeles and then to Cancun for Spring Break. None of them had a job, but there wasn't too much they wanted that they couldn't get. They made their living juicing guys the best way they knew how—by any means necessary.

Anytime Dana was preparing to go out of town, she made a habit of asking B.J. for a couple of hundred dollars. He always gave it to her too. He never wanted her to be out of town without enough money to truly enjoy herself. Call it intuition or just plain old knowledge, but B.J. knew this time Dana would not be asking him for anything. Even with his suspicions fresh in his mind, if she had asked, he would have still given it to her still, somehow he knew she wasn't going to ask. He was right.

"Won't you stay for dinner, honey. I got a roast in the oven."

"That is music to my ears. I'm hungrier than a hostage." Dana said.

Now that Dana was staying for dinner, B.J. wanted to go out to eat, but he wasn't about to let her make him miss his mom's mouth watering pot roast. The dinner conversation was humorous, like it usually was when the four family members got together. T.J hogged most of the conversation talking about how he couldn't wait to start high school in a few weeks. While Dana was in Miami, B.J. would be home taking his little brother school shopping. T.J. had enough clothes to dress an entire class, but B.J. still felt the need to take him shopping every other week. Dana knew about all of their shopping trips and wished she was given the same treatment.

Today was Tuesday and Dana and her crew weren't leaving for Miami until Thursday. Today was also the day Taye was scheduled to meet with his sweet new connect. B.J. hoped everything went well for his boy even though he wasn't too thrilled about losing one his longtime customers. It was getting late and Taye still hadn't called to tell him whether things went smooth or not. His mind was on his boy and how he should break the news to his family about the possibility of him becoming a father in the near future. That, particularly, was on B.J.'s mind throughout dinner, not to mention the fact that he was seated at the table with a thief.

Mama's roast, string beans, dirty rice, and corn on the cob was devoured and enjoyed by all. T.J. jumped up and rushed to get on the telephone. B.J. jumped up and rushed off to his room. Dana rose from the table, ready to leave. She still had to stop by the liquor store for Mike.

"What I told you about eatin' and runnin'? Only the cook can eat and run and I ain't got nowhere to go. Clear the table and put these dishes in the dishwasher for your mama, honey."

"Why can't B.J. do it?" Dana asked. She didn't want to risk missing the liquor store. Mike would be pissed.

"Because I asked you to." The truth was, Miss Janice could have easily asked T.J. to do it before he took off. She just loved to see Dana performing household chores. She genuinely missed having her only daughter around and anything she could do to prolong Dana's visit was reason enough.

"Okay, but under one condition," Dana bargained.

"Girl, you always tryna cut a deal wit' somebody. What condition?"

"You let me take a plate home." Like anyone who ever tasted it, Mike loved Mama's cooking.

"No problem, honey. And tell Mike I said 'this ain't no delivery service.' He's welcome to eat with us anytime."

While his sister and mother were having quality time; B.J. was in his room, on the phone with Taye.

"Did you go by her crib yet?" B.J. asked.

"Dawg, I don't even know where her crib is at. She always comes ova here."

"Damn, so you don't got no way of getting in touch wit' this broad?"

"Nope. I'm sick right now. Come thru cuz I don't even wanna talk about this on this jack no more."

"I'm on the way."

How could Taye trust a girl on a business level that he had no way of tracking down? Had B.J. known this, he would have told Taye not to deal with her until he found out where she lived; even if he had to follow her home. Now just like that, Taye was ass out.

He had gotten his $36,000 together and went to meet Jisella and her peoples at the designated spot, a movie theatre. Taye never once asked himself, what respectable business man would make a first time deal in the parking lot of a movie theatre? Granted, there would be people around, so if either party's motive was robbery, there would be no shots fired without witnesses. But what about privacy? How could the connect sit in a car and count out 36g's without catching the attention of nosey moviegoers? The connect had no intentions of counting out the money. Whatever was collected would be enough. More importantly, sitting in a dim parking, how could Taye get a good look at, or even test the product he was buying? He had nothing to go on except the word of a chick whose house he didn't even know the location of.

Taye had pulled up in the cinema parking lot on time, anxious to get on. He liked the idea of meeting in a public place because it decreased the chance of gunplay. Don't get it twisted. If Taye was robbed for his last $36,000 at gunpoint, he had every intention of going out blazing, but that was not the case. Taye was robbed without the use of force. Jisella had pulled up beside him in a green Ford Explorer with deep tints and New York tags. Like a lot of hustlers on the East Coast, Taye always looked forward to the day when he would have his very own New York connect. Jisella jumped in his truck carrying a plastic shopping bag and talking fast. She hopped in the passenger seat and then looked behind her to be sure they were alone.

"Where's the money, Baby? Dude said he ain't ready to meet no new faces, but dude said if everything goes smooth and your money is straight then he'll meet you next time."

"I can live wit' dat," Taye said, taking a peek over at the Explorer. He couldn't see past the tinted windows if he tried. "The money is straight," he told her with a cocky confidence, then added, "lemme see whatchu twirkin' wit' first."

"It's right here, baby." Jisella dug into the shopping bag that up until that point she had been holding as if her life depended on it, and pulled out a block that was about the same width, length and thickness as a thousand grams of compressed cocaine. The block was covered in thick, gray masking tape and appearance wise; it was a go. Taye grabbed the brick out of her hand and searched it for some type of opening. He found on one of the corners a place where he could begin to peel the tape away. As he did this, Jisella waited anxiously. Taye dug through the opening just enough to expose some powder cocaine. He dabbed his finger into the opening and then placed the same finger on the tip of his tongue. By the time he put the tape back over the hole, placed the brick back in the plastic bag and reached in the back seat for the shopping bag containing his money, his tongue was beginning to get numb. He handed Jisella the bag full of money and pushed the other bag up under his seat. "Call me when you get everything situated. I'm tryna see you later."

That was the last thing Jisella said to him before she hopped back in the driver's seat of the Explorer and drove off. Taye pulled out right behind her and jumped on the highway. His whole ride home was spent trying to ignore the funny feeling in his stomach. Something was telling him he should have punctured the second block as well. The only reason he didn't was because he wanted to trust Jisella. He was falling in love with her. She sexed him good, looked good and he couldn't get enough of the arroz con pollo she always came over his house to make. She was the type of girl he could see himself sticking with and he had been tricking on her some kind of ridiculous. Now he had been tricked.

Taye had been in a hurry to get to his apartment and break down his goods, careful not to drive over the speed limit. He grabbed the plastic bag from under his seat and rushed up to his

apartment, climbing two and three steps at a time. Once inside, he reached in his kitchen cabinet for a box of Ziploc bags and his digital scale. Then he took the first block out of the bag and sat it on the kitchen counter. He had never laid his eyes on a whole key.

Taye had been copping from B.J. for as long as he could remember and B.J. always brought him exactly what he ordered and nothing more. It wasn't that Taye couldn't afford a key. He could, but B.J. wouldn't sell him one. B.J. would just piece him off and make him come back for more. This way he could charge Taye whatever he wanted to without having to give him a good deal on the whole thing. To hear B.J. tell it, he couldn't even supply keys. The truth was, he could but chose not to. So for the very first time, Taye had his eyes on his very own key or so he thought.

He began to pull at the tape along the same side he had dug in to test it. The tape pulled back slightly, revealing another layer of tape. He realized he would have to go about unwrapping his purchase another way. With one of his butcher knives, he proceeded to slice around the edges of the taped up block, making a complete circle. He was then able to lift the top completely off like a shoebox. When he did, what he saw was enough to bring tears to his eyes. There were two 'Girls Gone Wild' VHS tapes taped together. In the same corner he had tested, there was some powder matted together and it appeared to be glued to the edge of the box. It wasn't even an ounce of powder in the corner. Frantically, he reached for the other block and opened it in the same fashion. There he discovered the same exact thing. He was devastated. For $36,000, he had purchased video cassettes of 'Girls Gone Wild', volumes 1-4 and less than two ounces of cocaine. He just stood there, staring, unable to believe what lay before his eyes. When he caught his breath, he picked up the phone to share his pain with his boy.

I knew it. I knew it, B.J. thought on the ride to Taye's apartment. *I knew something wasn't right about that chick when I saw her eyein' me at the club that night. She was there lookin' for a vic. Better him than me. Good thing I made him pay me my lit-*

tle scratch when he had it. Damn, Taye. Within minutes he was knocking at Taye's door.

"Now tell me again," B.J. demanded. He had a pretty good idea of what happened—his boy had been robbed with no gun. It happens everyday.

"Yo," Taye began. "I pulled it open, you know what I'm sayin'. Just to make sure everything was everything. It was all good there, where I pulled it open at. I tasted it and tested it. It was a go."

"So she must have known what side you was gonna open it at?"

"Yup, cuz I opened it where it looked like the tape was already startin' to peel a little suttin'. Damn, it just happened so fast and we in dis wide open ass parkin' lot and I ain't tryna be sittin' there all day."

"That's messed up, man. What's really messed up is you don't even know how to find dis chick. Damn, playa. We gotta smoke a blunt to dis one."

How could smoking a blunt help? Nothing could help. Not all the smoking and talking in the world. Nothing would bring back Taye's $36,000, not even an address to Jisella's place. His money was gone like the nineties and there wasn't much he, or anyone else could do about it. They sat right beside each other on the leather sofa, smoking and talking, but they were miles apart. B.J. had money and Taye was broke. Just like that.

B.J. did feel a little sympathy for his boy. He didn't think his prices were so high that Taye had to result to taking his business elsewhere. B.J. played fair so Taye had no justifiable reason for wanting to spend his money with someone else. He had been making money with B.J., but he thought of all the money he could be making if he was to holler at a new, sweeter connect. Greed. It'll get you every time.

Not only was Taye heated to the point he had smoke coming

out of his ears, B.J. was also in his feelings because he knew some type of lookout would be expected of him. He could offer Taye a little something, but it probably wouldn't be what he was expecting. B.J. didn't owe Taye anything, so whatever he did for him would be out of the kindness of his heart. B.J. decided he would front Taye four and a half ounces of powder, nothing more. Anything more and B.J. would be exposing his hand. Taye had no idea B.J. was copping up to four bricks at a time. All he knew was that whenever he called for something, B.J. had it. Say for instance, Taye called for nine ounces. B.J. would pretend he had to call someone else to go and pick it up. He never let on that the weight belonged to him.

If B.J. gave Taye four and a half ounces for free or fronted him nine ounces for a real cheap price, he would be putting his business in the street. To do that would create vulnerability and that was not something B.J. was about to do. Taye would have to fight his own way back from broke. The most B.J. would do was offer him four and a half ounces for a good price, on consignment. When Taye paid him, he planned to turn around and front him nine ounces. That was the most and the least he could do.

"So, you don't got no way of findin' out where shorty rest her head?" B.J. questioned a stressed Taye, who was seated on the couch with his palms to his face and his elbows on his knees.

"Nah, man. Unless..."

"Unless what?" Now, B.J. was not quick to give his money away, but he was down to ride every day of the week and twice on Tuesday.

"Remember when I first met shorty the night of that concert?"

"Yeah."

"Well, I sent shorty in a cab home that next morning. Maybe the cab company keeps records of where they drop people off at."

"Maybe." B.J. knew it was a long shot. "But that was like two months ago. You think they would still have a record of that? You don't remember where she told the cab she was going?"

"Nope. I already thought about that," Taye confessed. "I just remember hearing her say something about the Eastside. But money talks. For a huned dollars, I'm sure they could come up wit' a address, or a block or suttin'."

"Maybe, but we gotta get a girl to do it. They'll tell a girl before they'll tell a guy."

"Yeah, but who? What about that chick Kenya? Could she do it?" Taye must have forgotten that B.J. wanted to hear nothing from her.

"I ain't tell you about shorty?"

"No. What happened?" Taye lifted his face from his hands.

"So, I go ova dere to make her take anotha test. Sure enough dat joint come back positive. Man, listen. Then she gonna wait until after I give her the money for a abortion to tell me that she ain't getting no abortion. What part of the game is dat?"

"Seems like we shoulda just stayed home. Ain't nuttin' good come outta us goin' out dat night."

"I know dats right." B.J. chuckled. Bringing up Kenya lightened the mood in the room a little.

"So whatchu gonna do?" Taye asked.

"What you mean what I'm gonna do? What can I do? If she's havin' the baby, she's havin' the baby. I done did all I can do."

"Yeah, but what you gonna do about getting her to call the cab company for us?"

"Oh yeah, I'll get on that first thing."

They smoked a little while longer as they discussed Taye's

loss. Taye was tryin' to convince B.J. that maybe Jisella wasn't in on the scam. He was convinced that whoever the connect was had even tricked her. She trusted him and he trusted her. That was the way Taye wanted to look at it. Even after being robbed, he was still referring to the invisible person in the green truck as 'the connect'. Taye had been calling Jisella's cell nonstop and when he got no answer, he even went as far as to say, "I hope she's okay. Maybe the connect did suttin' to her so that she couldn't lead us to him."

Unbelievable, B.J. thought. *He still don't get it.* Taye was in deep denial. Somewhere in the back of his mind he knew that maybe Jisella was in on him being set up, but he didn't want to believe it. Even her not answering her phone hadn't convinced him. B.J. wanted to get out of there so when Kenya called and invited him over he told her he was on the way. He had no intention of going, but he felt like he needed a reason to leave Taye alone with his misery. Taye reminded B.J. to get Kenya to call the cab company and said that he would be calling him first thing in the morning for a lookout. They said their goodbyes and B.J. left. If he didn't know better, he would have sworn he saw a tear fall from Taye's watery eyes.

Within half an hour, B.J. was seated on his bed counting out all of his money. Every penny was where it was supposed to be. He sat back, grateful for his collection. Not wanting to put it away, he just stared at the eighty some odd thousand dollars. After about an hour of watching Comic View and spending time with his money, he grew tired. He put his cash back in its hiding place, under the radiator, and began to undress. It was about time for him to be getting ready to move out of his mother's house, but he felt so lonely. Living all alone was not something that he wanted to do.

Before B.J. went to sleep that night, he thought about his relationship with Kenya in great detail. He couldn't put his finger on it, but something about her did not sit well with him. She was pretty, but he did not consider her an absolute beauty. She had the appearance of someone who was well off, but he had a feeling she was struggling. He had labeled her as a gold digger early on and as it turned out, he was right. B.J. had no love for gold diggers and therefore he had no love for Kenya. There really wasn't too much to that.

His feelings for Kenya conflicted with his yearning to be close to someone. He wanted someone with whom he didn't mind spending his time and money. He wanted someone who was genuine and financially comfortable rather than someone who went out of her way to appear to be. For the first time in his life, B.J wanted something his money could not buy—love

Chapter 15

"Eight thousand six hundred fifty two, 8,653, 8,654." Eight thousand six hundred and fifty four thousand dollars. That's how much Free had collected after six weeks of hustling. She made that without even trying hard or giving it much thought. She had even taken herself school shopping for clothes and sneakers on two separate occasions, spending almost a thousand dollars each time. She had also already purchased all of her schoolbooks. It was Labor Day weekend; the last weekend before school was scheduled to start. Before the semester got under way, Free had a couple of things she wanted to talk to Nita about. Well, actually she had one thing she wanted to talk to her about. Nita came walking towards Free's bedroom door just seconds after she stashed her money in her top dresser drawer. No knocking, Nita busted straight in.

"Girl, we still goin' to the club tonight?" Nita had just let out one of her male companions. This one had left the apartment in a flash, leaving fifteen twenty-dollar bills on Nita's junky nightstand.

"I don't know. Listen, let me talk to you for a minute." Free patted a spot next to her.

"What's good?" Nita asked, taking a seat on the edge of Free's bed.

There was no easy way for Free to say what she had to say.

She just had to get it off her chest. "Why every time I look up you got a different guy ova here? What's really good?"

"What you mean?" Nita's attitude changed instantly.

"What I mean? Every time I come up in here you got company. I don't mind, but why it gotta be a different guy every time? Every dude in town gonna know where we live by the time the lease is up." That's right. Free was already thinking about how much time she had before the lease would be up. She had enough money to put herself in a decent one-bedroom apartment and planned to do just that.

"Why you so worried about who I got comin' ova here?" Nita's defensiveness was showing. "Don't be J cuz you ain't had no company since we moved up in this piece. You slippin', yo!"

Now why did she have to say that? Free hopped up off the bed. "Slippin'? Slippin'? I'm far from slippin'. Believe my feet is planted."

"Well, you need to plant your feet in some new shoes. You ain't been shoppin' but once this whole summer. Like I said, you slippin'. Too busy worried about how I'm getting' mine."

"What? What?" That's all Free could say. She was so close to exposing her secret and pulling out the many shopping bags that were hidden in the back of her closet. No, she wasn't about to go there. It took every ounce of willpower she had in her 127 pound body not to. Instead, she paced her bedroom trying to walk off the urge. "Oh, honey you need to worry about how you getting yours cuz I already got mines. Trust! You just worry about how you getting yours. That's what you do," Free said arrogantly.

The tension in the room was thicker than a pair of bifocals. There was no way Free was going to the club now. Her last comment had Nita staring at her, wondering how much she knew.

"I'm getting mine. You get yours." Nita stormed out of Free's room, slamming the door behind her.

Nita was super pissed! *Here I am tryna get money and my best friend is tryna knock my hustle. Dat lonely hater.* She forgot about Free and began making plans for her day. A guy she had met earlier in the week was suppose to be picking her up and taking her shopping. He had told her to call him first thing in the morning and even though it was the first thing on her mind when she woke up this morning, she still thought it was too early to call. Not wanting to seem like a thirst monster, she decided to wait until about one or two o'clock before calling. That gave her about three hours to kill and since she was not speaking to her roommate, time dragged.

Free was in her room upset as well. Her intentions were to have a heart-to-heart about her best friend's new sexual activity, but things didn't go according to plan. Now restless and bored, with nothing to do, Free wanted to go shopping. It was ten o'clock and the malls were just opening. She could get in there, spend a good thousand dollars and be back home before noon. Arguing with Nita made her want to spend and floss like crazy, but she was stronger than that. She grabbed her purse and in two minutes, she was pulling off in Ed's Sonata.

Nita fixed herself some breakfast and got on the telephone. She called up some of the guys she had been with recently, just to see what they were up to. Some didn't answer the phone and those who did, said they were either busy, sleeping, or would call her back later. Only one of the six guys she called engaged her in a conversation that lasted longer than five minutes. After Marco explained why he didn't have the time to drop by for breakfast, he asked her where Free was. The question didn't seem odd to Nita until she informed him that she wasn't home and he begun to inquire further.

"When she comin' back?"

"What you worried about Free for?" Here she was trying to call up people so that she could take her mind off of the argument she just had with Free and here he was asking her whereabouts.

"I ain't say I was worried about her. I just said I'm tryna holla at her, dat's all."

"Holla at her? Yeah, whateva. So when I'mma see you?"

"It's kinda early. I'mma call you a little later. But listen. Tell Free I'm definitely tryna holla at her."

"Holla." Nita hung up the phone with an attitude. Not only because she couldn't find anyone to come over for breakfast, but mostly because her ex-boyfriend wanted to holler at her best friend. If she was heated before, now she was on fire. She was tempted to call Free with 21 questions, but they weren't exactly on speaking terms. By the time she finished eating her cheese eggs, waffles, and turkey bacon, Free had returned home. In her hand she had her own breakfast from Mama Dot's, the local hangout/restaurant that specialized in soul food. Mama Dot's was only open from 1 am to 1 pm. It was a place that people went after partying all night or early birds went before starting their day. They sold the best fried potatoes and onions under the sun. Free went and picked herself up some with French toast, scrambled eggs and turkey sausage. She sat her food down on the kitchen table and poured herself some orange juice.

"So, what does Marco want with you?" Nita didn't waste a second before digging into her for information. The breakfast Free bought in from Mama Dot's made Nita's home cooked entrée look like Kibbles and Bits. This increased the animosity in the room.

"What do you mean?" Free needed to know how much Marco had told her. Nita went with the friendly approach. She wanted the scoop and she figured that she could catch more flies with honey than vinegar.

"Well," she started. "He called here and asked if you were home. I told him you wasn't and then he wanted to know when you'd be back. I told him I didn't know and then he said for you to call him back because he was tryin' to holla at you." She used her sweet, innocent voice.

"Oh, let me call him back." Free pulled out her Nextel, pressed her speed dial and began pouring syrup on her French toast. Nita found it very interesting that she had Marco's number stored in her phone.

"Whassup?" Free asked when he answered.

"You know whassup. I'm tryna holla at you like three times today."

"Dat's whassup." *That's $900.*

"I think my brother tryna holla at you too."

"Okay, I'll give him a call."

"Don't take all day to get around here either."

"I won't. One."

Nita was all over it. "What did he want?"

"Oh, nothing," Free lied. "He just told me that his brother was trying to holla at me." Well, that wasn't a total lie.

"Oh." Nita didn't believe it for a second. Marco had sounded as if it was a little more serious than that. Something was different about Free, but she just couldn't pinpoint what it was. For one, when did she start waking up and going to Mama Dot's? That was a place that was often frequented by hustlers. Not many women went there unless they were picking up breakfast for their man. "So when did you start going to Mama Dot's? And you didn't have to bring me none back," she said sarcastically.

"I know and you didn't have to fix me no breakfast either," Free quickly shot back. Just like that, the animosity had crept its way back into the room. Free continued to eat her breakfast while Nita was pretending to be busy cleaning the dishes she had used. Free was thinking about how as soon as she finished eating, she was going to her room to put her order in with Ed. Nita was trying to figure out the best way to pick her for infor-

mation. Free finished eating, cleared the table and went straight to her room. Nita went into her room and contemplated how much longer she should wait before calling her supposed shopping date. She hoped that any one of her guy friends called to take her somewhere. Anywhere. Free was on her way out the door when Nita stopped her in the hall.

"So are we still going to the club tonight?"

"Yeah, we could do that. I'll be back in a few hours."

"Where you going?" Nita asked. She was bored and a little offended Free hadn't invited her to ride with her wherever it was she was going.

"I'm just goin' smokin' and ridin' wit' my boy Ed. I'll be back."

"You sure are hangin' out wit' him right much. And he's lettin' you drive his car. Let me find out you hit dat and didn't tell me. How was it?"

"No I ain't hit dat." Free was annoyed at her friend's narrow-minded assumption. "I'll see you when I get back." She was out the door and on her cell making moves.

Nita was lonely in her apartment. There was nobody to call, meet or chill with. She was starting to notice how guys didn't want to have anything to do with her when the sun was out. But as soon as the sun went down, all sorts of guys started calling, wanting to come by or pick her up. She was restless in her room, then on their new sofa set and before long she found herself in her best friend's room.

Nita stared at her pretty face in Free's mirror. She looked around on her dresser and put her nose to the different designer perfume bottles that were arranged there. She loved Free dearly and desperately wanted to share her new lifestyle with her. She knew Free wouldn't approve of her promiscuity, but she wanted to tell her all about all of the money she had been making.

Nita wasn't looking for anything in particular in Free's room, but something told her to be nosey. Nita was naturally nosey, so that something didn't have to speak very loud. Next thing you know, she was rummaging through Free's dresser drawer. She didn't notice anything out of the ordinary in the underwear drawer until she looked all the way in the back. There she found close to $10,000. She picked up the separate g stacks and examined them with her mind racing. What was Free doing with that kind of money in her dresser drawer? She eyeballed the money one last time before putting it back where she found it. It blew her mind. What other secrets did Free have? She searched through both the socks and T-shirt drawers and found nothing unusual.

When Nita was finished with the dresser she went straight to the closet. In the back, tucked away behind her extensive collection of attire, she found over a dozen shopping bags. There were bags from everywhere; Foot Locker to Gucci. She began to pull clothes and shoes out of the bags and peek at the sizes. Everything was Nita's size, which was also Free's size. She put all of Free's purchases back in the closet as neatly as possible. There had to be an explanation for this, she thought. Free had obviously come across a nice piece of change. But how? Nita was fiendin' to find out. Could Free have robbed someone? Did she have a big baller looking out for her? Even then, Nita reasoned that she would have had to save every nickel that he gave her to have almost ten thousand dollars stashed away in her panty drawer. Yeah, there had to be some type of unethical explanation for this and Nita was making it her business to find out what it was.

She spent the rest of the afternoon sitting around the house sulking. The guy who was supposed to be picking her up to take her shopping hadn't answered her call and that didn't surprise her much. She was beginning to recognize the pattern in her dating behavior.

RRRING...

Nita almost broke her neck rushing to the telephone.

"Hello."

"Hey, Nita listen. I got that DVD player for you. Did your T.V. get delivered yet?"

"Yeah, it did." She hated to admit it, she found herself happy to hear from Stephen, even if she did consider him to be a nuisance.

"Are you busy? I'm gonna come over there and drop it off if that's okay with you." He was hoping that she would say it was okay and why shouldn't she? He was the first person that had called her all day.

"How are you gonna get here?"

"My boy is gonna drop me off. I'm leavin' campus in about five minutes."

"Okay. I'll be here."

Nita decided that Stephen wasn't worth beautifying herself for, so she just sat in front of the T.V. watching an infomercial with her mind on her best friend. She told herself that she would have to step her game up. Compared to what she found in Free's drawer, her $1,500 worth of savings might as well have been fifteen pennies. She had been offered a proposition to make an easy grand, but she had turned it down without thinking twice about it. Until now. Now, that thousand dollars was calling her and she felt like a fool for having turned it down. She rushed to her bedroom and picked up her cell off the charger on her nightstand.

"Hello. Can I speak to Lamell?"

"Yo."

"Is this Lamell?" Nita asked in a voice full of uncertainty. She wasn't sure she should even be making the call.

"Who dis?"

"This is Tanita."

"Tanita," he repeated her name and thought for a minute, remembering who she was. "Oh, what's goin' on, honey? What took you so long to call? I thought you forgot about me?"

"Now, how could I do that?" she teased. The jewelry he wore alone was unforgettable, never mind the candy painted GS on twenties he was seated in.

"So what are you doing tonight?" the attractive 6′3″ baller asked.

"I'm tryna see you, that's if the offer still stands."

"As long as I'm standin', it's standin'. What time are you gonna be ready?"

"It won't be 'til much later because I'm goin' to the club but, after the club I'll be ready to meet you," she explained.

"Is you tryna make money or party? Let me know...nah, you go ahead and get nice and drunk. Do you need to meet me and get some of the scratch ahead of time or do you already got enough for drinks and stuff?"

Nita thought for a second. From the way he phrased the question it sounded as if he wasn't planning on giving her any extra money, just a small portion ahead of time. "No, I'm good. I'll call you when I leave the club. You gonna be up, right?"

"Am I gonna be up? You just make sure you call. Don't be freezin' up on me. I'm gonna hold down my end of the deal."

"Alright, Lamell. I'll see you tonight."

"Cool."

That was it. The deal was made and there was no use in turning back now. Besides, Nita felt like she needed that thousand dollars. She convinced herself that she would save it since she would be stepping out of her character to earn every penny.

The rest of the day was spent anticipating the late night that lay ahead and contemplating what she would do about what she had stumbled upon earlier. Nita's first thought was that someone was paying Free good money to stash drugs in their apartment. If that was the case, Nita felt like she was entitled to some of that money because it was her apartment just as much as it was Free's. Yeah, she was gonna get to the bottom of it one way or another.

Stephen came over carrying a heavy Toshiba box. Nita let him stay long enough to hook up the DVD player and then she was dropping him back off on campus. She was tempted to pay for his cab ride, but she didn't want to appear rude. Besides, dropping him off on campus was a good reason to get out of the house. She was fed up with waiting for the guy who was supposed to be taking her shopping to call or pick up his phone.

After dropping Stephen off at his dormitory, Nita ended up in the mall with the $300 her early morning booty call left on her dresser. It seemed like her car had it's own navigational system and before she knew it, she was pulling up in the mall parking lot. Once inside, she purchased a pair of lavender strappy sandals from Aldo and a lavender lingerie set from Victoria Secrets. The sandals would match the floral, violet and lavender top and white Capri pants she picked up at BCBG. She stopped at Claire's accessories for a lavender hair ribbon and the MAC store for matching eye shadow and nail polish. She would look good tonight. By the time she made it to the food court, she had less than twenty dollars left. Meanwhile, Free was parked on a side street, sitting in Ed's Acura smoking a blunt with him.

"You movin' dem joints faster than I thought you would," he confided in her.

"That's a good thing."

"Yeah, it's always a good thing; we both makin' money. But you ain't about to have me runnin' to meet you every time you get a phone call. You know what I'm sayin'? Especially when I'm already lookin' out for you on the number."

"So what you sayin'?" she asked, squinting her sexy eyes and staring him in the face.

"I'm sayin' we gonna have to work suttin out. You gotta start payin' for dem joints up front. I ain't tryna be meetin' you to throw you the joints then meetin' you again to pick up my scratch. You tryna run me ragged. I do got otha custies, you know." Ed looked over at her in an attempt to determine what type of person she was. If she didn't want to roll, she could roll out and he didn't have a problem with telling her to do so. He was putting her on for cheaper than some of his closest boys and if she hadn't been saving her money like he had suggested then that was her fault, not his. Free wasn't giving up the ass, so why should he continue going out of his way to look out for her?

Free thought for a minute as she weighed her options. "Alright, give me ten of them joints," she told him, unable to hide her grin.

"Whoa!" Ed smiled back. He was proud of her. He figured Free for the type who would be spending more than she was saving, but she had proved him wrong. She took the first free sixteen ounces he had given her and turned it into enough to buy almost sixteen pounds. Ed was impressed with his new ten-pound customer. He hid his excitement and returned to business mode.

"When you gonna be ready?" he asked.

"I just gotta go pick up the money then I'll be ready."

"Pick up the money? From where?"

"From-" Free started but stopped herself. She wasn't about to reveal the location of her goldmine to anyone, not even the person who helped her make it. "Where can you meet me in like thirty minutes?"

"Just call me when you ready."

"Aight," she replied and was ready to pull off, anxious to

spend her money and make more. He stopped her before she got out of his smokey Ac. "It's your money you spendin', right?"

Ed couldn't let her go without asking. Either way he would be happy to take the six grand, but he had to be sure she wasn't getting them for someone else and then giving them that same cheap price. She was so secretive, he couldn't determine if she was hustling good or just wasting her time. As many times as she had called him in the past two months, he knew she was making something; with women there was no way of knowing. For all he knew, she could have been getting pimped for the pounds.

"Yeah, it's my money." She didn't want to tell him all of that, but she knew that it made a huge difference.

"That's what I'm talkin' about," Ed cheered her on then pulled off, still smoking. Free drove straight home to get her money.

"How do I look?"

It was later that night and the girls were getting ready for the club. Nita busted into Free's room for an opinion on her outfit.

"You look cute," Free told her. "I like those sandals." Free was wearing Michael Jordan's college Mitchell and Ness throwback jersey dress and a pair of baby blue Prada sneakers.

"You look cute, too." Nita wasn't as surprised about seeing the jersey dress as she should have been because she had already seen it earlier that day in the back of Free's closet.

On the way to The Drop, Free smoked a blunt. She was loving the freedom the passenger seat offered. It was a change from having to drive all around town delivering pounds. She reclined and smoked with her mind focused on the profits she was set to make off of her first re-up. Nita's mind was focused on how she planned to save the thousand dollars she would make later that night. Nita lowered the volume on the radio to pick with Free.

"So, who bought you that dress?" she asked.

"It's cute, right? I bought it. Why?"

"Oh, no reason. I just knew it was official."

"Yup. I just decided to treat myself."

You been treating yourself a lot lately, Nita thought.

As usual, The Drop was packed. Both girls slipped $20 to the guy who was selling fluorescent over-age wrist bands. They had a few drinks, took a few pics, collected a few numbers and were ready to leave in a few hours. Nita was trying to figure out the best way to tell Free why she would be dropping her off at the apartment and then leaving back out. Free wasn't surprised and really didn't care. Nothing Nita did concerning men could surprise Free at this point.

"I'll be back," Nita announced once they pulled up in their parking lot. Free didn't feel like inquiring or arguing. She didn't even say her usual 'don't do nuttin' I wouldn't.' Nita was her own woman and destined to do whatever pleased her.

"Do you," is all she said before slamming the door on Nita's Honda. Nita quickly reached for her cell and called Lamell. He was awake and waiting just like he said he would be. He told her what hotel he was at and she was on her way. She pumped the radio and sang her nervousness away as she approached the exit.

Nita reached the hotel parking lot and gave her face a once over in her rearview mirror. All of her make-up was still in place, but just to be sure she looked her best, she applied an additional coat of lip gloss before leaving her car. She left her keys with the Marriott valet and was soon in the elevator on the way up to Lamell's room. She knocked and a light-skinned semi-attractive female answered the door.

"You must be Tanita." The girl politely greeted her

"Yes and what is your name?" Nita asked, stepping into the room.

"My name is Tasha," the girl responded. She had an understated cuteness about her and the blue denim cut off shorts and bright orange tank top she wore accented her feminine curves.

"Where's Lamell," Nita asked.

"Oh, he's in the shower. He just got back from the club not too long ago. Did you go to the club, too?" Tasha was just trying to make small talk. She was actually relieved to have someone to talk to because Lamell had kept her cooped up in the room all day.

"Yeah, I went to The Drop."

"Oh, he went to Macho's." Tasha was starved for conversation. "So, did you have a good time at the club? I'm just in town for a few days. Lamell wouldn't let me go to the club with him," Tasha shamefully admitted.

"Where are you from?" Nita was thrilled to hear she was from out of town.

"I'm from L.A.," she said staring down at the floor.

"How cool is dat." Nita had never been to Los Angeles or met anyone from there. Now she didn't mind talking to the girl. *Maybe when this is all over, we can be cool. If I ever make it out to L.A. at least I'll know somebody there.* Nita wanted to know why the girl was so far away from home. She figured it was drug related. She was right. Just then they heard the water in the bathroom being turned off, signaling the end of Lamell's shower. The girls flashed each other nervous looks. In less than a minute Lamell stepped out of the bathroom wearing nothing more than a white towel wrapped around his waist.

Lamell was sexy beyond words. He was tall, dark-skinned and most of all fly. Everything about him was extra—his cars, clothes, jewelry, money.

"What's crackin?" He greeted Nita. He walked over to the end table for a lighter to light the Black-n-Mild cigar he had hanging from his lips.

"Hey," Nita replied. Lamell opened the night stand and retrieved a g stack from the money he had in there. He tossed it across the bed in Nita's direction and told her to get undressed. Nita liked his style. *That's what I'm talkin' about. Pay me mines up front.* Nita stuffed the grand in her pocketbook and did as she was told. Lamell took a seat by the window on one of the chairs that surrounded a small round table. Nita was nervous, but the money in her bag helped her to relax. Tasha watched closely as Nita undressed and she enjoyed every minute of it. Nita was now only wearing her lavender lace thong set. She stretched out on the bed trying to find a comfortable spot. *Think about the money*, Nita told herself. *Damn, she look good*, Tasha thought. Tasha removed her tank top and jean shorts and stood completely naked. Lamell sat back, smoked, and positioned himself to enjoy the show.

Tasha climbed onto the bed, sexy like a cat in heat. She went to kiss Nita on the lips, but when Nita turned her face she was forced to settle for her cheek instead. She moved from her cheek to her neck. She then straddled her like a horse and whispered for her to lift up so that she could unfasten her bra. Nita's erect nipples became exposed. Tasha teased her breasts with her mouth. She knew just what to do to arouse their one-man audience. She licked, kissed then sucked every inch of Nita's near naked body. *Just pretend she's a guy. It's not that bad*, Nita reasoned with herself. *Damn, her body is bangin'*, thought Tasha.

Nita's thong was pulled off by Tasha's slow, soft hand. Lamell warned Tasha earlier that Nita was a virgin, when it came to women, and to take her time with her. Once Nita was completely naked, both girls looked over at Lamell to be sure he was catching all the action. He was. He had set Tasha up with several different girls on various occasions, but none were as attractive as Nita. He felt like she was worth every penny he had paid her.

Lamell unwrapped his towel and continued to smoke as he listened to Nita moan with pleasure. She clutched at the sheets and jerked her head back and forth violently as Tasha's skilled tongue went to work between her legs. Tasha's hand was mas-

saging her nipples while her tongue was massaging her clitoris. Nita had never been eaten so perfectly, or so passionately and she felt like butter left sitting in the sun. The only thing she wanted in the world at that moment was for Tasha to continue and she showed no intentions of stopping anytime soon.

Nita came three times and could no longer take it. Her body wouldn't stop shaking and she was making so much noise, Lamell was afraid someone in a neighboring room would call the hotel security to investigate. Tasha lifted her face and climbed her way up Nita's body, meeting her head on. This time Nita welcomed the lips that had bought her so much pleasure and they enjoyed a full fledged French kiss.

Nita caressed Tasha's short blond hair, fondling her breasts with her free hand. She began to kiss on Tasha's neck and shoulders and take pleasure in the sight of her smooth body. Nita told Tasha to lay down so that she could return the favor. Tasha had turned out girls who were straighter than nine fifteen so Nita's willingness didn't surprise her much. Tasha knew her head game was official. She laid back flat on the king sized bed and relaxed as Nita opened her legs and kissed around her pleasure point.

"Yeah, baby. That's right. Don't be scared," Tasha edged her on. It didn't take long for Nita to figure out what to do. She used her tongue to make circles around her clit and the next thing you know, Tasha was reaching a climax. Nita was on her knees with her backside in the air, sucking on Tasha's inner thigh. Lamell took this opportunity to climb onto the bed and join the party. He propped himself up behind Nita and slid into her from behind. It took Nita by surprise at first, but at that point she was open for anything. Rather than sit and watch the couple doing it doggy style, Tasha made herself useful. By the time the ménage à trois was over, Nita had went down on Lamell and she and Tasha tasted each other's juices for a second time.

Nita showered before dressing and leaving. She wanted to exchange numbers with Tasha, but thought that it was inappropriate. She wouldn't mind going shopping or out to the club with her. Lamell told her that he wanted to see her again under the

same circumstances sometime soon before Tasha left town. Nita agreed. She drove home feeling a little guilty and sluttish, but she refused to let it get to her. *All in a day's work*. It was nearly seven o'clock in the morning and she decided to stop at Mama Dot's for breakfast on the way home.

Chapter 16

"Man, I told you not to mess wit' dude. Come on, man. You know betta den dat."

Taye was being reprimanded by B.J. for selling to a guy named G, a dude from the neighborhood who some labeled suspect. A hustler, who went broke behind sniffing heroine, ended up catching a bank robbery charge and came home in less than a year, raising suspicion. Some people still dealt with him regardless, but not B.J. Even though he went to high school with G, he didn't trust him. When a guy is down and out, more often than not, he couldn't be trusted.

"I know, right. I wasn't gonna deal wit' him at first cuz I heard he was funny style," Taye tried to explain his actions. "But, yo he kept callin' me and I charged him an extra G. He gave me $4,500 for the joint."

B.J. had given him an eighth of a key for $2,750. For a $1,700 profit, Taye went against his better judgment and was now passing B.J. stolen bank money. If Taye wasn't so desperate, he would never have dealt with G. A person who's drowning isn't thinking about getting bit by a shark.

"Man, you know dude is on the run," B.J. said before accepting the money. For all he knew, the money could have been marked. And what would happen once the police finally caught up with G? B.J. didn't want to imagine the scenario.

"I'm tryna get back, dawg. I gotta do what I gotta," Taye confessed.

That's what I know, B.J. thought.

B.J. left from around Taye's, but not before telling him not to bring him anymore stolen bank money. If Taye chose to still deal with G then that was Taye's business. However, B.J. was smart enough to know that if Taye dealt with G then it was his business as well. He had a busy day ahead of him and he couldn't spend too much time busting his brain over that situation. He had to get a shape-up, stop at his hair braider's house, see Papi to re-up, and he had several big sales waiting. Also, he promised to stop by and see Kenya. Lastly and most importantly, he was taking his mom to Red Lobster for her birthday. Just a typical day in the life of a hustler.

While at the barbershop, he picked up on some gossip that had an effect on him. According to some random guy, who was getting a shape up two seats over from him, G was on the run and running around town copping work to wash his stolen bank money. Supposedly, he was even giving people money with the bank band still on it. How smart was he? From the conversation, it seemed as if everyone in town knew his M.O. and it was just a matter of time before the cops caught up with him. What kind of person gets a mysterious reduced sentence on a bank robbery charge then comes home and robs another bank in the same town? What did he have planned when the cops caught up with him? Chances are he would give up all of the dealers he had been buying coke from in an attempt to receive another reduced sentence. That's just the kind of guy G was.

Lil' Momma was only 17, but she braided hair like a professional. It was common knowledge to many that she was HIV positive but, that didn't stop B.J. from paying her a visit every week to get his hair braided. She was a sweet person and B.J. enjoyed the time he spent over her house relaxing and getting his hair washed and braided. He didn't even know her real name, he just called her Lil' Momma and she answered to that. He paid her $50 per visit even though he didn't have to. She was

satisfied with a couple of grams of weed and some conversation. He left there with his hair freshly washed and styled in his six trademark cornrows.

Already in the neighborhood, B.J. stopped by to find Kenya half-naked as usual. They talked about how she was starting to get morning sickness. She was excited while he was upset. The more he talked to her the more he realized that she was really trying to have a family with him. The thought put a slight case of fear in his heart. B.J. was not ready to become a father, but the thought of children did give him a warm feeling inside. If the baby happened to be his, he had every intention of taking good care of it. What he had no intention of doing was taking care of Kenya. She wasn't going to get a free ride through life just because she had opened her legs and gotten pregnant.

B.J. stayed at Kenya's messy apartment until his blunt was gone. The only reason she called him over was to ask for money. She claimed that she had a prenatal doctor's appointment. When he asked about her medical insurance, she informed him that hairdresser's didn't have any.

"I hope you don't think that I'm about to pay for a rack of bills," he told her.

"Well, what am I supposed to do?" she turned to look at him.

"You betta come up with somethin'." And he left it at that. For all he knew she wasn't even pregnant. She was probably just looking for a come up. When it came to extra money from B.J., Kenya had nothing coming. He wasn't mad at her for trying. He was mad at her for not asking him on the phone; he wouldn't have come all the way over to her apartment just to turn her down.

When B.J. went home to get his money together for Papi, he found a lead in the case he was determined to crack. According to T.J., Uncle Leon had come over to the house looking for B.J. and had ventured into his room even after T.J. told him B.J. was not home. B.J. needed to know what Uncle Leon wanted with

him, or from his room. He would have called him to ask, but Leon didn't have a phone or permanent address, for that matter. Uncle Leon was a functioning alcoholic, who made a living off of liquor and made a habit of shacking up with various women. He and his good buddy, Ray, ran a small liquor house that didn't bring in much money, but gave them the opportunity to drink for free.

"Did he say what it was he wanted?" B.J. asked his little brother.

"Nope."

As fate would have it, B.J. didn't have any drugs in his room so if Uncle Leon was looking he would have been out of luck.

B.J. gathered his money, put in a phone call to Papi, and proceeded to make moves. His body was taking care of business, but his mind was on trying to figure out who had been stealing from him. He was starting to lean more towards Leon than Dana, which really got under his skin because he knew his Uncle was either abusing the drugs or selling them to buy liquor. Either way, B.J. was focused on the best way to discover the thief.

B.J. took care of almost everything he had to take care of for the day. He had stashed his coke away in his room when he stopped home to pick up his mom. They were now seated at Red Lobster, munching on lobster, steak, and shrimp.

"Well, Ma, it looks like you were right about that grandmother thing." He couldn't think of an easy way to lay it on her. He didn't even know if Kenya was really pregnant by him, but if she was he didn't think it was right he wait until the last minute before telling the would-be-grandmother. He hated to admit it, but if it was his he would spoil the kid like crazy.

"Come again." Miss Janice dropped her fork and looked up from her plate.

"Well..." B.J. started, somewhat embarrassed. "Well, this girl talkin' about I got her pregnant and now she about to have a baby."

"Wow, B.J.! Why didn't you tell me?"

"I just did. But, I'm not even sure if it's mine. You know what I'm sayin'?" B.J. was staring in his plate.

"So tell me about her."

"Just some gold diggin' slut bucket that mighta messed around and got lucky. I can't really be for sure at this point. I just know I ain't feelin' her enough to be wit' her."

"Well, son. It sounds like you were feelin' her enough to be wit' her."

B.J. thought for a minute. "I was wit' her like dat, but I don't wanna be wit' her like dat. You know what I mean?"

"Yeah, I know what you mean," his mom confessed. "Why would you get mixed up with a girl like that? How long have you known her? And with all these diseases and stuff." Miss Janice was cool when it came to things like this, still B.J. didn't feel like revealing the complete truth to her; like how he had met her and got her pregnant all within 24 hours. "I would like to meet her."

"I've known her for a while," he lied, "but I don't want you to meet her yet. Not until she has the baby and I'm sure it's mine."

"That's nonsense," Miss Janice said in disbelief. "Any girl that interests my son, interests me. Now, when can I meet her?" B.J. felt the need to tell his mother that he wasn't interested in Kenya. "Well, what is it you don't like about her?" she asked, her voice full of concern.

Where do I start? he thought as he cracked open an Alaskan crab leg and dipped the meat in garlic butter. "She just doesn't do it for me, Ma."

"Oh, nobody does it for you. You always been so picky and choosy when it comes to girls. Get it from your father." Miss Janice rarely mentioned Dana and B.J.'s father. B.J. never met

him and Dana could remember seeing him less than five times in her entire life. He was a rolling stone, left town long ago and hadn't settled since. He never called, or showed concern for the two children he had with Janice. Of course, there were other children by different women, but they were complete strangers to B.J. and Dana. T.J. was the product of a short-lived relationship Miss Janice had with another man, who also showed little interest in his child.

"I don't know, Ma. She's cute, but I feel like she wants me for what I can I do for her financially, not emotionally. She had some rich ex-boyfriend, who spoiled her and now she thinks I'm about to fill his shoes."

"I wonder why she would think that," she said with a curious grin on her face. B.J. turned away. "Either way, I still want to meet her."

B.J. savored dinner. He always loved spending time with his mom, even though he didn't always take the time to do so. His mom was his heart and if she wanted to meet Kenya, she would but first he wanted to make sure she was really pregnant. He would at least wait until she started showing.

When they returned home, T.J. was patiently waiting for their doggy bags. B.J. went to his room to break down and bag up some of the coke he had bought earlier. He was in such a rush to go out with his mom and give her the four carat diamond bracelet he had bought her, he hadn't had the chance to do so earlier. B.J. knew it was past time for him to start keeping his work outside again, but he felt like he was not about to let some trifling thief run him out of his own room. If he started keeping his coke in the Buick again, he would never know who had been stealing from him. He held off all of his customers until the following day. It was a little after eleven o'clock when he finally laid down, putting an end to a busy day.

Before going to sleep, B.J. gave much thought to what his mom had said earlier. Was he too picky when it came to women? Is that why he only had two girlfriends in his entire life?

While things were going well for him financially, he was a firm believer in the old saying, 'money can't buy love'. His money was the only love in his life and there were times when his heart felt empty. It was times like these that made him long for a warm body to cuddle up against after a long day. He wanted someone who would help him save his money, not someone whose only interest was spending it. Baby or no baby, B.J. wanted a girlfriend and Kenya was not her.

Chapter 17

"Are you serious?" Free spoke into her cell. Shamika had to be lying to her because there was no way what she was hearing was true.

"Girl, if I'm lyin' then the truth ain't in me. I ain't got no reason to lie. I wouldn't even call you up like dat."

Free was dumbfounded. "Aight. I'm gonna talk to her and I'll see what she has to say about it," Free decided finally.

"Yeah, you do dat," Shamika suggested. "But don't say you heard it from me. You know what? I don't even care if you say you heard it from me. I ain't neva scared."

"Bye, Shamika."

Free hung up and signaled her way back into the left lane. She had a pound of weed under the driver's seat, but that didn't stop her from speeding to get rid of it and get home to confront her friend. She needed to sit and have a long talk with Nita. This new information Shamika dropped on her had her furious with her best friend. According to Shamika, Nita was easier than a forth grade final and for the right price she was down for whatever. People were calling her a two-hundred-dollar-ho. Free was upset, not only because she sensed truth in the rumor, but because she could feel that she and Nita were losing the closeness they once shared. Why wouldn't Nita discuss her new

money making scheme? Free knew that there was some truth to every rumor. How many other habits had Nita picked up? If it was all about the money, Free would give her best friend a grand or two without even thinking twice about it. Free had secrets of her own; how mad could she really be at Nita?

Nita's bones were starting to creep their way out of her closet. During a visit to her mother's house, she found herself on the receiving end of one of her mom's rare lectures. Nita just stopped by to bring her mom some money and show off her newly purchased school books. It was Sunday and school was scheduled to start the following Tuesday. Now, Big Nita was not the type to look a gift horse in the mouth, however when it came to her daughter's newfound wealth, she was rightfully curious. How could her unemployed, 18 year old daughter afford to give her $100 a week? Although Big Nita was now successfully working her way out of credit card debt, she could no longer go on without voicing her concern.

"I want to meet some of these guys." Nita had told her that different guys she'd been dating were giving her money. "And Tanita, what exactly are you doing to get the money?"

This conversation only caused Nita to change her mind about giving her mom any money at all. She didn't feel the need to be reprimanded for displaying generosity. If her mom wanted to question the money, she wouldn't have to worry about seeing anymore of it. Big Nita figured her daughter would take this type of stance, but her motherly instincts warned her that Nita was doing something illegal or unethical.

"I don't have to do nuttin' for it, Ma. I've just been dating guys who can afford to spoil me. That's it and that's all," she lied.

"Is that so?" Big Nita was hearing none of it. Her suspicions had been proven true by her daughter's obvious lies. She witnessed first hand as her daughter weaved her way through the dating world in search of the big spenders. In fact, if she wanted an idea as to whether or not her daughter would be home late, she would look out the window and make a judgment based on

the type of car Nita's date arrived in. If it was an average or below average vehicle, chances are her daughter would be home at a decent hour, but if her date was driving an expensive vehicle then there was no telling what time her daughter would be back home. It was a sad, but dependable practice Big Nita had come up with when Nita was still living at home.

More than anything, she wanted her daughter to change her ways, but that kind of change wasn't going to happen overnight. What Big Nita failed to realize was that it was actually her who stressed materialism to her daughter at a rather young age. Whenever Nita would speak to, or spend time with her father, Tariq, Big Nita would always have one question for her as soon as she walked in the door: "Did he give you any money?" One time, Nita told her mom that her dad had called and said he would take her to the movies on an upcoming Saturday. "You need to tell him to come and bring you some money," Big Nita instructed. Tariq never did come and pick Nita up that day. He didn't even call to cancel.

As a child, Nita was taught the powerful value of a dollar. If a man loved you he would give you money and if he didn't, he wouldn't, she thought. For Nita, love was a green, rectangular piece of dirty paper. Now she worked the streets in search of love and brought some love back home to her mom. Nita told her mother if she didn't appreciate the money, she didn't have to take it. Big Nita didn't answer. She did appreciate the money but, she prayed for the day her daughter would change her ways and settle down with one guy.

Back at the apartment, Free had just walked in to discover her roommate was not at home. She entered her bedroom and was greeted by the same smell she had been trying to hide for days. Ever since she had started bringing more work home, the strong weed odor in her room couldn't be ignored. No matter how deep in the back of her closet or how many plastic bags she stuffed it in, her room still carried the odor. If she could smell it, she was sure her roommate could also.

Just then she heard the jingle of keys, signaling Nita's return.

Free decided ahead of time that the best way to get her to talk about the rumor she heard from Shamika was to get her to talk about money. If there was one thing Free knew about Nita, it was that she loved to talk about money. Before Free could get a chance to make her way out to the living room, Nita came waltzing into her room.

"Whassup, girl," she greeted Free.

"Nuttin. What you been up to?"

"I know what you been up to. You been in here smokin' all day it smells like," Nita joked.

"Yeah, suttin' like dat."

"So, Free what you been up to?"

Both girls had the same motive—pick each other for information. Free's cell phone rang and interrupted their interrogation session.

"Cool. I'm on my way." Free hung up. She had moves to make and no time to hang out with her best friend. That had been happening a lot lately. "I gotta go and holla at somebody. I'll be back."

Bingo, Nita thought. *That's probably the guy she's working for who just called. She probably gotta bring him something. I'm just gonna hang out in her room until she leaves. If I'm right, she'll try to get me to leave, so she can get to whatever it is she has to bring him.*

One of Free's customers had called and ordered a pound. Free was trying to see that $900, especially since it was all her's, now that she started buying from Ed upfront. She was just waiting for Nita to leave her room, so she could retrieve the one pound from the four that were stuffed in the back of her closet and really be on the way like she had told her customer.

"Where you off to?" picked Nita.

"I just told you. I gotta go holla at somebody."

"Who? Let me find out you keeping secrets." She shouldn't have said that.

"Are you keeping secrets?"

Silence. The truth was, for the first time ever, they were both keeping secrets from each other. Something in Free's eyes told Nita that there was more to the question than what appeared on the surface. They stared into each other's eyes. Nita broke the long gaze first when she walked over to Free's full length mirror and began fingering her hair. She had a tendency to do that when she was nervous. Free sat on her bed and watched, waiting for Nita to leave her room. When it was evident that Nita was neglecting to do so, Free had no choice but to bring up what Shamika had told her. If Nita was put on the spot, she would leave the room just to avoid an uncomfortable conversation. Other than that, it appeared as if she planned on sticking around until Free left out the door.

"Listen," Free started, "you been getting down lately. I been hearin' a lot. All I gotta say is 'say it ain't so'."

What could Nita say? Half of her wanted to ask Free what she had heard and then deny everything. The other half of her wanted to play defense and ask Free how she had been getting down lately. She went with the latter.

"How you been getting down lately? Let me find out some dude got you throwin' bricks at the pen. I thought you was smarter than that."

"What you said?" As brown as she was, Free's cheeks began to redden. Normally, Nita was the rowdy one and Free was laid back but the truth was Free had the bad temper. Nita mumbled her last statement out of the side of her mouth, but Free's reaction made her turn around from the mirror.

"Did I stutter?" she raised her voice.

"You know me betta than to be beatin' around the bush. Speak ya mind, hustla." Free's tone showed her anger. She felt no shame concerning the money she had accumulated over the summer.

"All I'm sayin' is if you keepin' somebody's drugs or money up in here den you need to let me know. In case you forgot, this joint is in my name."

"No, I ain't forgot. There ain't nuttin' up in here dat ain't supposed to be up in here. Why? What you know dat you wanna talk about? Let me know." Free took a step closer in Nita's direction.

"I don't know nuttin', but if you wanna tell me suttin' or talk to me about suttin', I'm right here," said Nita, lowering her voice.

"Well, since you mentioned it..." This was Free's opportunity. She took a seat on the edge of her bed. "Why do I keep hearin' about you sleepin' around? They say you out here prostitutin' ya self for a lil' bit of nuttin'. What's up wit' dat? Holla at ya girl." The look she gave Nita emphasized the sincerity in her voice.

"What you heard?" Nita started to panic. She needed to know what she would be denying.

"They say you sexin' anyone who can afford to pay you $200. They say you out here actin' pressed for cash and you lettin' dudes have there way wit' you for a lil' bit of nuttin'." Free stared in Nita's face, awaiting a response. She met Free's gaze for a few seconds and then turned away out of embarrassment. As soon as Nita opened her mouth, she regretted what came out.

"Well, I'm sorry we all can't have thousands of dollars tucked away in our dresser drawer. I'm just tryna get mine and I-"

"Who the hell got thousands tucked in their drawer?"

"You. I was lookin' for some batteries and I went…"

"You went in my drawer?"

"Like I said," Nita continued. "I was lookin' for some batteries for the remote control for the DVD player and I couldn't find any anywhere and you wasn't here so I just peeked through your drawer and I found all this money. I don't know whose money you holdin', or who you robbed, or what you got goin' on but whatever it is, I know it ain't legal." Feeling like she was winning the argument, Nita folded her arms and gave Free a 'take that' look.

"And sellin' your body is? First of all, since when do I keep batteries in my drawer. Second of all…" Free was so hot, she couldn't even finish her sentence. She was insulted that Nita would go snooping through her room when she wasn't home, but she was more insulted by the fact that it had never crossed Nita's mind that maybe Free was stashing her own hard earned money. Free should have kept her savings in a more discreet hiding place. Nita shouldn't have invaded her privacy. "Second of all, what are you doin' goin' thru my stuff when I ain't here?"

"That ain't the point." Nita knew she was wrong and did her best to change the subject. "The point is, if you got somebody's illegal shit up in here, I need to know about it cuz this joint is my name!"

Nita was right, but at the same time she was wrong. Free thought she was going to leave the room with her last statement, instead she started walking to the closet, as if she already knew what was in there.

"Dat ain't the point I'm tryna make either!" Free yelled back. "You so worried about what I'm doin' for money. Tell me, Nita. How have *you* been making your money? Yeah, I guess you don't want to talk about dat, huh?"

When Nita didn't answer, Free walked over to the closet, nudged Nita out of the way and slid open the door. Nita was so interested in what Free had in her closet, she failed to respond to the initiation of physical contact.

"You want to know what I been up to?" Nita was talking fast as Free dug in her closet. "I been getting' wit' dudes den takin' there money. I'm gettin' money and I don't gotta worry about no cops or nuttin'. You betta get right and get wit' it."

Free pulled the four pounds out of the back of her closet. Nita had come clean, so shouldn't she. She was tired of stalling. "Oh, I'm right!" she retorted, sprawling her work onto the bedroom floor. Nita gasped as if someone was squeezing her throat. Free snatched up her Tommy book bag and threw one of the pounds inside. "You wanna know what I been up to. This is what I been up to. I been getting paid while you been getting laid." She grabbed the other three pounds from off of the floor and threw them back in her closet. Nita watched closely with a shocked, jealous eye. Free strapped the bag onto her back, stepped into a pair of red Diadoras and walked over to the doorway.

"If you'll excuse me, I got moves to make."

Nita was impressed with envy. For the first time it dawned on her that the money she had found in Free's drawer was her own. Instead of being proud of her friend's financial achievements, she was jealous. When she finally closed her mouth and reopened it again, her words heightened the situation to an extreme.

"Well, I'm not sure I want to be livin' wit' a drug dealer." She mumbled loud enough for Free to hear.

"What?" Free knew she didn't hear what she thought she'd just heard. Her rebuttal was thoughtless and cruel. "Well, I'm not sure if I want to be livin' wit' no hooker. Every time I come home you got a different dude ova here. You takin' this whole sleepin' wit' guys and then takin' their money thing a little too far. I might not get my money the best way in the world, but I don't have to worry about catchin' nuttin' either."

"You betta be worried about catchin' a bullet," Nita warned. Her words echoed through the room.

"I got money waitin', so I'm not about to sit here and argue wit' your jealous ass. Now get out my room," she directed.

Nita looked at Free like she had two heads sitting on her shoulders. *No she didn't just kick me out of her room.* Free moved to the side of the doorway, giving Nita just enough space to exit. "I know one thing," Nita stated once they were in the hallway. "You betta get dem drugs outta here if you know what's good for you."

Free's response was sharp and meaningful. "No! You betta stay da hell outta my room before I have to whip your ass. If you know what's good for you." SLAM. She was out the door.

I can't believe she came at me like that, Free thought on her way to Ed's Sonata. The argument with Nita gave her the urge for independence. If Nita didn't want her staying there, she would get her own place. She could afford it. If Ed didn't want to sell her his little hoopty, she would get her own car. She could afford it. If she met some new guys and they were trying to cop weed from her, she would sell it to them. She had it.

Nita sat in front of the big screen, trying hard to concentrate on a movie. She was livid; the last thing she wanted was for Free to move out. In all honesty, she was more aggravated that Free hadn't told her about the drugs in the house then she was about the actual drugs being in the house. Nita wasn't the most honest person in the world, but still she resented Free's secrecy. She wouldn't have had a problem with it, if Free had told her about it and then offered to put her in on the action. There wasn't too much Nita had a problem with when it came to making money. Her thoughts drifted from jealousy, to her friend's safety and were interrupted by the ringing of the house phone.

Free handled her business and was on the way home. She was smoking and zoning on the highway. Unlike Ed, she wouldn't smoke if she had a large amount of weed in the car, so now that she had gotten rid of her package, she took the opportunity to do so. She focused on how much money she had made over the summer and how much she was willing to do to keep it. She

knew Nita wasn't crazy enough to take or mess with her money, but still she wouldn't be able to rest until she found a new hiding place for it. Still, she would keep her money in her drawer for a few days, daring Nita to touch it. She started remembering all the stories she'd heard about people getting killed over money and drugs and she recognized that someone would definitely kill to get their hands on her earnings. Even though she knew all of her customers well, it was an unpredictable game. By the time she reached home, Free was convinced she needed a gun.

Free entered the apartment, walked past Nita on the couch and went straight to her room. She put her money away, kicked off her sneakers, and went back out into the kitchen to grab an ice-cream sandwich out of the freezer. Nita watched and tried to decide whether or not she would give her the message. She chose not to be petty and spoke up.

"Ya boy Ed called here for you."

Free didn't want to talk to her. If Nita hadn't mentioned her connect's name, she would have ignored her and went straight to her room.

"He called here? What did he say?" Why hadn't Ed called her cell phone?

"He called collect. He's locked up. He said he's gonna call back between 9:30 and 9:45. I wouldn't have accepted the call, but I recognized his name and I know you got his car so I figured it was important."

"What?" Free almost dropped her ice cream. "What else did he say?" Her voice was full of panic.

"That's it. He thanked me for accepting the call even though you wasn't here and he said if you wasn't home by 9:00 for me to call your phone and tell you to get home so you wouldn't miss his call."

Free looked at her watch. It was 8:45. She wanted to sit and

download her thoughts with her best friend, but the fight they had earlier was still fresh in her mind.

"Thanks for the message," she said, heading back to her room to wait for his call.

Chapter 18

"Where's T.J.?"

"He's not here, baby. I'm not sure where he went," replied Miss Janice.

This was the second time B.J. had come home early looking to spend some of his extra time with his little brother. B.J. had to realize that T.J. was getting older and he was not always going to be sitting around the house playing video games. B.J. had just returned home from a one night stand with a girl he had met a couple of nights ago. She was a pretty girl, who had given it up too easy and was not his type. Still, he had needs to fulfill, so he called her up and took her to a hotel.

B.J. had coke to sell, but he didn't feel like doing much of anything this Monday. He just wanted to chill and enjoy his money. He wanted to turn his phone off, hit the highway and ride out of town with someone special. He wished he had a girl he could take down to the beach, maybe do a little shopping. Unfortunately, he did not have a special female in his life. He thought of Kenya and gave her a call.

"Hey, I was just about to call you," she answered, happy to hear from him. B.J. could hear a lot of noise in the background, male voices in particular.

"Where you at?"

"I'm in the house. Why? You tryna stop thru? I need to talk to you."

It sounds like you got enough company. "Yeah, I might do dat. I'll give you a call a little later."

Poor Kenya. She couldn't win for losing. The one time that B.J. called her to spend time with her, she had a house full of men. *It just ain't meant to be,* he thought. In the kitchen B.J. found his mom seated at the table with her brother; just the person he wanted to see.

"What's goin' on Uncle Leon?"

"Nephew, man you're busier than downtown at five o'clock. I been tryna get wit you for a minute, Big Man."

"No, you da big man. Talk to me."

Miss Janice took that as her cue to get up and leave the kitchen. She knew that the men didn't have anything of great importance to discuss, still she wanted them to have their privacy. As soon as Uncle Leon started the conversation, B.J. stared at him trying to determine if he was the culprit who had been stealing from his room.

"Listen here, young'n. I need ya help wit' a little suttin', ya dig. I got this thing. Well, me and Ray, ya see, we 'bout to expand, ya hear. We got some things we tryna do, ya see."

"Well, it ain't nuttin' wrong wit' dat." B.J. had a good idea what he was getting at—money. Whenever Uncle Leon wanted to talk to B.J. it was always about money. He didn't ask very often, so if he came with a reasonable purpose, B.J. usually granted his wish.

"Yeah, couldn't nuttin' neva be wrong wit' dat," Leon agreed and fingered the brim of his cap before getting to his point. "Well, I need about $100 to get this plan into action. Get the ball rollin', ya know."

He wanted a hundred dollars. That's a small thing to a giant. B.J. swiftly reached into his pants pocket, peeled off two fifties and handed them to his Uncle. B.J. did this with such speed to emphasize the fact that if his uncle wanted something he had, all he had to do was ask. If Uncle Leon was stealing from B.J., he would not have been bold enough to stand before him asking for money. Over a thousand dollars worth of cocaine had been stolen from B.J. in the past two weeks and here comes Uncle Leon asking for a measly hundred dollars. It didn't add up. Uncle Leon was not slick enough to outsmart his nephew by stealing from him and then asking of him in an attempt to disguise the thievery. No, if Uncle Leon was the thief, he would have avoided B.J. as best he could.

"Thanks a lot. I appreciate it, young'n." That still didn't explain why Uncle Leon was in B.J.'s room the other day. As if he could read his mind he said "Listen here, I was wonderin' if you had any old sneakers you wasn't wearin' too much." That wasn't a problem. B.J. was in the habit of giving his used sneakers to his Uncle. Even though B.J. wore a size 10½ shoe and Uncle Leon wore an 11 that didn't stop him from coming and asking for B.J.'s old sneakers every month. B.J. would often sit them in a garbage bag outside of his closet. Perhaps that was the reason his Uncle had went into his room that day.

"Yeah, no problem. I'll put them together for you. Stop by tomorrow."

After Uncle Leon left, B.J. went to his room to get his work together for his customers. So much for taking the day off. When he dug into his stash, he discovered that once again the same petty thief had robbed him. This time there was a whole ounce missing. What was supposed to be four and half ounces was now only three and a half. B.J. was highly upset. He slammed his work down into his Diadora shoe box and left the house in a flash. Because Dana was still in Miami, the thievery upset him more this time. She wasn't scheduled to return until the following morning. He sped to the nearest drug store and purchased a pack of 5 volt batteries. The batteries in his scale had to be going bad because there was no way someone in his family was bold enough to be stealing whole ounces from him.

He returned home in less than ten minutes, switched the batteries in his scale and reweighed the short sac. Just like he figured, there wasn't anything wrong with his scale. There was something wrong in his house. He was fuming. Uncle Leon had just left the house and he hadn't entered B.J.'s room once during his visit. What was really going on? B.J. continued to reweigh and rebag his work. He was taking shorts, left and right, and there had to be some type of explanation for it. He gathered enough work for the sales he had waiting and left out the house to meet with his customers. This time, rather than putting the remainder of his work in a shoe box, he put it in the numerous pockets of his three puffy North Face coats. He wasn't trying to take another loss.

B.J. contemplated shorting each of his customers three and a half grams until he made up for the ounce he had just lost. He later decided against it based on the fact that some of his customers weren't as discreet as he needed them to be. They would call him right back and say wide open on his phone, "Man, you shorted me three and a half grams." When he looked at it from that perspective, it wasn't worth the trouble. He didn't talk in detail about drugs or prices on his cell phone. He would just have to take the loss. More than anything, he needed to keep his phone as clean as possible. He used his phone to call Papi and he had no idea what type of heat Papi was generating.

As he rode hittin' switches, he got an unexpected call from Taye. B.J. was starting to fall back when it came to Taye. Now that he was broke, Taye was a natural live wire and there was no telling what he would be willing to risk to get back on his feet. B.J. planned on giving him his space. They were still cool, but B.J. had given him all that he could give him as far as lookouts were concerned. Now, here was Taye on B.J.'s phone asking him for another lookout; asking him to take another short.

"Yo, I got this dude tryna holla at a heezy. Where you at?"

Whoa! Now all of a sudden Taye knew somebody who was trying to cop a half of brick. B.J. felt a bad vibe instantly. Who was this person?

"Where you at?" he asked, preferring to discuss it with him in person.

"I'm at my joint. Come thru."

"I'm on the way."

B.J. had one more switch to hit before he would be able to stop at Taye's house. See, B.J. wasn't in the business of selling half of bricks, he had it but he didn't sell such large quantities. He would rather sell his customers a couple of ounces here and a couple of ounces there, he came out better doing it that way. He didn't care who the person was, he wasn't putting a half of brick in Taye's hands. B.J. was just cautious like that. He didn't even like the idea of Taye thinking that he could call him up for a half. Taye and B.J. were cool, but they weren't friends. No, B.J. wasn't feeling the sale. For all he knew it was a set up. B.J. stayed paranoid like that.

"See, I know you don't want to see dude's face so you could ride in the truck wit' me. I'mma park around the corner from where dude be at and get out. That way you don't have to worry about him seein' your face." Taye had it all figured out.

"And what dude want?" B.J. asked. He had a way of asking questions he already knew the answers to.

"He want a half. He's ready to get on today cuz he been tryna holla at me for a few days now. I told him fifteen and he was cool wit' dat. So, if you put me on for like thirteen, well it's a go."

Thirteen? B.J. reflected. *Since when do I got halves for thirteen? And fifteen?* Who the hell would pay fifteen? B.J. was now thinking Taye was trying to get the coke for G. Taye probably had a plan to switch the money so that he wouldn't have to bring him bank money. B.J. was no fool. He was a successful survivor, who did his best to never go against his better judgment.

"Man, I can't get my hands on no half," he lied with a straight face.

"For real?" Taye asked, recognizing a lie when he heard one.

The truth was, Taye felt like B.J. wasn't looking out for him like he should have; like he could have. Taye felt B.J. was being selfish. There was no half key customer. Taye had every intention of taking the half and saying he got robbed again. He would have his hoopty parked around the corner, where he planned to stash the work. He even had a guy he had been beefing with for some time that he planned to pin it on. He went as far as to have one of his girl's change her voicemail from her personal message to just plain music, he then told her not to answer the phone when his number appeared. He planned to call her phone and leave all sorts of messages as if her number was the number of the guy that robbed him. Yeah, Taye had all the answers. He was even going to bust a few shots in the air before he came running back around the corner and say he tried to catch the guy, but missed. Taye had it all planned out, but he didn't plan on B.J. being one step ahead of him.

One doesn't really know a person until they see that person very rich or very poor. Money, or lack there of, is a consistent truth exposer. Now, if it was his boy Slim, B.J. would have thrown Slim the half and told him to call him when he got on his feet and got himself together. B.J. knew Slim, but he didn't know Taye like that.

"For real. I couldn't get my hands on a half right now if I wanted to. It ain't sweet like that," B.J. told him.

"Well, I'mma talk to dude. I'm sure he'd be willin' to wait on dat. How long do you think it might take?" Before, the dude was in a rush. Now, without even speaking to the dude, Taye was sure he'd be willing to wait.

"I gotta call up my peoples. I'll get back to you in a few days on dat." Who did B.J. have to talk to? That was all game. He had more than three half of bricks in his house already.

"You do dat cuz I'm tellin' you dude's good peoples and he got the money to spend all day."

B.J. didn't trust Taye's judgment. To hear him tell it, Jisella was good peoples. They smoked for a while longer and played a few games of Madden football. Just when B.J. was beginning to wonder who really had his back, he got a call from his boy, Randy. At a time when B.J. wasn't really sure who he had in his corner, he was glad to hear from him.

Randy and B.J. went back like a recliner. B.J. used to cop from Randy back in the day when he was just a youngster getting his feet wet in the game. B.J. would re-up with Randy, grind up a decent profit and then turn around and spend every dime he owned with Randy. That was loyalty.

One winter night, several years ago, B.J. was robbed at gunpoint for an eighth of a key. As it turns out, the robber was one of Randy's customers. When the shady customer came back to Randy bragging about his conquest, Randy pistol whipped the young boy and robbed him for the seven grand he was looking to spend. B.J.'s beef had turned into Randy's beef and the thieving youngster wanted no trouble with Randy. Randy gave B.J. back an eighth of a brick and ever since then there was nothing B.J. wouldn't do for him. Randy later caught an assault charge due to an unrelated incident and B.J. kept his commissary stacked throughout his 18-month bid. They didn't speak much these days, but whenever B.J. changed his cell number he always made sure Randy had the new number and vice versa.

"What's good, baby? Long time no hear from," B.J. smiled.

"Can't call it. Ain't nuttin' changed but the bullets in da burner and da day of da year."

"I know that's right," B.J. laughed then asked. "Where you at? Lemme smoke witcha like I joke witcha."

"Yeah, I gotta put a bug in your ear anyway. Come to the barbershop. How long?"

"Gimmie fifteen."

"Aight."

B.J. hung up then looked over at Taye, who appeared to be hanging on his every word. B.J. smoked the rest of the blunt he and Taye were passing and then left to meet his boy. When he arrived at the barbershop, he spotted Randy's Excursion parked across the street. The barbershop was closed and Randy was seated outside in his truck. B.J. hopped out of his Cadillac, locked the doors and jogged across the street to jump in the white SUV.

"Whassup, Big Bank Hank?" Randy teased. Randy was fond of calling B.J. 'Big Bank Hank' in appreciation of all the money he had watched him accumulate. It was his way of letting B.J. know that he still remembered his broke days and now that he had a little paper, he didn't want him to forget where he had come from.

"Dat's you, neva me," B.J. smiled as they gave each other dap.

"Roll up. Take a ride wit' me, hustla."

"No doubt."

B.J. was breaking up some dro on a CD case as Randy initiated the conversation. It had been a few months since the guys had sat and smoked with each other.

"You know I let some bitches get me for like seven g's."

"Say what?"

"Fo' sho'." That in itself was a mouthful. Both men could remember clearly the day Randy had robbed an unsuspecting customer for seven grand on B.J.'s behalf. Now, several years later, due to an ironic twist of fate, Randy had been robbed for the exact same amount.

"Who was it dawg?" B.J. asked ready to return the favor. As far as he was concerned, Randy's beef was his beef.

"Some bad lil' young broads. I mean, some bad lil' broads I

was lettin' give me some action up at the room. So, I pays 'em what I said I would pay 'em but they done seen all the money I had on me and they feel like they wanted more. Dey got greedy. I turn my back and dem lil' bitches was gone, money and everything."

"Where did you have the money at?"

"It was in my book bag. It was my fault for lettin' dem see all that money anyway."

"Where did it happen? Where can we find dese broads?" B.J. was more than ready to offer his services.

"Man, I been at dese hoes all summer. It happened in the beginning of the joint," Randy revealed. "But peep dis," he continued. "Word on the street is one of dem chicks is getting a lil' money now. Heard she slangin' dem pounds for dem Jamaicans."

"Okay, okay." B.J. was there to help. Nobody was going to rob his peoples without having a price to pay. He was just taking it all in.

"See, you know, I ain't sweatin' the money. But it's the principle. There's rules to this thing of ours. When you hit a lick, you stay quiet and if they woulda did dat, I coulda lived wit' da loss. Now shawty out tryna make a million dollars off my cheese. Nah, I can't live like dat, you know."

Yeah, B.J. knew exactly what Randy was saying. It wasn't that the girls had stolen the money. It was the fact that they had stolen the money and were trying to do the right thing with it. B.J. wasn't one to knock a hustle but at the same time, a wrong could never be made right.

"So, dey getting money, huh?" B.J. wanted more information. Female hustlers turned him on.

"Not dey, just one of 'em. Heard she makin' moves like a shoe and I ain't 'bout to hang like a lace while she gets paid off my scratch. No sir."

"I hear you dawg. So, what the broad lookin' like?"

"She look good. She black but she got a Chinese thing goin' on. Nice hair, nice shape, she cuter den a thousand dolla bill. Real jazzy broad. Real, real jazzy broad."

"Where she from? Who she be wit'?" B.J. asked in a voice full of interest.

"She be wit' da lil' broke chick who brung her up to the room. I don't even know where dey from. I ain't even catch her name but da otha girl name is Tanita."

"Don't sweat it, playa. I'll do my best to run across her. Maybe put the word out that I'm tryna buy a coupla pounds or suttin'. It's nuttin'."

"Exactly. Keep ya ear to the street and ya eye on your money, playa. Oh, this is what I wanted to tell you. Ya boy Taye, they say he doin' terrible. Dey say he lookin' for a vic, like a fiend lookin' for a fix. Watch ya boy."

"Good lookin', baby. All I could do at this point is watch shawty. I done did all I could. I can't help 'em," said B.J.

By this point, they had pulled back in front of the barbershop. B.J. took one last toke before throwing the blunt out of the window, signaling the end of their conversation.

"Dat's right. Just keep ya ear to the street and ya eye on your money," Randy repeated his warning.

"Fo' sho'. Take ya time, hustla."

"Fo' sho'."

B.J. returned home later that night and had a hard time falling asleep. Kenya had been calling his phone constantly and now it was to the point where he wasn't even answering. He figured that she wanted something because that was the only time that she blew his phone up. Unable to sleep, he ventured into

the kitchen for a midnight snack. There he found his mom, seated in near darkness, smoking a Newport.

"What you doin' smokin'?" The question startled her. Miss Janice had quit smoking cigarettes the same year she gave up her drug addiction. B.J. hadn't seen her pick up a cigarette in years.

"Just got stress on my mind, is all."

"Stress like what, Ma? What do you need?" B.J. closed the refrigerator and took the seat at the table closest to his mom. He was thinking the worst. His mom had used cigarettes as a crutch when she was fighting her addiction. B.J. began to wonder about his missing cocaine and curse himself.

"Just got myself a case of the old folks blues. I'll be okay. Don't you worry about me, son."

B.J. eyed his mom closely, in search of any signs of abuse. "But you don't need dem cancer sticks. Mom, are you okay?"

"I'm fine, honey. You go back to sleep. I'll see you in the morning. Goodnight, B.J."

"Goodnight, Mom." B.J. kissed her on the forehead and headed for his room.

Chapter 19

Close to three weeks had passed and Nita and Free were well into their first semester of college. They shared three of the same classes and for the most part, they were keeping up with their studies. Nita had tried to cut back on some of her male company, but she was still spending many nights away from home. Free, who was experiencing a drought, was spending more time in the apartment than she preferred. There were times when Free couldn't even study or really enjoy a movie because guys were calling the house all times of the night for Nita. There were so many different men calling that Free had to start writing the names down just so that she could keep track.

Nita had went on another adventure with Lamell. When he had called, she went over to the hotel expecting to see Tasha. Instead, Lamell was there with one of his boys. Supposedly the guy had just been released from prison and if it hadn't been for the grand Lamell threw her way when she entered the room, Nita would have turned him down. Nita had never had sex with two guys at the same time, but for $1,000 she was willing to give it a try. When she tried to squeeze an extra two-fifty out of Lamell, he said she was being outrageous and that it was a gift for his homie. She had already accepted the money so she undressed and made preparations to block what would happen out of her mind.

Free's paper chase was halted. When she spoke to Ed, he

explained his situation. Ed was pulled over in his Acura for failure to stop completely before making a right turn at a red light. The police officers smelled weed and asked if they could search the vehicle. Luckily, Ed had only five pounds of weed on him. He was accustomed to riding around and smoking with much more weight than that. He was being held without bail in the city jail and charged with possession of marijuana with the intent to distribute. He was more worried about whether his baby's momma would spend the money he had stashed over in their house than he was about the 24 months he was looking to serve. He had told Free to hold it down and not to forget about him. She sent him a $200 money order with promises to do the same the first of every month. Ed expressed his appreciation and continued to call once a week.

In the meantime, people were calling Free's cell phone on a daily basis, asking for weed she could no longer supply. Free had adjusted her study time and leisure time around the meetings she had with her customers and now that she had no product to sell, her lifestyle was beginning to change. She had more than enough money to buy her own vehicle but without a connect, there was no way she was willing to spend that kind of money. She had gotten quite comfortable with buying a new pair of sneakers every week and smoking as much weed as she could fit into her lungs. All of this was taken from her overnight and her customers continued to call questioning her about when she would be back on. She had to do something.

Nita and Free were back on speaking terms, but neither of them had forgotten about their big dispute. They would come home and study together or just sit around the apartment in front of their big screen. Nita would often try to pick Free for information about her money making lifestyle and in turn she was offended when Free neglected to show interest in her cash collecting affairs. Nita yearned for Free to let her in on her hustle. As much as she warned Free about the negative aspects of being a drug dealer, if given the chance, Nita would try to sell whatever Free put into her hands. But Free wasn't going that route. The game is to be bought not taught.

"A yo! Nita." Free had just hung up the phone with yet another unsatisfied customer. "Yo Nita," she called from her bedroom. Nita paused the movie she was watching and went into Free's room to see what it was she wanted.

"What?"

"Listen. You remember that day when I went out of town with Ed and I saw that white Excursion and I got all scared."

"Yeah. How could I forget? I was worried sick. Why?"

"Well," Free continued, silently praying the answer to her next question would be 'yes'. "Remember when you said you would remember the address I gave you? You didn't write it down somewhere, did you?"

"No. Why?"

"Damn! No reason." Free's long shot had missed. Her last hope was that Nita had wrote down the address of Ed's connect. She had already tried to purchase weed from other sources, but no one could provide the quality, quantity, and price she desired. She was now desperate and ready to visit Ed's connect without him. She remembered the exit and if she racked her brain hard enough she could probably get to the correct vicinity but without an exact address, she would be lost.

"Why would I need to write the address down if I memorized it?" Free looked up from her phone. She could have kissed Nita.

"You memorized it? And after all this time you still remember it?"

"Yup. 3218 Towson Parkway."

Free threw her phone down and jumped up off the bed. Her best friend had come though for her. If only Nita knew what the address meant to her. Three months had passed and still Nita had the address in her head. That's what friends are for.

"Girl, I could kiss you right now." Now that she had the exact address, she could easily search the internet for directions. Free was pacing her bedroom, putting her plan into motion. Nita noticed the change in her mood.

"What's the big deal?" she asked.

"Oh, it's no big deal," Free lied, changing her tune. If she didn't know better, she would have asked Nita to ride with her. This would be Free's solo mission and if things didn't go well, she didn't want to be responsible for putting anyone in jeopardy. If things did go well, she didn't want to have to look out for anybody, but herself. Either way, she planned to buy Nita a pair of Prada sneakers just for remembering the address.

Nita, after noticing how Free was not going to elaborate further, sensed the end of their brief conversation and left the room. She figured that whatever Free needed the address for was her business, especially since Free didn't plan on sharing the information. *The worst thing that can happen is they tell me 'no' or that they don't know anyone named Ed.* She thought deeper. *No, the worst thing that can happen is that they think it's a set up and that I'm working with the police.* Her thoughts drifted even deeper. *No, the worst thing that could really happen is Randy answers the door. Yeah, that's the worst thing that could happen.* She rolled a blunt then sat back and smoked as she weighed her options. By the time the blunt was finished burning she would have a plan of action.

"Where you goin'?" Nita asked as Free whizzed past her reaching for the front door knob.

"I'll be back, sweetie."

"Alright. Be careful."

Nita was getting a gut feeling that something was about to happen to her best friend, but she couldn't quite put her finger on it. Even if she could, it was too late. Free was out the door.

Free's first stop was to Kinko's to access the internet. She

could have gone to her mother's house to use the computer over there, but Kinko's was on the way to the Interstate. Deja vu hit as she stopped at the same gas station she and Ed stopped at the very first time she made this same trip. She filled her tank, grabbed a soda and was on her way.

Free spent the hour long drive in contemplation mode. What if nobody was home? What if that really was Randy's truck she had seen parked outside and he answers the door? What if they tried to rob her? What if a girl answers the door? What if they turned her down and the trip was for nothing? She wouldn't know unless she tried and it was worth the trip. If not, she would never know what was on the other side of that door.

It was indeed a bold move on Free's part, but Free was a bold girl. She traveled with $6,000 inside of her purse. Worst-case scenario: she'd get robbed. Still, she had another six grand at home to get back on her feet with. Just as she was approaching the Harristown Parkway exit, her concentration was interrupted by the sound of her cell. From the caller ID, she could see that it was Nita calling from the apartment.

"Whassup?" Free answered, ready to gun down the call.

"Where you at?" nosey Nita asked.

"I'm in the middle of suttin'. Lemme call you right back."

"No. You don't gotta worry about callin' me back cuz I'm not gonna be here. I'm getting ready to go out. You don't gotta rush me off da phone either. I just called to tell you your mother just called for you. She said for you to call her right now."

"Alright. Thanks, babe. I'll call your phone in a little while." Free closed her cell phone and reached over to the passenger seat for the print out containing the directions. Reading and following them required her full attention and she decided that she would call her mother back when she was finished taking care of business. Once she exited the highway and began following the instructions, it all came back to her. She recognized the church at the corner where Ed had told her to make a left.

Passing the Wendy's and movie theatre, she knew she was close. All that was left to do was make a right onto Towson Parkway and look for the house that read '3218'. Her nerves were shot and mind was racing. She didn't know whether to turn around and go back, or continue on. She approached the block, made the right turn and now there was no turning back.

When Free scanned the block for anything suspicious, she was pleased to see no sign of the Ford Excursion. *So far, so good.* She parked directly across the street. She thought about circling the block first, but decided that straight forwardness was her best approach. Grabbing her purse full of money, she headed for the house that read '3218'. She had also thought about leaving her money in the car until she knew things were copasetic, but she took a chance and brought it with her when she went to ring the doorbell. *I only live once. Either it is or it ain't.* Free climbed the four steps leading to the porch and rang the doorbell. The sun was beginning it's descent to the other side of the Earth and when she peeked through the front window, she was able to see that lights were on in the house. She heard the footsteps walking towards the front door and she started shaking in her Air Forces. It was too late to turn around and walk away.

"Who?" a male voice yelled from the other side of the wooden door. She didn't answer right away. If she did state her name, would they know who she was and grant her an entrance? She was starting to think the trip was a bad idea. "Who is it?" the voice repeated, only this time it sounded as if it was directly in front of her.

"It's Free. I came to holla at you about suttin'," she heard a voice inside of her say.

"Yo, who's dat?" another voice asked. This male voice sounded as if it was coming from a little further inside of the house.

"I don't know," the first guy answered.

Fear engulfed Free as the door unlocked and opened before her. She stared into the eyes of a middle aged, dreaded,

Jamaican man with a Mack 11 in one hand and a Backwood cigar in the other.

"What can I do for you?" he asked. Finding such a beautiful girl on his doorstep was a pleasant surprise, but he didn't loosen his grip on the gun. Free stared at the Mack and then back into the eyes of the man who had the potential to take her life right where she stood.

"Well," she started her pre-rehearsed speech. "I'm close friends wit' Ed. You know Ed that drives the blue Acura? He bought me out here wit' him a few times to cop and I know I shouldn't have come out here like this but..."

"Yo, who's dat?" the second voice appeared in the doorway. This man was much older than the first and bare-chested with locks that hung to the middle of his back. He too was smoking on a Backwood.

"This here is Free. She said she's lookin' for Ed," the first guy missinformed him.

"No, I'm not lookin' for Ed. I'mma good friend of Ed's and he bought me up here wit' him a few times and-" Free had to get to her point soon because both men's patience was wearing thin. "Well," she continued in a more confident tone. "I'm tryna cop a few of dem thangs." Wheww, finally she said it. Just in case they were unaware of it, she neglected to comment on Ed's current whereabouts. It seemed like a full minute passed as the two men looked at each other and then at her, assessing the situation. The second guy, who seemed to possess an air of authority, spoke first.

"Wait here." BOOM! The door slammed in her face. She waited on the step a full two minutes before the door reopened and she was commanded to enter. The second, older looking guy took control and introduced himself as Rico, passing her his blunt and although she was not fond of Backwoods, she accepted the gesture and began to smoke.

"So, you Ed's girlfriend?" Rico quizzed. Although it was a

casual question, nothing about Rico was casual. His mannerisms were that of a seasoned street veteran and his physique was enough to put fear into the bravest of men.

Free batted her eyelashes and played with her healthy, shiny hair. "No. We're just cool."

"Okay, just cool. What can I do for you?"

Within minutes, Free was back in business. Things went well for her on her first solo, out of town re-up. Rico supplied her with ten pounds of good green and only charged her $5,500. She left with an unexpected $500 in her pocket, a smile on her face and a new connect. Rico gave her his cell number and told her to call before her next visit.

"You neva know what you might stumble upon. Didn't ya mother teach you to call before you come?" Rico joked, but was dead serious. "Always come alone. I'll have ten waiting for you, but if you need more you'll have to let me know ahead of time. I don't deal in funny money or funny business. We'll keep this between you and me. Agreed?" His accent was so thick, she had a hard time understanding him.

"Fo' sho'." Free shook her head in the affirmative.

"Give ya keys to my bredren and he'll bring your weed to the car for you."

Free did as she was told and the guy who answered the door with the Mack 11, left out the house carrying a navy blue medium sized duffle bag. When he returned, he handed her back her keys and just as she was leaving out the door, Rico grabbed her arm and smiled.

"And, Free. You don't have to only call me for business, you know. If you want I can come to the city sometimes and take you out to dinner or somethin'." Free knew it was coming sooner or later. Rico had been undressing her with his eyes the whole time his boy was counting her money.

"That could work," she returned his smile then turned to leave. She had discovered a long time ago that as long as a man thought he had the possibility of getting some, he was satisfied. One didn't actually have to give him any, but as long as he thought he could get some, he would remain interested. If Rico wanted to look at Free's pretty face and use it as an excuse to look out for her, she would let him go right ahead and do so. Free wasn't one to cut her options and she was all about doing what she could to please her new connect. Some may say she was leading him on, but as long as he continued to give her the pounds for five-fifty, he could say whatever he wanted to.

Free's ride home seemed much shorter than the ride out there. She drove without music and she kept her eyes glued to the rearview mirror. That was a habit she picked up ever since she started hustling. She remained conscious of all cars and drivers in her vicinity. She did this especially when she was smoking or driving with a lot of weed in the car. Free made it off the highway and to her apartment safe, but her stress was not over.

"Where you been? What you got in that bag?" Her roommate was all over it.

"Damn, can I live? I just got in the house," Free snapped. She wasn't answering any questions. She was walking straight to her room, lugging the heavy duffle bag full of weed.

"I know one thing. You betta not have what I think you have in that bag. Yeah, I know dat much," Nita stated slickly.

Free stopped in her tracks, thinking for a few seconds and continued to walk down the hall. Nita was on her heels and Free slammed her bedroom door right in her face.

"Yeah, whatever it is, you need to get it up outta here," Nita yelled through the door. Free slid the bag under her bed and went out into the hall to confront what seemed to be her number one enemy.

"Yo, get this! I'mma ask you one more time to fall back. I coulda stayed at home if I wanted to be told what to do. Man lis-

ten, I don't give a damn who name this apartment is in. What I bring up in dis joint is my business. Fuck you and dis apartment!" Free screamed.

"That's how you feel? Well ya mouth can say anything. All I know is you know what I'm talkin' about. Act stupid if you want."

"Get a life." Free went back into her room, leaving Nita standing in the hall. She didn't have time to sit and argue with her roommate. She wouldn't even be mad if Nita was anti-drugs, but Nita would scope out perspective dates in hopes that they were dealers. In fact, if a guy wasn't a drug dealer, she probably wouldn't date him. That was the reason Free had a problem with her argument. Nita was being a hypocrite and the only reason she had a problem with Nita bringing drugs into the house was because she wasn't making anything off of them. Simply put, Nita was a hater.

Free unzipped her very own duffle bag and ogled at the sight. Ten pounds of bright green ganja. There was no mistaking it, this weed was better than the stuff she had been getting from Ed. The ten pounds were basically sold, but she was now thinking about raising the price. She changed her mind. If she kept her price the same her customers would probably spend more with her. Either way, the package would be sold the next day and her connect would be impressed. That was always a good thing. By the time she made sure everything was what it was supposed to be it was too late to start calling her customers. She planned to start spreading the word first thing in the morning. Tonight she just chilled, sampled her new batch and recounted the $6,000 she had hidden in her panty drawer. She was smitten with her new life and there was nothing Nita could say to steal her joy.

Just when Free was good and relaxed, Nita came banging on her door. She went to answer and Nita practically threw the cordless phone in her face and marched off.

"Hello," said Free.

"Hey, honey. What have you been up to? I've been tryin' to call you all day. Didn't Tanita tell you?" Free had been so focused on her business, she had forgotten to return her mother's phone call.

"Yeah, she did, mom. I'm sorry I forgot. Is everything okay?"

"Yeah, I'm fine but Mathew is not doing too well, baby."

"Why? What happened?" Free asked, sincerely concerned.

"A boy he used to go to school with was killed. Poor thing, they shot him three times. The cops don't even have a suspect. Your brother's taking the whole thing pretty hard. He doesn't want to talk or anything. I'm probably gonna have to get him some counseling or something."

"Oh, mom. That is terrible."

"I know. And the worst part is that Mathew insists on going to the funeral and I can't take him I've got three important interviews I've gotta conduct. There's no way I can reschedule. I have to be there."

"How can I help? When is the funeral?" Although she didn't spend much time with him, there wasn't much Free wouldn't do for her little brother.

"It's tomorrow, Freeda. I know how much you hate funerals, but I need you to take him. He won't consider not attending."

"No problem, Ma." Free thought about how much she did hate funerals. She hadn't been to one since her grandmother passed away.

"Okay, honey. Be dressed and ready to go first thing in the morning. I'll call and wake you up. Okay?"

"Okay."

"Thanks, Freeda. You're a lifesaver."

Chapter 20

B.J. couldn't do it. As much as he thought he wanted to, he just couldn't bring himself to do it. He removed his beloved Beretta from his head and placed it on the bed beside him. Who said suicide was the easy way out?

It had been a long week. Just when B.J. was beginning to believe that his own mother had been stealing from him, the identity of the thief was revealed—T.J. He'd been stealing small quantities of cocaine from him all summer long, bagging the uncut coke into oversized $20 sacs and hitting the block. His bags were larger and more potent than the other dealers in that neighborhood and needless to say, T.J. was developing a growing clientele. T.J. didn't need the money, he just wanted to sell drugs; just like the fiendin addict who murdered him in cold blood, just wanted to get high.

Now, the day of young T.J.'s funeral, B.J. was cooped up in his room with his Beretta, contemplating suicide. He could no longer live with himself, knowing that he was the indirect cause of his only brother's death. Had he not been keeping his drugs inside of the house, T.J. would not have had access to them. B.J. never flaunted his illegal lifestyle before his little brother's eyes, but still he blamed himself for what happened and now wanted to take his own life. The fact that he didn't want his mother to suffer the grief of losing both of her sons in the same week was the only thing stopping him.

Miss Janice was heartbroken. Her baby was about to be placed into the earth and she knew her eldest son was somehow involved. Her first reaction was to kick B.J. out of the house and tell him to take all of his drugs with him. This morning she was undecided. Her body was filled with the indescribable sorrow that only a mother who has lost a child can experience. Her eyes carried a sadness, the dark and heavy bags under them matched her dress. It was indeed a devastating day for the Jennings household.

Dana arrived in a black pants suit, ready to ride with the family in the limousine. She and her mother had made all of the arrangements, which B.J. paid for. Both women had questions that needed answering. How could this happen? How did the 30 little baggies get into T.J.'s sock? What was he doing in that part of town? Why weren't there any suspects? The questions were endless.

It was 6:45 am, on a Thursday morning. The limo was scheduled to arrive at 7:00 and the funeral would start at 8:00. Dana sobbed quietly on the couch, while Miss Janice tried to keep herself busy by cleaning her already spotless kitchen. T.J.'s biological father, who had relocated to the West Coast many years ago, sent his sympathy and expressed regret regarding his failure to attend. T.J.'s father had been absent his entire life, so Miss Janice was not surprised by his not being there when it really mattered. What did surprise her was the fact that her eldest, and now only living son, hadn't left out of his room in almost three days. When the limo arrived, she sent her daughter to check on him.

KNOCK...KNOCK...

"B.J. open up. It's me."

"What do you want?" Not only was he not dressed, he hadn't even showered.

Dana entered and cleared a seat amongst the frenzy of clothes, shoes and junk scattered across the room. There wasn't much to be said. It would be just the two of them now. At the sight of his sister, B.J. began to cry uncontrollably. She removed the gun from his hand, placed it under his pillow and moved closer towards him. She embraced him like he was a baby in her arms. He felt as if he had let her down, as if he had let his entire family down.

"Let it out," Dana whispered. She, herself, was in tears. She stroked his frizzy braids and urged him to pull it together. "He's in a better place," she spoke up over his weeping. Up until that point, B.J. hadn't expressed any grief, only anger. "Pull together," she whispered through her tears. "We have to be strong for Mom. Come on B.J. We need you to get dressed, honey."

Like the soldier he was, B.J. got up and was in and out of the shower in five minutes. Dana left his room, but not before laying his suit out on his bed for him. Initially reluctant to leave his room, he quickly dressed and eventually joined the rest of the family.

"He's takin' it hard," Dana relayed to her mother, returning to the living room.

"I'm sure he is, Dana. I'm sure he is." Just as Miss Janice was looking at the clock on the wall, B.J. appeared in the doorway.

"Boy you look a mess." Miss Janice went right to work, buttoning his jacket and adjusting his tie. "Dana honey, grab me my pocketbook. We need to be going now." The family was on their way.

"Freeda, you awake?"

"I am now, Ma. What time is it?" she growled into the phone.

"It's after seven. We are on the way. Get up and get dressed."

"Okay." Free still had her eyes closed. She hung up the phone, picked at the crust in her eyes then looked over at the clock. She laid back down for another five minutes before finally crawling out of bed and into the shower. Today, she decided

to wear a simple dark grey linen dress and matching Jimmy Choo pumps. By the time she combed down her wrap and applied a light coat of make up, Mrs. Harrison was ringing the doorbell to deliver Mathew.

"Thank you so much, Freeda." Her mom kissed her on the cheek.

"It's no problem, Ma. How are you doin'?" she greeted Mathew.

"I'm fine. Are you ready?" her skinny little brother asked. He was dressed in one of his many church suits.

"Uhh, let me just grab my purse."

"Alright. I'm gonna go now. I'll call you when I get off work," Mrs. Harrison said. She walked over to her son, rubbed his cheeks and bent over and kissed him on the forehead. "It's gonna be okay, Mathew, honey. I'll fix you something special for dinner tonight. Okay?"

"Okay," Mathew agreed.

"Freeda, won't you join us for dinner?"

"Yeah, that sounds good." Free gave her mom a kiss on the cheek and watched her leave. Truth be told, she didn't want to take her little brother to the funeral. She had people to see and money to make. She was having a hard time remembering that family should always come first, as she started to tabulate all the money she would be missing out on today. "So, Mathew. Tell me something about your friend before we get there. What's his name?" she asked once they were seated in the Sonata.

"His name was Thomas, but everybody called him T.J. He was real cool. He was in my science class and his homeroom was right next to mine. I think he used to live not too far from here."

"Really? So were ya'll close?"

"No, not really. He was a year older than me. He just graduated, but he was still cool though. One day when somebody stole my lunch money out of my coat pocket, he bought me lunch. The next day, when I tried to give him the money back, he told me don't worry about it. Yeah, he was real cool." Mathew was staring out of the car window.

"That was nice of him," Free admitted. "So, what happened to him?" she asked. Miss Harrison had neglected to fill her in on any information on how the kid died.

"I don't know what happened," Mathew revealed sadly. "They say somebody shot him in the projects, but he didn't live in the projects. I think the police said on the news that it was drug related or somethin' like that. I'm not sure."

"That's so sad. How old was he?"

"I'm 12 so he had to be 13. Yeah, 13."

"Oh, poor thing." She began to feel bad for her brother and his deceased friend. "Well, you know God knows best," she started in. "Everything happens for a reason, Mathew. He is where he is supposed to be. He's resting and he is stress free."

"Yeah, I know, but I still wish he didn't die."

"I do too."

The entire Jennings family arrived in style. B.J. rented a navy blue Rolls Royce and several other dark colored luxury vehicles for the extended family and friends to arrive in. The reception was to be held at a community center not too far from the burial site. The church was filling up with mourners dressed in black. Supporters of all ages were present to see the young boy put to rest.

"It is always a shame when a life is taken," the elderly black preacher began, "but, when that life is a young adolescent, a tender child such as the many young faces I see before me today, it's a tragedy. Ladies and gentlemen, I ask you to dig deep into

your soul. I ask you to reach into your inner being. Ladies and gentleman search yourself for a place where a tragedy can be transformed..."

The meaningful sermon was followed by Dana's tear jerking eulogy and an extended prayer session. There wasn't a dry eye in the building. T.J. lay in his cherry wood casket in an all black, silver-trimmed, three-piece, Tom Ford suit. The gunshot wounds in his shoulder, neck and abdomen had been concealed well, giving an appearance that he was only sleeping. Uncle Leon sat beside his sister, offering his shoulder for her endless tears. Dana was in shambles; B.J. was in a daze.

"Free, are we going to the cemetery with everybody else?"

"Do you want to, Mathew?"

"Yes, please can we go?"

"Oh, okay."

Mathew was only a kindergartener when his grandmother passed away, so this was his first memorable funeral experience. He was soaking it all in. Free was more than ready to leave, but she did feel deep sympathy for the family and was willing to take part in the entire service, to please her brother. She couldn't imagine what it would feel like to lose him.

They drove towards the back of the processional leaving the church headed towards the cemetery. Outside with the other grieving attendees, Free and Mathew stood watch as T.J.'s body was lowered into the ground. It was a still, cloudy morning with over a hundred people present. The body of Thomas Jennings had spent its last seconds above ground and his medium sized casket was now being covered with dirt.

"Free, can we go with everyone else to the reception?"

"Do you really want to, Mathew?" Obviously she didn't.

"Oooh! Please, can we? After that we can go home. Please," he begged.

"Oh, alright."

Free wanted to leave and get her busy day started, but it didn't seem like that would be happening anytime soon. Aside from the serious eye contact she was making with a handsome stranger, Free had no interest in staying. Her cell phone was vibrating off the hook and she had a fresh batch of weed sitting in her room waiting to be sold. She had much respect for the dead and much sympathy for the family, but if it hadn't been for her little brother urging her to stay, she would have opted to leave immediately after the church service. Now, here it was going on one o'clock and she was on her way to a local community center for the reception.

"I am kinda hungry," she informed Mathew, who was silently staring out the car window. He didn't respond. "Are you okay?" Free asked

"Yeah, I was just wonderin', that's all."

"Wonderin' what?"

"I was just wonderin' why someone would get involved with drugs and they know it's gonna kill them."

"What did you just say?" She took her eyes off the road and looked at him, wanting to be sure she had heard him correctly.

"I said, why would somebody get involved wit' drugs and they know it's gonna kill them. Either it's gonna kill them or they gonna end up going to jail. Everybody knows that. I use to think T.J. was smart, but I guess not."

Free almost choked. She felt as if his statement was aimed directly towards her like he somehow knew all of his sister's dirt. His words soaked into her subconscious as if it were a sponge. She wanted to defend her lifestyle, but the truth in his statement weighed heavy on her heart.

"The dead shall remain above our judgment." That was all she could manage to muster.

They arrived at the reception and Free was surprised to see that the event was being catered by one of her favorite soul food restaurants. It was obvious that someone had spared no expense for the entire service. Everything was top quality with a touch of class and well taken care of.

Throughout the day, Free was taking notice of who T.J.'s immediate family members appeared to be. It was obvious who T.J.'s mother was, from the stream of tears that soaked her pretty face. His siblings were easy to spot as well—comforting and never leaving the side of his grieving mother. The glamorous woman called her 'Mom' on more than one occasion and based on that, her first conclusion was drawn. The handsome male she had been exchanging looks with all morning, who was being offered condolences by many, must have been T.J.'s older brother. However, she wanted to be sure.

"Did T.J. have an older brother or something?" she asked her little brother once they were seated and digging into their healthy plates.

"Yupe, he did. He had a older sister, too."

At that instant, as if he heard himself being discussed, B.J. walked passed their table. Mathew stopped him to introduce himself and offer his condolences.

"How did ya'll know T.J.?" B.J. asked after Mathew expressed deep sympathy.

"We went to school together. He was a grade higher than me."

"Oh, okay," B.J. responded, then looked over at Free for the umpteenth time that day. He had been admiring her ravishing, natural beauty. Just as Free was about to speak up and introduce herself someone called B.J. away from the table.

"Thanks again for coming." And just like that he was gone.

So B.J. is his name. Free shifted in her seat, trying to avoid the dampness that had suddenly found its way into her panties.

Chapter 21

Free spent the day after T.J.'s funeral hittin switches. She sold all ten of her pounds and profited $3,000 before the sun even set. She was definitely feeling herself based on her accomplishment. She was also feeling the guy, who called himself B.J. Free wasn't use to having such an immediate attraction towards a stranger but something about B.J. was unlike any other guy she had ever laid eyes on. She convinced herself that with the death of his brother there was no way he would be interested in meeting someone new. Next, she figured that someone as handsome as B.J. probably already had a girlfriend and wouldn't be interested in her. She even went as far as to tell herself that it didn't make sense for her to try to meet or show interest in him because he had already seen her and showed no signs of interest. She wanted to ignore the butterflies that danced in her stomach every time she pictured his face, but never would she forget the way he stared at her. It was as if his eyes pierced through her and into her soul. Free and her roommate were still not on the best of terms, but she had to share her feelings with someone.

"I mean, it's like he was the sexiest thing I've ever seen in my life. He had the thickest eyebrows and the longest eyelashes. He's brown skin, like my complexion and he's so tall and kinda built. I can't stop thinkin' about how he was starin' at me. All day, I'm thinkin' B.J., B.J., B.J."

Nita was doing something out of the ordinary today—spend-

ing the night at home without any male company. "How did he look at you?" she asked, stretched out on the sofa with the cordless and her cell right beside her.

"I can't even really describe it. It was just so...so intimate, like we knew each other already. It was kind of weird, but at the same time... I don't know I can't call it."

"Yeah and you can't call him either. It's not like he was gonna be givin' out his number or tryna collect numbers at his brother's funeral."

"I know," Free admitted. "I feel so bad, like I should'ntve been lookin' at him like that there. But every time I'd turn away then looked back at him, he'd be starin' all in my face. It was like somebody told him suttin' about me or suttin'."

"Mmh. So what are you gonna do?"

"What can I do? There is nothin' I can do. If I really wanted to get the number to his mom's house I'm sure I could but, I mean, what would I say? No, I wouldn't go thru all of that, but damn he was fine."

"Yeah, he musta been if you tried to pick him up at a funeral. He kinda sounds like this dude I met at the mall the other day. He was light skin, short and kinda rough lookin'. So, he was coppin' dem new black and white Huraches, right. So, he tried them on and was askin' me how I think they looked. So, I told him they looked good, but they'd look even betta on my feet. Girl, why he asked me what size I wore then told the girl to go and get them in my size. He bought me the sneakers then asked me for my number, talkin' about he wanna take me outta town. Girl-"

"Where dey at?" Free asked cutting short Nita's never-ending story.

"Where what at?"

"The Huraches. Let me see 'em." Free always was a sucker for the latest Nikes.

"Oh girl, please. I left the store wit' dem and walked around for a little while. Man, then I went right back in there and returned them. Shoo! For dat huned and nineteen dollaz."

"Damn, you shoulda kept 'em. I woulda bought dem off of you."

"Girl, you know I wasn't even thinkin' like dat, but we could go to da mall now. I'm sure dey still got some in your size," Nita suggested.

It was a good idea because Free wanted to spend a couple of dollars anyway. She had been making a lot and spending a little. She owed herself a trip to the mall, but promised she would only buy the Huraches. To be sure she would keep her promise to herself, she slid $200 in the back pocket of her jeans. Nita grabbed about $500 from the $2,200 she had saved up and slipped it into her Fendi book bag. They were on their way.

Twenty-five minutes later they were browsing the racks of the Atrium. Free had already made her intended purchase and was cruising the aisles, looking for nothing in particular. Nita was picking out pieces to try on in the fitting room.

Right before her eyes, there he was. *It can't be. My eyes have to be playin' tricks on me.* Free's eyes were on point and so was B.J. as he rummaged through a pile of Enyce t-shirts. Her heartbeat was going a 100 mph and she couldn't take her eyes off him. Caught up in admiration, she watched him pick out about four different colored t-shirts and drop them off at the register. He was now on his way to a rack of velour sweat suits, totally unaware that he was being watched.

Free came to the conclusion that if she didn't approach him she may never get the opportunity again. She swallowed her fear of rejection and smoothly walked over to him. He had his back turned as she tapped him on the shoulder. B.J. quickly turned around to see Free. They stared into each other's eyes, neither of them wanting to end the gaze.

"Your name is B.J., right?"

"Yeah, didn't I see you yesterday. You're Mathew's sister, right?"

"Right. You remembered." She was thrilled. "I just wanted to come over and introduce myself and to express my deepest sympathy. I didn't get a chance to speak to you yesterday and I just wanted to come over. It's such a coincidence that I ran into you today."

"What are you getting' ready to do?"

"Uhh. Nothing. Whassup?"

"You tryna come hang out wit' me? I know I don't know you like dat, but well, I don't do too much beatin' around the bush. You tryna hang out, get somethin' to eat or suttin'?"

"Sure we could do dat," Free agreed. "So, where you tryna go?"

"It doesn't matter." B.J. looked around the store and remembered where he was and what he was doing there. For a minute he had been lost in Free's eyes.

"Let me just get this stuff. You see anything you want?"

Free didn't even bother to glance around the store before answering. "No, I'm good. But thank you anyway."

He respected that. "Okay, Baby. Give me a second."

Free walked back to the fitting room to find Nita. She left B.J. searching through the racks.

"Nita, which one are you in?"

"I'm right here." Nita opened the door, in her panty and bra set. "Girl, these jeans fit so good. They not too small, but they fit so tight, they look like I grew up wit' 'em on." Nita beamed, holding up a pair of dark blue Diesel jeans. "And they on sale for $80!" Free was not impressed.

"Listen, why the guy I was tellin' you about is here."

"Who?"

"The guy B.J. I was just tellin' you about."

"For real?"

"Yes, girl. And he talkin' about he wanna go and get suttin' to eat."

"Are you gonna go?"

"Is money green? I'll call you later, alright?"

"Have fun. I wanna come out there cuz I wanna see what he looks like."

"Alright, come on, but don't be starin' all in his face like he's some kinda specimen."

Free left Nita in the fitting room and went back out onto the floor just in time to see B.J. paying for his clothes.

"You ready, Ma?"

"Yeah, you ready?"

B.J. waited for his change and reached for his three shopping bags. He realized something as he turned to look at Free.

"I'm askin' you to ride wit' me and I don't even know your name. What's your name?"

"I'm Free," she informed him.

"Free. That's a beautiful name. It fits you."

"Thank you. Is B.J. your real name?"

"No, it's not. It's just a nickname."

"So, what's your real name?" she smiled, cherishing the conversation.

"Ah ha. All information will be given out on a need to know basis."

"What if I said I feel like I need to know?"

"Anything you need to know, you'll find out in due time," he smiled back at her.

"I see you got all the answers."

"No, not all the answers."

Nita came from the back of the store and switched her way over to the counter, laying her jeans down. She approached Free and B.J. unnecessarily loud.

"Ooooh! Don't ya'll look so cute. Free, let me find out you found yourself a twin."

It took them both a couple of seconds to find out what in the world she was talking about. After they looked each other up and down, they realized what she was referring to. As if they had planned it ahead of time, they had on the same exact outfit. Plain white T-shirt, blue jeans, and brand new all white Air Force Ones. They looked as if they were meant to be together.

B.J. was speechless. When he saw Free for the first time, he was attracted to her. Now, he wanted to ask her 21 questions and analyze her answers. He wanted to listen to her life story. He pictured her in a floor length, black ballroom dress, with pearls around her neck and her hair in a bun.

"Yeah, I saw you peekin' in my window this mornin' when I was getting dressed," Free joked.

"Yeah, you got dat," B.J. answered back. He was still speechless. He knew it when he saw her yesterday. He was positive about it when he just so happened to run into her today. He was staring into the eyes of his soul mate and he wondered if she felt the same.

"I'll see you later," Free told Nita, who was waiting for an introduction she would not receive.

"Have fun," Nita spoke to the couple as they exited the store and left her at the register.

"Who was that?" B.J. asked.

"That was my best friend, Nita. We live together."

"Is that right?"

"Unfortunately. Right now she's startin' to work my nerves."

"I can see how that could be possible," he laughed. They reached his Cadillac and he walked around to the passenger side to unlock and open the door for her.

"A gentleman. How nice."

"I'm a gangsta and a gentleman," B.J. confided while walking around the back of his vehicle to the driver's side. When he reached his door handle, he was pleased to see that Free had already unlocked his door for him. He hopped in and took off.

Although Free didn't spot any ashes or any type of tobacco residue, she smelled a faint weed aroma. She pulled a Phillie out of her purse. She just felt right at home in his comfortable passenger seat.

"What you rollin' up?" he looked over and asked. He hadn't smoked in days.

She pulled out a sack, which was a little less than half an ounce of her personal stash. She didn't even get a chance to pass the bag over to him before he started questioning it.

"What is that? Regular?"

"It's not regular. It's some fire mid-grade," she stated, in the habit of promoting her product. He took the bag from her, peeked inside, then passed it straight back. Next, he reached in his jeans pocket and passed her about a quarter ounce of Hydro.

"Roll that up instead. No stress, no seeds."

B.J. decided to drive to a somewhat secluded park, often frequented by the teenagers in the city. They parked under a huge oak tree, overlooking the glistening lake. That is where they smoked their first blunt together. The conversation flowed like a faucet. They shifted from the classic Phillie versus Dutch Master debate to a friendly argument over the greatest MC of all time. By the time B.J. got around to asking his million dollar question, the blunt was long gone.

"So, Free. Are you a queen of hearts or a queen of diamonds?"

She sat with the question for a minute, in search of an answer that was equally clever.

"Queen of hearts," she answered truthfully. "But, don't get me wrong. I love money just as much as the next man, if not more. Love is priceless, but if you sleep on money, you're gonna wake up broke."

He was impressed beyond words. It was getting late and restaurants all over town were closing, but still the conversation continued long after the last pull on their second blunt. For the first time ever, B.J. admitted to someone the role he played in T.J.'s murder. He felt so natural and at ease around Free. He was just dying to put a voice to the guilt that was eating away at his insides.

"And that voice inside of my head, it was tellin' me it wasn't a good idea. But what do I do? I bring the stuff in the house anyway. And I'm watchin' it. I'm watchin' it come up missin' and I'm all over it. Every day I'm getting madder and madder. And I'm frustrated, like 'who would have the nerve?' I'm heated, but still I don't move it. I know somebody's on to me, but still I don't move it. I just keep it right there." At this point his eyes were watering. Free ran her fingers through the parts in his cornrows and listened. "How could I not know?"

"How could you know?" she spoke softly.

"It's only right. I tried to make sure he didn't want for nuttin'. He didn't need anything he just wanted to earn his own. What's killin' me... what's killin' me is I know the example I set, the example I set wasn't about nuttin'. Why couldn't it have been me? Why him and not me?"

"You know how it is," she offered. "God knows best. He has a plan for us all. You know what they say."

He looked up at her. "What do they say?" he asked in search of her wisdom.

"They say the same thing that makes you rich will make you cry. Every time." He felt the truth in her statement wholeheartedly.

"Tell me about it. Tell me all about it."

Three hours later, they were still seated in the Caddy and had smoked up a decent appetite. Unfortunately, most restaurants in the town were closed for business. One of the few places that was still open was T.G.I. Friday's. Since it was a Friday night, it was sure to be jam packed with hip hoppers. Despite the desire to avoid a crowd, their hunger pains had them on the highway headed towards Friday's. They parked in one of the few empty spaces and entered to an array of twenty-something party goers. Girls were made up, with heels and high priced outfits. Free could care less. She was dressed identical to her date so he obviously approved of her outfit. For lack of a better option, they took a seat beside each other at the crowded bar. Too young to order drinks, they munched on buffalo wings and mozzarella sticks and spoke over the crowd. They were cracking jokes about each other's sarcastic approach to life when B.J. was mushed lightly in the back of the head.

"What the hell are you doin' up in here?" Kenya asked, squeezing herself in between B.J. and Free's barstool. Here we go, Free thought. She had been enjoying B.J.'s company so much, she never thought to ask whether or not he had a girlfriend.

"What's good?" he replied smoothly.

Kenya accepted his inch and took a whole yard by leaning over and giving him an over exaggerated hug.

"Hey, Baby. What you doin' up in here? You got time to chill wit' these off brand ass chicks, but you ain't got no time for me," Kenya said loudly then turned to look in Free's face to be sure she had caught the comment. She did. Kenya was taking full advantage of the situation and Free wasn't having it. She looked behind her, then to her left and right side and spoke past Kenya to her date.

"Yo, who she talkin' to? I know she ain't talkin' 'bout me!"

Kenya turned to face Free so that she could fully assess the girl she had been eyeing from across the room. The girl was prettier than her, there was no denying that. Kenya quickly searched her for a flaw but couldn't find one. The only thing she did notice was that she was better dressed than the girl. "Bum ass bitch," she mumbled under her breath. Free heard her loud and clear. As Kenya whipped her head around to face B.J., Free's adrenaline began to rush. She looked past Kenya, to B.J. for a better understanding.

"Yo, I'm in the middle of suttin' right now. I need you to fall back," B.J. spoke up. Kenya was all in his face trying to say something about seeing him later. She had no plans of walking away a loser. Free jumped down off of the barstool. She wasn't comfortable with her positioning or the way Kenya's backside was all in her face. Kenya kissed B.J. on the cheek and when she leaned back to slide from in between the two barstools, she stepped on Free's foot. Free gave her about three seconds to excuse herself and when she didn't, fuel was added to the fire burning in Free's chest.

"Excuse you," Free said with a no nonsense attitude.

Kenya looked down at the stain she'd just put on Free's sneaker and then back up into Free's face. Free was doing the same thing, looking down at her sneaker and then up into

Kenya's face for an apology or some type of explanation. Kenya breathed heavy, as if to say 'whatever' and then whipped her head around to face B.J. again. When she did, her long black hair, brushed past Free's face. That was all it took. B.J. looked at Kenya to see if she realized what she had just done. It didn't matter. Neither apology, nor explanation could stop Free's hand as she mushed Kenya hard in the back of the head. B.J. was shocked. Kenya turned back around and pushed Free back onto the barstool. There was nothing anyone could do to stop them now.

Free stepped from in between the two stools, leaned back and punched Kenya in the face in record speed. B.J. hopped off of his barstool. Kenya reached out to grab Free's hair, but came up empty handed and found herself getting stole in the face again. Free was throwing all kinds of blows. By the time Kenya did get a hold of hair, Free had blackened her eye. Now they had a firm grip on each other's hair, but Free was losing the hair pulling battle. All she had was a handful of tracks.

"Let go of my hair, you bald-headed scalawag!" Free screamed.

One of the bartenders had called the police and B.J. was steady trying to break up the fight. Nothing could loosen the grip Kenya had on Free's long, thick hair. Finally, Free grabbed one of Kenya's breast and dug her nails into it like she was trying to separate it from her body. It worked. Kenya let go of hair and took a step back. That's when she was punched in the side of her head so hard, she lost her balance. She stumbled and Free's left fist reunited with the left side of her face. There was now a sufficient amount of space for B.J. to step between them. It took him and two other waiters to separate them. It was Free who got the last hit. She kicked Kenya super hard in the mid-section.

"Where's my pocket book?" Free yelled out as a waiter had her high in the air carrying her out of the restaurant. The majority of people inside had stopped eating and drinking and were gathered around watching the action. They were cheering and confirming the victor. One would have thought it was fight night in Las Vegas.

"I got it right here," B.J. yelled back, holding up her bag and following the small disorderly group out of the door. Kenya was being escorted out as well. Now, the girls were out front screaming threatening insults at each other. One of the waitresses came outside and mentioned to her coworkers that the police were on their way—that was all B.J. needed to hear. He ordered the man holding Free to let her go. When the man didn't budge, he raised his voice, threatening the man. The man moved out of his way and let his girl go.

Free was steaming. She wanted more of Kenya and she cursed herself for not driving her own car. She was mad that she had allowed herself to be put in a predicament where she would be fighting the girlfriend of a guy she was out on a date with.

"Gimmie my shit!" She walked over to B.J. and snatched her pocket book out of his hands. Kenya was being walked to her truck to be sure she left the premises.

"What?" B.J. wasn't even sure how to react.

She looked him up and down and rolled her eyes as she flipped open her cell phone. B.J. stared at her in admiration. He was still in a daze from what had happened.

"Girl, where you at? Come and get me. I'm up at Friday's and I just had to punish dis chick and..."

"Man, hang up the phone!" B.J. shouted with all kind of bass in his voice. Free ignored him and kept talking. "Man, if you don't hang up dat phone. They said they called the cops up here. Stop playin', Free."

The mere mention of the police brought Free back to her good sense. She immediately started following B.J. to his Caddy.

"Get dressed. I'mma need you to come pick me up. I'mma call you right back," she told Nita before hanging up.

Once they got to B.J.'s car, they pulled off with the distant sound of sirens behind them. Free was in the mirror checking her

face for any marks or scratches. B.J. couldn't help but look over at her. *Unbelievable*, he thought to himself.

"How the hell you gonna tell somebody to come and pick you up? If you ridin' wit' me, you ridin' wit' me 'til I say so." He wanted to push her buttons. He had a weakness for feisty broads. She gave him one of her famous 'you can't be serious' looks as she pulled back her ruined wrap. She reached over and slid his ghetto money clip off his wrist and used it to hold her bun in place. She couldn't hold back her laughter. His last statement was hilarious. They laughed until they were near tears.

"Who was that broad?" Free was starting to get serious again. Before he came up with an explanation, she warned him. "Don't lie to me either."

"That wasn't even my ex-girlfriend. I can't front, I did sleep wit' her one time earlier this summer. That's it. We ain't serious like dat. Shawty was over steppin' her boundaries and you put her right back in her place. Free, I haven't known you long. In fact, I just met you, but I want you to know that I would never put you out there like dat. I don't do mines like dat."

"Yeah, how you do yours?" Free was in the mirror again double checking her face for any evidence of defeat.

B.J. reached out for her chin and used it to shift her gaze in his direction. He took his eyes off the road for two seconds. "I take care of mines." Oh, how she wanted to believe him.

After he hung up on her the first time, Kenya continuously called B.J. He had answered and she screamed threats directed towards Free. Free was calm now and determined not to let Kenya get her riled back up. B.J. was getting hype for her.

"Look here. Get this straight. You ain't my girl; never was, never will be. It don't matter who she is. She's wit' me. What?" He held the phone away from his ear because she was screaming at the top of her lungs. "I'm not 'bout to sit here and listen to this. Stop callin' me. I don't have nuttin' for you." He hung up and within seconds his phone was ringing again. He had to turn it off.

They rode around for almost an hour, joking and reliving the brawl. B.J. started calling Free Iron Mike. He said she had fists of steel, as he spoke of the beating she gave Kenya. It was over and Free had calmed down so they were both able to find humor in the situation. She wanted B.J. to understand that the reason she had hit Kenya had everything to do with the fact that she felt disrespected and nothing to do with B.J. He understood fully.

"I got to make sure I don't get on your bad side," he joked.

They laughed at each other's comments and fed off of each other's observations. They were so engrossed in each other, it took them a while to realize that neither of them had picked a destination. When there was a two second break in the laughter, they looked into each other's eyes and spoke simultaneously.

"Where we goin'?"

Chapter 22

B.J. made it home at four-thirty in the morning. At her request, he had dropped Free off at her apartment and made plans to spend the weekend with her. He was digging her like a shovel, there was no doubt about it. The more he thought about her, the more intrigued he became. Not to mention the fact that she lightened the load on his heart.

The house was completely dark. Granted, it was late but his mom would normally leave the light in the hallway on throughout the night. When he opened the door and was unable to focus his vision due to the pitch blackness, he knew there was something wrong. On edge, he flicked on the hall light and walked into the kitchen. What he saw there was enough to break him down worse than the death of T.J.

"What's goin' on, Ma?" Miss Janice had been sitting at the kitchen table in complete darkness, awaiting her son's return. Since T.J.'s murder, she had spent every day searching for the real cause of his death. Where did he get the drugs discovered on his body? She knew in her heart who the source was, but she needed proof before she would start pointing fingers. Miss Janice had searched B.J.'s room and found all the evidence she needed. Two and a quarter kilos sat on the kitchen table.

"I think you can tell me what's goin' on betta than I can tell you." Her eyes were pink and puffy. She had been up all night, crying and waiting for B.J. to come home.

B.J. silently took his seat at the table. He didn't want to say the wrong thing or cause his mom to do something crazy with his drugs. He couldn't think of the right thing to say. There was really nothing that he could say.

"I knew it was you all along," Miss Janice spoke slightly above a whisper. "I knew it was you who bought this death into my house, but I didn't want to believe it. I've been watching you coming in and out of the house. I've noticed a change in you over the years. I seen it from day one, but I didn't want to believe it. You dealin' the same stuff that almost took me out. You saw me sufferin'. You lived through that and still you bring this death into my house." She nodded her head towards the coke on the table. "How much is this worth to you?"

B.J. had already done his speedy mental calculations. He had a little over $70,000 stashed away in his room. That was a little more than what he had started the summer with. The two and one quarter kilos was what he had profited. He could live with only seventy some odd thousand, but he didn't want to. How much was the coke on the table worth to him? Everything and nothing at all.

"Why?" he asked, his voice weak and shaky.

She stared into his eyes. "Was it worth T.J.'s life?"

"Mom, you know the last thing I wanted was for something to happen to T.J. I loved him just like you loved him. There wasn't a thing I wouldn't give or do for that little guy. Nothing. Did I give him any drugs? No. Did I know he was selling? No. Were those my drugs they found in his sock? More than likely. Do I regret ever bringing them in the house? Of course. I would give anything to change the way things went. I would live broke for the rest of my life if it would bring T.J. back, even just for one minute."

"Am I supposed to be impressed because you would live broke to right your wrong?" she said through her teeth. "Tell me suttin', son. If you didn't give him the drugs, how did he get them?" All signs of her sadness were replaced by outright anger.

"I think he was stealin' from me," B.J. admitted shamefully.

"And so do you think you are not to blame because you didn't put it directly in his hands?"

"Mom, I know I am not innocent. I am guilty and I know I am. Everyday I'm livin' wit' regrets about the decisions I've made. The pain in my heart runs so deep you wouldn't believe it if I told you." B.J.'s words were sincere.

She leaned back in the wooden chair and crossed her arms across her chest. "I ask you again. How much is this worth to you?"

"Why?" he repeated, avoiding her question.

"B.J., you are my only living son and I will always love you, but I can't have you living under my roof another night." As lonely as Miss Janice would be in that big house all alone, seeing B.J. run in and out would be a constant reminder of what had happened to her youngest son. "You have until sunset, tonight, to get your belongings and leave my house. You have damaged this family and this household beyond repair."

B.J. was crushed. He had every intention of moving out of his mom's house, but not under such bitter conditions. There was no time like the present. He immediately started planning his relocation. Looking into his mom's face, searching for some type of leniency or remorse, he saw her bend down and grab a bottle of Clorox bleach from the floor beside the table. His heartbeat pounded and instincts told him to grab his cocaine.

"Stop playin'," he yelled as she untwisted the cap and lifted the bottle into a pouring position. He grabbed for the coke as she stood and turned her back to block him and give herself a better opportunity to aim the flow of the damaging liquid. It happened so fast. Before B.J. knew it, he had pushed his mother aside and snatched up the two and a quarter kilos. The bleach Miss Janice poured missed the coke, splashed onto the table and was now dripping on the floor.

Miss Janice regained her balance and pulled B.J. by the collar. He had nearly pushed her to the ground. He turned to face her, protecting his goods as if he was being robbed by a stranger in the street.

"You remember this day! This is the day you chose your lifestyle over your family. You only get one family and when you're no longer livin' your illegal lifestyle, who's gonna be here? Huh? Who's still gonna be right here?" B.J. understood what she was telling him, but he didn't want to hear it. He turned to walk out of the kitchen and his mother continued to yell after him. "As long as you're sellin' drugs you'll never be happy, no matter how much money you get." Truth spoken.

B.J. opened the front door to leave back out. "I'll be back for my things," he announced humbly. Now where was he going? The sun wasn't even up yet and he hadn't been to sleep, but he had to get his work out of his mom's house. B.J. drove straight to a hotel, checked himself in and tried to get a few hours of sleep. He didn't want to think about anything, or make any important decisions until he was well rested. Sleep didn't come easy. When his phone started ringing a few hours later, he was up and on the go. His first agenda was to sell the coke he had in the stash box of his Cadillac. He planned to meet with all of his customers and in no time he would have a stash full of cash.

His phone was ringing off the hook. Customers were calling non-stop. He hadn't sold a gram since T.J. died and everyone was past ready to re-up. Taye had been calling, worrying him about the fake half-key sale. Kenya had been calling all morning shooting him all kind of profanities. Although he was tempted to, he could not afford to turn his phone off this morning. The one person he was fiendin to hear from hadn't called.

Hours passed, drugs sold, money collected and thoughts gathered. The hard part of Free's day was over. Now she just had to go home and count her money. She was sure it was all there because she had counted it as she collected it. She reached home to find Nita sitting in the living room hugged up with a new friend. He was a cutie. Even Free, who was in no mood to

be introduced to unwanted company, had to admit that. He was the color of a starless, midnight sky. He looked mean, real mean and his black leather Timberland boots had seen better days. His black hoody and jeans had a worn out "please wash me" look. He was a stick up kid, who had just hit a big lick and was spending his cash with Nita. She could care less how he made his money, as long as he had it to spend. They called him Virgil.

Free came into her apartment and went straight to her room without saying a word. She had been back and forth to the apartment several times that morning, dropping off wads of cash and retrieving pounds of weed. Now all of her weed was finished and she had a drawer full of loose money she had to sort and separate. She pulled out all of her money, laid it out on her bed and picked up her cell to call Rico.

"Hello, Free darling."

"Hey, baby. I'm tryna come see you."

"So soon? That's great. When can I expect you?"

She thought for a minute. It didn't seem like she would be hearing from, or making plans for the weekend with the new love of her life. Her customers wouldn't be ready to holler at her for another day or two, but she still wanted to ready when they did call.

"Is tomorrow morning cool?"

"Sure. What time will I see your pretty face?"

"How 'bout 11 o'clock?"

"Cool."

"See ya then."

"Bye, honey."

Free profited three grand in one day, bringing her grand total to $15,000. She was so proud of herself. When she finished

counting everything up, she thought hard for another place she could hide her money. Now that Nita was on to her dresser drawer, she didn't feel safe keeping her goldmine anywhere near there at all. She decided to unscrew the back of a wooden grandfather clock that hung on the wall above her bed. Inside the back of the clock was enough space for her goldmine to fit comfortably. She replaced the clock on the wall and plugged it back into the outlet. There was no noticeable difference. With that done, she was restless and ventured out into the living room. To her surprise, there was no one there. Nita and Virgil were in Nita's room getting their foreplay started. Free was fed up.

B.J. was fed up. How long was this chick gonna wait before she decided to pick up the phone and call him? Who did she think she was? How long did she think he was going to wait on her call? He was pulling into his sister's apartment complex with a carload of clothes and shoes. Dana had agreed to let him keep his clothes at her place for as long as he needed. B.J. and Dana's boyfriend, Mike didn't wear the same size shoes, but still B.J. didn't want to leave his gear there for too long. He still had a gang of jeans, shirts, boxers, sneakers, and fitted caps at his mother's house even after he had filled his car to capacity. He could barely see out of the rear window as he backed into a parking space. He felt so homeless. It was as if everything he owned was riding around with him.

"So, Dana. You think you could do dat for me?"

Dana had heard the full story from her mom. She wasn't surprised that B.J. had lugged his things over to her place and was now asking her to get an apartment in her name for him. B.J. had stated that he didn't really care where the apartment was located, but Dana knew better than to believe that. B.J. would be pickier than an afro comb when it came to his new residence. Dana wasn't going to get the apartment for free. She was already plotting on how much she could get out of him in exchange for signing the lease. Nothing was free of charge when it came to Dana.

"A favor for a favor," she bargained.

"A favor like what?" B.J. asked. He was desperate and offended at the same time. He really needed her for something and all she was thinking about was how much she could gain.

"Well, my rent and phone bill is kinda-"

"How much, Dana?"

"A g should cover it."

"A g?" *So she just gonna tax me like dat.*

Dana stared him right in the eye and repeated her request. "A g."

He had to think about it. A thousand dollars was a high price to pay, especially when he would have to pay his own first month's rent, a security deposit, introductory bills, and other household expenses. He hated that she was even charging him. If she had just asked him for a grand he probably would have gave it up to her, but since she was charging him, he didn't want to come up off it.

"Let me think about it. I don't really got it like dat," he told her. He had just spent a grip on the funeral. One would think Dana would have taken that into consideration.

"Okay, just let me know," she replied.

B.J. left shortly after storing his things in Dana's hall closet. As he was walking out to his car, his phone rang. It was Free. *Took her long enough.*

"Hey Ma," he answered on the first ring, happy to be finally hearing her voice.

"Whassup, Boo? How was your day?"

"Coulda been betta. It's almost over now. Why am I just now hearing from you?"

"Huh?" she asked.

"You heard me. Where you at?" He was putting his foot down. He wanted the girl and he had to make her know it.

"Who you talkin' to like dat? Where you at?" She was playing hard to get.

"Stop playin' wit' me, ma. I'm comin' to pick you up. I need you to come wit' me to do suttin'. I'll be at your joint in fifteen minutes. Be dressed." He hung up before even giving her a chance to answer.

Take charge, Daddy. Free jumped up off of her bed to look in her bedroom mirror. She looked cute, as usual, but she wanted to do a little something extra. The last time he saw her, she had on her usual everyday white T-shirt and blue jeans. Today she felt like doing a little more than that. She searched through her wardrobe for something appropriate and decided on a red denim Girbaud dress and a pair of red wooden Candies. She felt cute as she filled her red Kate Spade bag and waited the arrival of her date. B.J. gave her his classic 'I'm outside' phone call and she was on her way.

Free and B.J. spent the evening together and were now sitting in his car outside of her apartment smoking on a blunt. They had just left the tattoo shop where B.J. had got a huge portrait of T.J. along with the letters R.I.P. tattooed on his back. The tattoo also had the phrase 'The Good Die Young' along with T.J.'s birth and death dates. The tattoo cost B.J. $500 and was the most physical pain he'd ever thought he'd have to endure. In the process, Free's poor little hand didn't have a chance. He had squeezed it until her blood stopped circulating.

Earlier that day, B.J. had reserved a Penthouse suite at one of the better hotels an hour away at the beach. He was going through a lot and needed a mini vacation. He didn't consult with Free before making the reservation. He just assumed she would be available and willing to join him. She was available for the night, but since he hadn't called her earlier, she had already

made plans for the following morning. There was no way she was going to be able to break those plans to go with B.J. As much as she may have wanted to do that, she had something very important set up for the next morning.

"What, you got somethin' to do?" B.J. was irritated. He planned to drive Free to her apartment complex so that she could pick up whatever she would need to spend the night with him. She waited until they were in front of her apartment before announcing that she would not be available for the weekend.

"I already told you. I got some business to take care of," Free said seriously then smiled, diluting the harshness of her words. She wanted to spend the rest of the weekend at the beach with B.J., but she had already given Rico her word that she would be there in the morning. Should she disappoint her new connect to please her new love interest?

B.J. recognized a familiarity in the urgency in her voice. The way she declared her plans to take care of business sounded like something he would say. What kind of business did an unemployed college student have to take care of on a Saturday morning? From out of nowhere, a conversation he had had with one of his boys popped into his head. *"She look good. She black but she got a Chinese thing goin' on. Nice hair. Nice shape. Real jazzy broad. Real, real jazzy broad."*

Free definitely fit the description. It couldn't be. He never asked Free what she did for money. She said she was in college and he settled for that. Now, he felt like he needed to know more. He wasn't a corner cutter so he came straight out with what was on his mind.

"You hustle, ma?"

"I do what I gotta. Why? You need somethin'?" Free was feeling herself, unaware of whom she was talking to. All she was thinking about was the fact that she had money to get and B.J. could either help her out or slow her down. She played right into his hands.

"Yeah, I might," he thought for a moment. "I got this guy, one of my boys actually and he's tryna get on wit' some weed. Not no dro like I keep. See, I keep dro but he havin' a hard time getting his hands on some decent regular. He don't buy no ounces, though. He sell those. He's lookin' for some pounds. Do you know anyone?"

Free couldn't believe her luck. Another customer just like that. She was already mentally calculating her profit and at the same time wondering how much B.J.'s friend had to spend with her.

"Yeah, I know somebody," she answered greedily. "He won't be ready 'til tomorrow. How many of dem thangs you think your boy gonna need?"

Listening to her talk, B.J. watched his dream girl transform into just another chick, right before his eyes. Up until that point, she was flawless in his eyes. Regardless, if she was the same female Randy had referred to, he wanted to tell her to go upstairs and lose his number. He played it cool.

"It depends. What's dem things goin' for?"

"Dey goin' for nine hundred, all day." Free was not about to lower her price no matter how much she liked dude.

"That ain't too bad. I'll call my people and let them know. So that's what you gotta do? Get wit' your peoples in the mornin'?"

"Let me find out you da police," Free snapped. "Like I said for the third time. I got something to take care of in the mornin', but if you want we can hook up so I can holla at ya peoples." Free had all the answers. B.J. sat back and listened smoothly. There was only one way for him to find out what he needed to know.

"Far from the police. I'll get wit' my boy in da mornin' and we'll give you a call. What time will you be ready?"

"Give me 'til around three cuz I gotta coupla things I gotta do first."

"Yeah, I know. You gotta take care of suttin'," B.J. snapped back.

Free could only smile at him. He was so cute to her, not to mention the fact that he was now talking about spending money with her. B.J. never did go into detail about the arrangements he had made for the two of them. What she needed to take care of in the morning was now important to him as well. He didn't want to spend the night alone, but he had to watch her walk away. He refused to get any closer to Free until he discovered whether or not she was the female hustler who had slept with his boy then robbed him.

Free walked up the short flight of steps leading to her apartment door. Like the gentleman he was, B.J. waited patiently for her to get safely inside before driving off. Before Free could get her front door open fully, she swung her head around and yelled softly downstairs to B.J.

"Goodnight." He watched her hair toss in the wind as she turned back around to enter her apartment.

What a sweetheart. I hope I'm wrong about her.

Chapter 23

Next morning. At the last minute, Free called Rico and told him that she wanted to double her order. Twenty pounds. She knew if she only got ten, they would be sold in one day and why should she keep running up and down the highway? It was just a matter of keeping them hidden in her room until she got rid of them. More and more, she was considering finding an apartment of her own. She could afford it and she needed her privacy. Rico was happy to hear about the unexpected increase and told her to come through; he would be waiting.

As soon as B.J. woke up, he called Randy.

"What's crackin', playboy?"

"Ain't nuttin'. Check dis. I think I ran across one of dem broads you was tellin' me about. I set up suttin' wit' her for three o'clock today. Call me around two and we gonna ride and go check her out."

"Dat sounds cool. Where you ran into shawty at?"

"I'll put you on to all of dat when I see you. Make sure you hit me up."

"Fo' sho'."

B.J. had spent the night at some random hotel after stopping

by Dana's house for a change of clothes. For the second night in a row, he didn't get much sleep. He gave a lot of thought to his living condition. For lack of a better option, he went ahead and paid Dana the grand she was asking for. In return, she promised to wake up first thing Monday morning and start collecting applications. She said she already had a good idea of the type of place he wanted and she even knew a place that would easily accept her. Once she got the thousand dollars in her hand she was extremely helpful and told him that he could probably move in by the weekend.

As soon as he hung up with Randy, his phone rang. It was Kenya. He didn't know why he answered it, but he did.

"Who was dat hood rat you was wit?!" She started screaming and questioning him as soon as he put the phone to his ear.

"Look-"

"Well, you need to tell me suttin' about her cuz I need to know what name to put on the police report."

B.J. hated the word 'police'. "What report?" he asked. She had his full attention.

"I'mma charge dat lil bitch wit' assault and attempted murder. I think she killed our baby. I got all kinda cramps and I started bleedin'. I'm not supposed to be bleedin'. I need you to come wit' me to the emergency room."

"Emergency room? You don't got no pills you could take?"

"No, I don't. And I'm in pain, so can you please give me the girl's name or her number or suttin'. I'm serious."

"Alright. Lemme call you back." There was no way he was going to do what she was asking of him.

She was still rambling on when he hung up, but he didn't do it on purpose. He didn't necessarily want her in pain, however a miscarriage didn't sound like bad news to him. Silently, he prayed that she was having a miscarriage.

B.J. showered, dressed, checked out of the hotel, and then drove past his mother's house. He was hoping that his mom's car was not parked outside, so that he could go inside without any difficulty and put away the money he had been riding around with in the stash box of his Caddy. It was the same money he collected after selling the coke his mom had tried to ruin. He felt like he needed to get it out of his car and store it somewhere safe. When he pulled onto the block, he didn't see her car so he parked, grabbed his money and went inside.

B.J. walked past the kitchen to his room and had a flashback of the confrontation with his mom. He didn't intend to shove her as hard as he did, but he was out to protect what was his. He wished he hadn't been forced to make such a decision. B.J. was overly protective when it came to the things that he risked his life everyday for. In his room, he reached under the radiator and removed one of the tiles to get his hands on his collection of cash. He put it all together and counted it all out. His total was almost $130,000. He grabbed two grand and put the rest back in his well thought out hiding place.

Like most mid-level hustlers in the game, B.J.'s goal was to get his hands on a quarter of a million dollars. Once he got a quarter mil, he would be satisfied and ready to retire. He figured that would take him roughly six months, depending on his spending habits and how often he went to see Papi.

B.J. walked past T.J.'s closed bedroom door on the way outside to his car. The sight of the closed door jump started the pain in his soul; more and more he felt like the game owed him something.

Free was on the highway to meet with Rico. She didn't have a problem finding the house and she was back on the highway going in the opposite direction in no time. She decided that the smartest thing to do would be to go home and put some of the weed away before riding around and meeting her folks to start selling it. She already had customers waiting but that didn't stop her from picking up her phone to call B.J. when she was within fifteen minutes of her apartment.

"Yo, meet me in fifteen minutes. Who you wit?" she questioned him.

"I'm wit' dude I was tellin' you about. Why? Where you at?"

"Oh, alright. Well, don't come to my apartment then. I don't know dude like dat. Where you wanna meet me at?"

Listen to her, B.J. thought as he started running his game. "Look here, Boo. If I'm ridin' wit' somebody den dey good peoples. It really ain't too much to dat but I'mma respect ya gangsta. Where you wanna meet me at?"

"You know where the McDonald's is at as soon as you get off the exit by my house?"

"Yeah, dat'll work. Listen, my dude is real cool peoples. As a matter of fact he's tryna get hooked up wit' one of ya girls. What's your friend's name again?"

While they were waiting on Free to give them a call, Randy and B.J. had discussed the situation in great detail. Randy revealed that one of the girls was named Tanita. The more they talked, the more B.J. began to realize that more likely than not, Free and her roommate were the girls Randy was speaking of. The physical descriptions they compared had an uncanny resemblance. Both men agreed on that. What they didn't agree on was what should be done to the girls in terms of Randy's revenge.

"She got more than enough guy friends, let me tell you," Free said. "She don't need no more. But how long before ya'll get to the McDonald's."

"Like ten minutes. What you mean she got enough friends? How you know what she got? My dude is tryna get at her."

"Hear what I tell you. But I'll see you when I get there, baby."

"Yeah, aight." B.J. hung up. Randy was all in his face.

"What she said her name is?" he eagerly asked.

"She didn't say, but she'll be at the McDonald's in fifteen minutes."

B.J. was steady trying to convince Randy to see his point of view. "All I'm sayin' is kidnappin' shorty ain't gonna get you your money back. There's other ways to do things. If she don't see you then we'll have the upper hand. It don't make sense for us to put all our cards out there. All you gotta do is wait inside the McDonald's and get a good look at the chick. I'll be outside polyin' wit' her. If it's her, just call me and let me know and I'll handle it from there."

"Man, I ain't waitin' in no McDonald's! What you in love wit' dis chick or suttin'? I know you ain't goin' and getting soft on me. If it's her, I'mma work her 'til I get my scratch back den I'mma make her pay some more. I'm tellin' you dese broads robbed me for seven grand and you tellin' me dat you wanna hear dere side of da story. Are you serious?"

Randy didn't realize it immediately, but B.J. had started driving in the opposite direction of the McDonald's. Upon second thought, B.J. was glad Free was smart enough to decline them an invitation to her apartment. Randy was talking about kidnapping, robbing, and possibly raping a girl he had feelings for. What kind of sense did that make? He had to think fast. He owed his boy honesty, but at the same time he owed Free something as well.

"Look, dawg. I am serious. I already told you, I'm feelin' shawty. Now we gotta figure out how we gonna do dis before we get up here cuz I ain't tryna see nuttin' get outta control."

"You already outta control, playa. I know you ain't no sucka for love, playboy."

"Neva dat." B.J. made the left turn that would lead them back in the direction of the McDonald's. He didn't want to admit it, Randy was absolutely right. He was stuck between love and loyalty. "I just think there's a betta way to go about dis, is all I'm

sayin'. Kidnappin' dis chick is not gonna get you ya money back. Give her a chance to explain herself. Give her a chance to pay her debt. If she is who you say she is, then she knows she robbed you. If they did it together then she owes you thirty-five and her girl owes you thirty-five. We not kidnappin' her. Maybe rob her, but we ain't takin' all her weed. I already told you, I'm feelin' shawty. If anything, we'll take $3,500 worth. That's about four pounds."

Randy just looked over at his boy. He wanted to argue, but he figured B.J. was not going to pull up at the McDonald's until they came to some type of agreement. He had already coughed the seven grand up as a loss, so if it was returned to him it would be considered extra money. He was already thinking about using it to buy a Grand Prix he had seen advertised in the Auto Trader.

"Damn, her head must be da bomb," Randy commented as they finally approached the McDonald's parking lot.

Free had already stopped at home and was sitting in the drive thru ordering a milkshake, awaiting B.J. and his friend. She had put fourteen pounds away in her room, under the bed, and the other six were in the car with her. She planned on running around all day making deliveries. If B.J.'s boy didn't want the six pounds she was riding with, she knew quite a few people who did.

"That's her, Dawg! That's her!" Before they even pulled all the way into the parking lot, Randy was confirming Free as the thieving hooker.

"Be easy. Let's see what's she's gonna do when she sees you."

Oh shit! Free's heart skipped a beat as soon as she looked into B.J.'s car. She instantly recognized the passenger. *Say it ain't so,* she thought. She wished she had only bought one pound out of the house with her. As the guys pulled up and parked, she had about thirty seconds to decide what she would do. She knew she couldn't run very far or for very long. B.J. already knew where she lived so if he wanted to find her, he could. Free began to wonder if she had been set up all along and if B.J. knew who she was since the first time he laid eyes on her. Perhaps that was the reason he had stared at her so deeply. Then she thought to their chance second meeting at the shopping mall and leaned towards the idea that seeing Randy in B.J.'s car was just a devastating coincidence. Like the grown woman she was, Free parked directly beside them and hopped out. No shame.

"Lock your door. Take a ride wit' me, ma." B.J. addressed her through the rolled down driver's side window. She looked over at Randy, who was staring straight ahead.

"Aight," she answered coolly, with no fear.

It came time for B.J. to make an important decision. It is customary for a lady to sit in the front seat when riding with a gentleman. Randy had no intentions of moving. As if everything was normal, B.J. made the request.

"Yo, dawg. Let the lady sit in the front seat," he said, giving Randy a 'work with me' look.

Free was far from a 'backseat broad', but she didn't like the idea of Randy sitting behind her either. By the time Free locked her car and made her way to the passenger side, Randy was seated in the backseat. Free got in, adjusted her seat and kissed B.J. on the cheek.

"Whassup," she greeted both of them calmly.

"How you?" Randy replied. B.J. pulled off.

"Could be betta," Free answered. She was beginning to realize that B.J.'s friend wasn't interested in getting any weed from her. If he was, he wasn't planning on buying it. While the vehicle should have been a hostile environment for Free, it wasn't. She felt a sense of security when she was around B.J. She looked at Randy one more time before she turned her back and worked on normalizing her heartbeat.

"So you got anything you wanna talk about?" B.J. asked her.

Free didn't want to play stupid with either of them and from the way B.J. phrased the question, it was obvious that he knew the history between his two passengers.

"That depends on what you wanna talk about," was the best response she could come up with.

"You should know what I'm tryna talk about. I'm tryna get me some get back," Randy answered her.

"Look, you know it wasn't my idea." Free tried to cop a plea. "I mean, we did come thru on our part of the deal. We did what we was supposed to do and then you tried to gyp us out of our money. We had to do something."

Free felt awkward discussing one of her lowest points in B.J.'s presence. She had never prostituted herself or robbed a guy before Randy. She always kept the notion in the back of her head that one day she would have to face Randy again, but never did she imagine that it would be under such circumstances.

"What you mean I tried to gyp you?" Randy yelled. "I gave you what I said I would give you. What are you talkin' about? Ya'll got me for seven grand. What part of the deal was that?"

"We got you for five grand," Free calmly corrected him.

"So, you gonna sit right here and call me a liar," Randy asked. Free turned around to face her accuser.

"I ain't callin' you a liar," she raised her voice to match his. "Okay, there was only six grand in the bag plus the one you already gave us. That's seven altogether. But you already owed us two of dat seven, so really we only took five," she explained.

"How you figured I owed you two?" Randy asked.

"You said you would give us a g a piece."

"Like I told you that day and I'll tell you again, I was only givin' ya'll a g to split between ya'll and I told your girl, Tanita,

that on the phone before ya'll even got up to the room. I wasn't tryna get ova on ya'll. Shawty was tryna get ova on you."

Free was quiet for a few seconds. What Randy said was believable. Nita knew Free would not be willing to sleep with a stranger for a measly $500, but a thousand dollars sounded a little more convincing. Could her best friend have lied to her to get her to go along with the plan? It sounded like something Nita was capable of.

"She told me you said you was gonna pay us a g a piece."

"Well, she lied to you. Did she tell you dat ya'll was gonna rob me too?"

"No. She didn't tell me nuttin' like dat. That part wasn't planned. To be honest, I didn't know she was gonna take your bag until she actually took your bag. We did split the money fifty-fifty though."

B.J. took his eye off the road long enough to look in his rear view mirror and make eye contact with Randy reemphasizing the point he had made earlier about the girls having separate debts. Still, he didn't say a word. It was for the two of them to discuss and come to an agreement.

"Yeah, well what now? Suttin' gotta give," Randy told her.

Free turned back around, to the front. She just stared out the window not wanting to say anything that might make the situation worse. After a while, B.J. looked over at her and she spoke up. "I'll give you $2,500. That's my half of the five g's. Otha den dat, there's nothing I can do. I was expectin' a thousand dollars, not five hundred. So, I feel like, we took five g's from you, not six. I'll give you back my half of the five, but you gotta give me some time to pull it together." B.J. was impressed with her assertive resolution. Randy was not.

"I really ain't tryna wait. You know, I been waitin' all summer as it is. How much time is we talkin' about?"

"Not too long," Free answered. She knew what was coming next.

"What dat weed lookin' like? I'll take a coupla dem joints instead. I got bills like you. I need suttin' now."

"I don't got nuttin' now. What I brung to show ya'll ain't mine? It's my peoples and dey ain't goin' for dat. I'll get ya money together in a minute. It won't be long," Free held her ground.

Once again, B.J. looked into the rearview mirror and made eye contact with Randy. Free had defended herself, but at the same time she admitted to her wrongdoing and accepted responsibility. B.J. was as proud as he could be of a girl who had slept with one of his boys. At the same time he was upset and disturbed. He knew there was now limits as to what he could allow himself to feel for the girl. Even with the freshly uncovered skeleton hanging out her closet, B.J. glanced over and loved the view.

Free looked over at B.J. using her eyes to ask 'what does this mean between us?' B.J. broke away from her stare and turned onto the street that would lead them back to the McDonald's. He turned the radio on full blast and rode without saying a word to either passenger. Yeah, he was in his feelings.

As they pulled into the parking lot beside Free's car, B.J. turned down the radio just enough for Randy to hear Free say. "Ya boy knows how to get in touch wit' me."

"What about ya girl? How do I go about getting in touch wit' her," Randy asked.

"I'll let her know you're lookin' for her."

"Yeah, you make sure you do dat."

They were now parked beside Free's car and she was opening the door to get out. She was stalling, moving extra slow, hoping B.J. would say something to her before she left his car. He noticed, but had nothing to say to her.

"Call me later," she told him. He simply lifted his chin towards her and said nothing. Free got out, Randy got back in the front seat, and B.J. pulled off.

When Free was seated safely in the Sonata, she wanted to pick up the phone to call Nita and see what she had to say about the situation but she couldn't. She still had the weed under her seat that needed to be promoted and sold. She picked up the phone and began calling customer after customer. The twins had introduced her to a few new customers and they themselves continued to cop from her every time she re'd-up. Business was booming, but now she had this $2,500 debt hanging over her head.

Free knew she didn't have to pay Randy back. She did, but she didn't. People took losses everyday. There was no way Randy was ever expecting to see his money again. What if she didn't have it? What if she was an average Jane who didn't have access to that kind of money? Because they knew she hustled, they figured she had a way of coming up with the money. She didn't want to appear broke in B.J.'s eyes so she decided to pay Randy back his money. She knew the only reason things had went so smoothly was because of B.J.'s influence over Randy. She had feelings for him and didn't want him disappointed. She would pay her debt.

Her first customer of the day, an older Hispanic fellow she had met through the twins, noticed the change in her mood right away.

"You okay, Mami?" he asked once he got in the car.

"Yeah, I'm aight." She pulled three pounds from under her seat and sat them on his lap. He reached in both of his pockets, pulled out a total of $2,700 and passed it over to her. He examined the weed as she counted his cash.

"I don't know, Mami. You look like somebody made you upset. Just let me know. I can't have nobody upsettin' my girl."

"I'm good, baby."

The transaction was complete and they went their separate ways. Free met with two other guys and got rid of the other three pounds. She was now headed home to confront her roommate. Free had called Nita and told her to meet her at the apartment because she had something important to talk to her about. When Free arrived home, Nita was nowhere to be found, so Free called her right away.

"I'm out wit' Virgil," Nita announced.

"Well, when you think you gonna be home cuz I told you I gotta talk to you." Free didn't want to reveal over the phone what she needed to talk to Nita about. Seeing Nita's face when she mentioned Randy's name was the only way Free would be able to tell whether or not Randy was telling the truth. Free knew Nita like the back of her hand and she could spot a lie on her friend's face from a mile away.

"I'm around his way wit' him. I shouldn't be too late. Why? Whassup?"

"I'll talk to you when you get here." CLICK. Free hung up the phone and went about her business.

Chapter 24

He didn't even see them pull up behind him. Even if he had spotted them, there wasn't much he could do at this point. The blue lights came on and his short run was over. When G first saw the car pull up behind him, he didn't know whether to run or stop. He was looking at serious time for conspiracy to commit bank robbery. There was no way he could avoid incarceration and even a fifty percent sentence reduction would leave him serving every bit of ten years. He knew they would catch up with him one day, but why today? He had his son and his gun in the car with him. G pulled off the highway and onto the shoulder. He looked at Lil' Gary, sitting in his car seat, and reached in his back pocket for his last hope.

"Can I see your license and registration, Sir?" the state trooper asked.

G pulled out his fake driver's license then reached in the glove compartment for the registration to his baby mother's car.

"Keep your hands where I can see 'em," the trooper yelled into the vehicle.

"I'm just reaching for the registration," a nervous G pleaded.

One look at the fake driver's license and Trooper Dave called for back up. He thought he recognized the driver of the vehicle when it sped past him. Now upon closer examination he was

sure he was looking into the face of one of the city's most notorious bank robbery fugitives. What a catch this would be. He instructed the driver to remove the keys from the ignition. G turned his head and looked at his little boy in the backseat. If he ran, he knew there was a chance that neither of them would make it. As the officer waited with his hand held out, G continued to stare at his son and curse his baby mother for making him baby sit today.

"Is there a problem, officer?" he asked, hoping for the best and trying to remain calm.

"No Sir. There's no problem. I'll just need to go and run this information. I'm gonna have to ask you again for your car keys."

G did as he was told. He took Lil' Gary out of his car seat and held him close. He was tempted to sit him on the side of the road and pull off. The fact that he no longer had car keys was the only thing stopping him. He held his son tightly along with the small piece of hope that perhaps the officer hadn't recognized him. His gut told him, he didn't have a chance.

Four hours later, DEA agents were kicking in Taye's apartment door thanks to two search warrants. The agents found a 9mm, nine ounces of cocaine and a little over a quarter ounce of Hydro. They also had an arrest warrant in the name of Dante Briggs a.k.a Taye. Both warrants were granted based on incriminating statements federal drug agents received from a cooperating confidential informant. An unsuspecting Taye, was somewhere across town trying to talk his way into the panties of a minor and would be returning home shortly.

Free had just settled in for the night when Nita arrived. She had sold nearly all of her weed and finished counting and storing her money when she heard the key in the lock. She jumped up off the sofa.

"Hey, chica. What's goin' on girl?" Nita greeted Free on her way in the door. She had an armful of shopping bags, so it was no surprise that she was in a good mood. "Look at these boots I

made Virgil buy me," she practically shouted before Free even got a chance to answer her semi-rhetorical question.

"I saw Randy today."

Nita dropped the Chanel shoebox she was holding. It landed on the floor but she didn't reach for it. Instead she took a seat on the edge of the couch.

"Where? What happened? What did he say?!"

Free watched Nita's face closely. Nita twisted her nose the same way she did whenever she told a lie. It was becoming apparent to Free that she was guilty of some thing so Free decided to tell a lie of her own.

"When I left the apartment this morning and went outside, he was right outside. He was just sittin' in his Excursion waitin' for one of us to come out."

"Are you serious," Nita asked, rubbing her fingertips across her eyebrows. Another nervous habit.

"Yes, I'm serious and he said he's comin' here tonight at twelve o'clock for his money. He said if we're not here, he's gonna have his boys run up in here. And then after that we're still gonna have to pay him."

Nita jumped up off the edge of the sofa and began pacing the floor. Free took a seat and just watched Nita's cool melt.

"What are we gonna do?" Nita asked frantically.

"Well, I know what I'm gonna do. I'm gonna pay dat man."

"What else did he say?" Nita took note of how calm Free was acting.

"What else should he have said?" The question escaped Free's mouth through clenched teeth. Watching Nita fidget triggered Free's temper.

"Oh, I don't know. I was just asking." Nita was lying and Free had spotted it.

"Nita, how much did Randy say he was gonna pay us to have sex wit' him?" Walking over to the window, Nita's eyes began to swell with tears.

"Why would you ask that? You know how much he said he was gonna pay us. It wasn't what he gave us. He tried to gyp us out of our money. We did what we had to do to get ours. Why? What did he say?" Free walked over to Nita and got in her face, but kept her cool.

"I'mma ask you one more time and I don't want you to lie to me. Randy is goin' around tellin' people that he was only supposed to be payin' us $500, not a g. You gotta help me figure out why he would lie like dat."

Nita nervously contemplated her best response. The look in Free's eyes told her that whatever she came up with, it had better be good. "What are you talkin' about?"

She should have come better than that, thought Free. "I'm talkin' about dude comin' here in a few hours to take us for all we got! I'm talkin' about us robbin' dat man for no reason!! He didn't gyp us. You just got greedy. You know if you said he was payin' a grand, I would be down to do it. You got all the sense. Then when I told you what he was workin' wit' in da bathroom, you just got greedy. You took his book bag, not me and now you got me involved in dis crap. I don't got time for dis."

"Oh, so I did this all by myself?" Nita shouted, taking a step backwards. Free was so close she could smell the weed on her breath. "I know you ain't tryna stand here and act like you ain't spend his money right along wit' me. For all I know, you're still spendin' his money!"

"Yup," Free proudly admitted. "Believe I am. And what you spendin'? Whateva it is, you betta be ready to come up off it before he gets here. He knows where we live so we gotta pay him." Free didn't know exactly where she was going with the lie, but it sounded believable, so she stuck with it. She knew Nita would be lax about paying the debt if she heard the real story; she needed to add a sense of urgency to the scenario. She wanted to see how Nita would react under the same pressure she had been under when she was in B.J.'s car. Would Nita crack or come clean?

Nita grabbed her pocket book and shoebox and took off for her bedroom. "Well, I'm getting out of here," she announced. "I don't got no money for him and I ain't tryna be here when him, his boys, or whoever gets here."

"What about me? Cause you leavin', I gotta leave too. Nita they gonna get us for whatever dey can get. And then he's still gonna want his money back. Don't you get it? We gotta pay him somethin'." Free was really enjoying this game.

Starting to panic, Nita kept walking to her room with Free on her heels. She had every intention of taking everything of value with her when she left and never paying Randy back. *I'll call Virgil from the car and tell him to meet me at the Ramada,* she thought. In her mind, a trick is trick, a vic is a vic, and a lick is a lick. "I don't gotta pay him nuttin'," Nita protested. "Just because you're rich. Man listen, I don't got it like dat."

"Suttin' gotta give," Free found herself quoting Randy. "I can't have his boys thinkin' dey could run up in here wheneva dey feel like it. You gotta come up off suttin' cuz I can't have none of dat."

"Well, you betta pay dat man den."

Free shoved Nita's Prada duffle bag off of her bed and onto the floor. "So, you just gonna buck on dat man. You started all of dis, Nita. You are so foul. Where do you think you're goin'?"

"I'm goin' out wit' Virgil. I'm not about to sit here and wait for Randy. If he wanna get gangsta, well Virgil is as gangsta as dey come. I ain't scared of Randy. I mean... I might got a coupla dollars for him, but $7,000? That's crazy."

"No. What's crazy is the way you lied about this whole thing in the first place," screamed Free as she stormed out of Nita's bedroom. "Now, that's crazy! I can't believe you would set me up like dat." Nita never did deny the trickery.

Free marched back in the room with a point to prove. She had in her hand twenty-five hundred dollar bills. Not only did she plan on paying her debt, she would pay it in style.

"I got my $2,500 right here. You gotta g to add to this? Where's it at?" she asked, looking around the room for where Nita's stash might be.

Maybe Free was lying and Randy wasn't coming to collect at midnight. Nita knew there had to be some truth in what Free was claiming. She had to at least have spoken to Randy. How else would she know that Nita had lied to her? She never once thought about Free's safety or how the conversation with Randy went. All she was thinking about was how she was going to get back the grand she was about to give up. She reached in her top drawer and counted out a thousand dollars from the $2,300 she had there.

"Look, this is all I got," she offered and squinted her pretty brown eyes at Free. Nita was analyzing her facial expression, trying to determine whether or not she was telling the truth. "This is a g. If he can't settle for that for right now, well I really don't know what you gonna tell him. I really don't even got this to give."

Free took the money out of her hand and recounted it. "Yeah. This'll hold him off for a while. I still have no under-standin'. You straight lied to me. You been doin' a lot of wild stuff lately. I need you to get yourself together. It's like I don't even know you no more."

"Look, Free. Save the sermon." Nita picked her duffle bag off the floor and continued to pack her overnight bag. Virgil had instructed her to go home and cook while she waited for his arrival. Now she would have to go out and pick him up. "I'm the

same ol' Nita," she continued. "Am I not to do me? I know you gonna let me live. I'm tryna do the same thing as anybody else. Get money and stay alive. Who are you to judge me? Now if you'll excuse me. I got moves to make cuz I ain't tryna be here when ya boy gets here."

"Leave me to clean up your mess," Free said, before leaving out of her room with a handful of cash.

Now that Free had a decent amount of money for Randy, she felt comfortable calling B.J. She hadn't spoken to him since getting out of his car earlier. Even if he was no longer interested in her, she still wanted the opportunity to explain herself along with trying to justify her actions. She didn't want to just call him for that reason alone. Well, now she was calling so that she could get in touch with Randy and pay him his money.

RRRING...RRRING...

B.J. looked at his phone and saw that it was Free calling. He had been sitting in his hotel room thinking about her as well as other things and wondering when she would call. He picked up feelings behind the situation with Randy, but still he wanted to hear her side of the story without Randy present. She called at a good time. B.J. was laid back on his bed, relaxing and watching a little T.V.

"Hello," he answered as if he didn't know who was calling.

"Listen, I need to see you."

"Oh yeah?" B.J. asked in a manner that questioned the purpose of her wanting to visit.

"Yeah. Where you at?" Free was confident in her request.

"I'm up at the Marriott. Why? You comin' thru, or do I need a thousand dollars?" That was a cheap shot but based on his attitude, Free was expecting to hear something like that.

"B.J., I ain't tryna hear dat. You judgin' me based on my past

and I'm tryna make you a part of my future. We need to talk. What room are you in?"

"Room 1634. How long are you gonna be?"

"Not long. I'm leavin' my house now."

"Can you bring me suttin' to eat?"

"Yeah, I got you."

Within the hour, Free was knocking on B.J.'s hotel room door with a order of shrimp and broccoli and a pint of shrimp fried rice in her hands. She knew B.J. loved Chinese food and she hoped he would be satisfied with her choice.

"Special delivery," Free joked as she entered the room and placed the plastic bag containing the food on the dresser.

"For me? Thank you. How much do I owe you?"

"You good, baby. I think I can afford to feed you." Free took a seat on the king size bed while B.J. started digging into his food.

"Shrimp with broccoli, my favorite. Did you eat yet?" he asked, trying to get some type of conversation started. Free sat quietly staring at a music video.

"Yeah, I ate already," she lied. The truth was, Free hadn't had much of an appetite today. Her mind was elsewhere.

"What did you eat?" B.J. asked in between bites.

"I stopped and got a slice of pizza. I really haven't been hungry."

"Oh, okay."

B.J. had a lot on his mind, as did Free. He wanted to hear her side of the story. He wanted a reason to believe her and forget about any mistakes she had made in the past. It was so quiet in

the room, you could hear a mouse urinating on a cotton ball. When B.J.'s cell phone rang, it startled them both.

"So, you just gonna leave me here for dead?" Kenya yelled into the phone. She had a horrible habit of yelling to get her point across. Up until when he saw her name on the caller ID, B.J. had totally forgot about Kenya and her begging him to take her to the hospital.

"You didn't call back, so I didn't think you still needed to go." She had called him back several times and each time B.J. had looked at the caller ID and didn't answer the phone.

"You a damn lie!" Kenya shouted. "You got me pregnant and then you gonna just ignore me when I told you that I need to go to the hospital. This is serious, B.J."

Kenya had been bleeding all day. The pain in her abdomen was so severe, she was sure she was suffering a miscarriage. She didn't want to spend hours in an emergency room waiting area, but she was willing to do anything in order to spend a little time with B.J.; convinced that if he spent time with her, he would develop an interest. She was so wrong.

"I got you pregnant? You got yourself pregnant. Nobody told you to jump on my dick raw dog, first thing in da mornin'. I tried to stop you but it seems like you had your own agenda."

Free almost caught whiplash; spinning her head around to face B.J. What was he talking about? As far as she knew, he didn't have any kids. Now, just a few days had passed and he was on the phone arguing with some chick, who claimed to be carrying his child.

Their conversation lasted a few more minutes and Free listened carefully to every word he uttered. The only reason he stayed on the phone with Kenya was to clear the air. He figured when he hung up, they would put all their cards on the table. Keep it real with each other, so to speak. Free knew exactly what he was doing. *He has a secret and I had a secret. How could I be mad at him? How could he be mad at me?*

"I'll call you later," B.J. ended the call and turned his phone off. He knew Kenya would call right back. The conversation he had with Kenya was for Free. He said things like 'I don't got a girlfriend yet. I don't gotta answer to nobody' and 'maybe it's for the best you lost the baby because I don't think we'd be good together. That was just one night together and I got somebody else I'm tryin' to get wit'." He knew Free was listening to every word.

Free looked over at him, waiting for him to explain. She had a way of getting her way with him.

"That was that chick from Friday's." B.J. threw his phone on the dresser and sat next to Free on the bed. "She talkin' about you made her lose her baby and she's gonna charge you wit' attempted murder."

"I didn't know she was pregnant." Free was shocked. "She shoulda thought about that baby when she was getting all up in my face." Free's voice changed from sassy to sympathetic. "Was that your baby?" she asked.

"Yeah, she claims it was but, I have no way of knowin' for sure. Remember, I told you we were together once?"

"Yeah, I remember."

"Well, that's when she claim she got pregnant. I don't know what to believe."

"B.J., I'm sorry if I embarrassed you today. I'm sorry you had to find out about the situation with Randy like that. There's a few things I want you to know."

"Like what," he asked. He wanted to hear everything she had to say.

"First of all. That was a once in a lifetime thing. Me and Nita was pressed about goin' to see 50 Cent when he came here back in June. We needed something to wear and we needed to pay for the Escalade we rented. I know that's no excuse, but we was desperate."

"Go 'head," B.J. urged her to continue.

"Well, I can't lie and say I didn't do it, because I did. It lasted about three minutes and I hated every second of it. I only did it for the money and then afterwards it turned out that I wasn't even getting what I thought I was getting. Next thing you know, Nita snatched up his bag and we was out the door. That's the whole truth. I really like you, I feel like I at least owe you that much." She was nervously pleading but, she had gotten it off of her chest and it felt good.

B.J. looked away when Free was finished speaking. He stood up from the seat and turned his back to her. B.J. had a habit of staring out windows. Whenever he was in any kind of room, if there was a window, he was keeping a constant watch out of it. If he ever found himself in a room without a window, he became noticeably uncomfortable. B.J. watched from his room on the 16th floor as cars sped by on the Interstate below.

"I guess nobody's perfect. We all have our flaws. I just wish it wasn't with my man. I feel like I'm stuck and tryna play both ends. I'm feelin' you but, you know, I got principles. My boy really wanted to do you dirty today. You know dat, right?" She knew. B.J. heard a noise from behind and turned to find Free reaching for her purse.

"I know and I appreciate you looking out for me. I make bad decisions just like anybody else, but I pay my debts." She laid the money on the bed. "This is my twenty-five and this is Nita's grand. She said she gonna do her best to get up da rest."

B.J. walked over, picked up the cash then looked into her eyes. *She works fast,* he thought. He picked up his phone and turned it on to call Randy.

"Yeah, dawg. Get at me in da mornin'. I'm here wit' shawty and she gave me some paperwork to pass you."

"Fo' sho'." Randy agreed then hung up.

"That's taken care of," B.J. told Free then sat the money atop

the dresser. Almost everything about her was impressive. He took a seat on the bed and then tapped the space beside him, gesturing for her to join him. She slid over, closer to him.

Being so close to him was better than Free thought it would be. The subtle smell of his cologne and the look in his eyes was more than she could bare. She brushed her manicured hands over his cornrows and looked him in the eyes. All it took was for him to lean inward and they were locking lips. He liked the way her lips felt but he liked the taste of her tongue even more. They kissed for what seemed like hours and. B.J. felt himself surrendering control. He pulled away and stood up from the bed. Walking slowly back over to the window, he felt like somebody was trying to steal his heart out of his chest and there was nothing he could do to stop it from happening. So, he went along with it.

"Free, you know you my girl, right?"

The nerve, Free thought. *So he just gonna tell me I'm his girl. Who does he think he is?*

"I know," she said with a sexy smirk.

"But if you slept wit' anymore of my boys den you need to let me know right now. I'm not dat type of dude. You know, cause I don't..."

"Miss me wit' all of dat. I'm not dat type of chick either. So, if you got anymore girls pregnant then you need to let me know right now."

"Yeah, I see we gotta work on your smart ass mouth."

"I'm right here. Come work on it," she flirted.

B.J. took his seat beside her on the bed and they went to work on each other's lips.

Chapter 25

Things happen fast in the drug game. Changes occur overnight. B.J. and Free met each other and within three days they were a happy couple. When a person is right for another person, it doesn't take long to figure that out. The same applies when a person is not right for another person. When it is real, there is no need to question it. Free saw in B.J. a guy she would be willing to spend the rest of her life with. B.J. looked at Free and saw a beautiful girl he could never grow tired of. They were lucky to have found one another.

After they sorted through all the problems that might arise in their relationship they spent the night at the Marriott cuddled in each other's arms. Free had one last test for B.J. She didn't figure him for the type that would press to get in between her legs, but she had to be sure. If he could spend the night sleeping beside her without making an aggressive sexual pass at her, then he was a keeper in her eyes. B.J. had one last test for Free, as well. B.J. would often spend the night with various good looking females. When you're about to go to bed at night and you have sex on your mind, it doesn't take much for a person to look attractive. The trick was for a person to still be considered attractive the next morning. Morning came and both, B.J. and Free, passed their tests with flying colors. B.J. did no more than rest his arm on Free's stomach as they slept. When they awoke, he noticed she had the most beautiful 'wake-up face' he had ever seen.

Still, there was big trouble brewing in paradise. A snitch anywhere is a threat to hustlers everywhere. Taye called B.J., first thing that morning, talking fast and wanted to meet with him. B.J. agreed to do so within the hour. Free, who had made herself comfortable with the plush hotel accommodations, opted to stay and sleep while B.J. went to handle business. After a short shower B.J. left to go and meet with Taye. He left behind $150 on the nightstand for Free to go and purchase the room for an additional night.

It had been about a week since B.J. spoke with Taye, he never did sell Taye the half of key he had been so desperately begging him to provide. B.J. lied and said that his connect was experiencing a drought. Taye didn't believe it and he shouldn't have because it was just an excuse. When Taye first went broke, he gave him a decent price. Since then, no drugs or money had passed between their hands. That is not to say that Taye did not continue to call with a mouthful of requests. That he did, but it was to no avail. B.J. had cut him off.

B.J. pulled out of the Marriott parking lot with a strange feeling in his stomach. He was still dealing with his grief and beginning to feel good about the fact that he had a new girlfriend and soon a new apartment. He was taking a step in the right direction towards maturity. But that wasn't the cause of the feeling in his stomach. He felt like he was missing out on something. He thought about T.J. and the last time he had seen his mother. Those thoughts made him uneasy; however that wasn't the cause of the turmoil he felt in his gut. As he rode, he returned Taye's phone call.

"Listen," Taye spoke with urgency. "Where you gonna meet me at? I need to see you like now. I gotta a coupla dollaz and I need to see you like now."

B.J. had no desire to see Taye or his money. He told himself that he would go ahead and meet with him and then get his phone number changed later in the week. B.J. was an expert when it came to cutting old ties and making new ones.

"Where you at, man?" he asked, quite annoyed.

"I'm in the house. Come thru my joint," Taye commanded.

"I'm on the way."

"Listen," Taye added. "I got like five dollars to spend wit' you so be straight wit' dat when you come thru."

Huh? B.J. was confused. Taye had never spoken to him like that on the telephone before. If Taye had money to spend, he would just say that he needed to see B.J., or he wanted to holla at him. Now he was on the phone talking crazy and putting in specific orders. That wasn't what caught B.J.'s attention. Taye had been acting strange and breaking all sorts of rules since he went broke. What struck B.J. as odd was not the wide open manner of the request, but the actual request. B.J. sold an eighth of a key for $3,500 and a quarter for $7,000. Five thousand dollars did not fit right in that equation.

"Five dollars?" B.J. asked the first question that popped into his head.

"Yeah, five grand," said Taye, loud and clear.

Whoa! thought B.J. Taye was talking super reckless. "I'll be thru there," he said before hanging up.

Now, B.J. knew where the strange feeling in his stomach was coming from. When discussing drugs on his telephone, never had anyone discussed dollar amounts in such detail. Now here was Taye, not only making a strange request, but he was too vivid with his order. He may as well had called B.J.'s phone and said, "I have five thousand dollars to spend on some powder cocaine." That wasn't how B.J. handled business and Taye knew it. B.J. felt the set up, still he didn't want to believe it. He hadn't heard anything about Taye being picked up by the Feds, so he ignored his hustler's intuition and tried hard to convince himself that it was nothing more than a case of paranoia. Anything to avoid the realization that the time had come for drastic measures.

B.J. went ahead and drove over to Taye's apartment that day, but he was no fool. His mind and his heart could remain in denial but there was no denying what his ears had heard. Taye's mouth was out of control. B.J wanted to believe that he had been drinking, but it was the first thing in the morning. Perhaps he had been up all night on one of his ecstasy highs. Whatever the case was, B.J. felt like he needed to see what was going on with his own eyes. He was in cautious mode.

Normally, B.J. would enter Taye's complex through the front entrance. Today he came in through the back entrance. He drove through the complex, slowly scanning all the parked cars and the few residents he passed. He wasn't looking for anything in particular; just anything out of the ordinary. He was so into what was going on inside of the complex, he paid no attention to the white van he passed on the way in. The van was parked at a neighboring Food Lion, adjacent to the apartments.

B.J. didn't call to say he was outside like he would do under normal circumstances. He just went upstairs and knocked on the door. Taye answered the door right away. He didn't appear to be high or drunk. Actually, he looked perfectly sober.

"Come in, Dawg," Taye instructed.

That was the first thing out of the ordinary that B.J. noticed. B.J. was already halfway in the house when Taye invited him in. Such a formality as inviting people to enter your home, was not Taye's style. It was too formal. The second thing that B.J. noticed was the fact that Taye wasn't smoking. Taye was the type who woke to a blunt in the ashtray and today it smelt as if he hadn't smoked in his apartment in days.

"You ain't smokin' nuttin'?" B.J. asked before looking around, deciding where he would sit. He was experiencing a serious case of the paranoid criminal syndrome.

"We can."

We can, thought B.J. *What does he mean 'we can'?*

Any other day Taye would say 'roll up' or he would mention something about the reason he wasn't already smoking. B.J. allowed the scene to soak in as he reached in his pocket and pulled out a bag of Hydro, tossing it over to Taye. Taye caught the weed and went over to one of his kitchen drawers to retrieve a cigar. B.J. found himself a seat on the recliner. They smoked the blunt Taye rolled and conversed back and forth about nothing in particular. Taye didn't bring up the subject of his intended purchase and B.J. was beginning to sense that he was nervous about something.

B.J. was over there for a full twenty minutes before Taye brought up the telephone conversation that had initiated the visit. Even then he was hesitant and not as excited as he had been over the telephone. Taye reached in the same drawer he had dug into for the cigar and pulled out a stack of money.

"Like I was sayin', here's the five g's dat I got to spend wit' you." Taye walked over to the recliner and extended his arm to pass B.J. the money, but he didn't dare reach for it. B.J. stared into his face.

"What you talkin' about, yo?"

"You know what we was talkin' about ova da phone. I said I was gonna need to holla at you. What can I get for five g's?"

"What you was tryin' to get?" B.J. chose his words carefully.

"For five grand I figure I should be able to get a four and a half and a 62. What you think?" he asked.

"Yeah, I think you should be able to get that for five grand. That sounds about right."

"So whassup," asked Taye. He was ready to get the whole thing over with and he felt like if he held out his arm any longer, it would fall off.

"You tell me whassup. I'm chillin'. Ain't nuttin' goin' on ova here." B.J. sat back further.

Taye knew what that meant. The trust was lost. When one dealer refuses to sell to another, there is usually a very good reason behind it. For B.J., something just didn't feel right and that was reason enough to decline the sale. His instincts told him that it was not safe and that was all it took for him to shoot down Taye's request.

"What?" asked Taye. He really needed the sale.

"I said I'm chillin'. I don't got it like dat."

"You chillin'?" Taye had a look of desperation on his face.

"Yeah, man. I ain't been doin' too much of nuttin'."

"Really?" he asked sarcastically. Taye knew he was being lied to.

"Really," B.J. repeated. Taye walked back over to the kitchen counter and returned the money to the drawer. And, since when did Taye offer his money before seeing what he was buying? That wasn't his style either. B.J. knew something was up. Not dealing with Taye today was the best thing he could have ever done. B.J. rose to leave. Taye tried to make him stay.

"Where you goin'?" Taye jumped up.

"My sister's house."

"Make sure you call me when you get straight," Taye pleaded.

"I ain't gonna be straight no time soon. I'll let you know if I hear suttin'."

"Alright. Good lookin'. Be easy."

B.J. didn't know it, but if he had taken that five grand out of Taye's hands, his whole life would have changed. He left the apartment with the same queasy feeling in his stomach, but now he knew what had caused it. At first, he didn't notice the dark green Impala, occupied by two federal drug enforcement agents

following him onto the highway. Once on the entrance ramp to the Interstate, B.J. looked in the rearview and spotted the Impala two cars back. It was the only car in his rearview that made him feel uncomfortable. When he stayed on the entrance/exit ramp and got right back off of the highway with the car still tailing him at a distance, he knew there was trouble.

B.J. panicked on the inside while remaining visibly cool. His thoughts were swift and thorough. The first thing he did was assume everything: his phone was tapped, the feds were the cause of Taye's wild phone call. He thought hard and drew quick, accurate conclusions. Since they hadn't pulled him over, they must have been surveilencing him while they built a case. He drove down one of the city's main streets in search of a fast food restaurant. He would go there to stall for time and rack his brain for clues.

That was the vehicle that would have pulled him over had he served Taye. Since he hadn't, the car had to be just tailing him, trying not to lose him. By the time B.J. pulled into the Wendy's parking lot, he recognized that he had two choices. He could take off and expose the fact that he knew the car was following him. This plan could result in an unwanted car chase. If they had an arrest warrant with his name on it, he would already be in custody. Option two, drive at a normal speed and outsmart the officers by ditching them slickly. Either way, B.J. knew he had to get the Impala out of his rearview before he did anything else.

The two seasoned agents did not follow B.J. into the Wendy's parking lot, instead they had a good view of his caddie from the Racetrack gas station across the street. Their orders were strict: Don't lose him.

Pulling out of the Wendy's, B.J. snacked on his spicy chicken sandwich with cheese combo. Next stop was the closest shopping mall. He drove and ate, putting his simple plan into action. He cruised along at a safe speed, keeping a close eye on the police in his rearview. He arrived at the mall, which was less than ten miles away, parked near the front entrance and went inside. He appeared to be paying no attention to the Impala as

it positioned itself perfectly to watch the movement of his vehicle. Cooly, B.J. walked into the mall and strolled the short distance to the Macy's department store. Here, he took the escalator to the bottom floor and found his way to the men's restroom. When he was sure he hadn't been followed, he slipped two quarters into a pay phone to call Free.

"Hello," she answered on the second ring.

"Hey Boo, listen. I need you to do me a favor."

"What's that?"

"I'm havin' car trouble. I need you to pick me up from the mall."

"The mall? Which one?"

"I'm at Greenview Commons. I need you to come right now, though."

"Okay, baby. I'm on the way."

"Alright good, but don't call my phone. Just pull up in the back at the food court entrance. I'll see you when you pull up."

"Are you okay?" Free asked, sensing that there was more to the story than she was being told.

"I'm okay. Just come right now, okay."

"Okay." Free hung up and was out the door to get her man.

Meanwhile, Nita was seated in the driver's seat of her Honda, waiting for Virgil to come outside. She had been sitting outside of the project apartment for going on fifteen minutes now. Just when she was about to pick up her phone to call him, Virgil came jogging to the car, clutching at his hip.

"My bad," he offered, as he climbed in. "You know people always tryna talk me to death. I forgot I got dis dude waitin' up da street. Why you still sittin' here? Pull off!"

Nita liked Virgil. She liked the rough look of his face and the smooth feel of his body. He didn't have a lot of money, but she respected the way he woke up every morning trying to get more. He was a hoodlum, a straight-up thugged out individual and that was attractive to her. She loved laying in bed with him, listening to his war stories of brutal street life and then riding around with him and actually catching a glimpse of it for herself. Virgil didn't have a driver's license; Nita was his chauffer, taking him all the places that he needed to go.

"Make a left," Virgil instructed, with a Black-n-Mild cigar stuck between his lips.

"Where we goin' now?" Nita asked.

"Didn't I just tell you I have to go meet dis dude?"

Nita found herself driving towards the heart of one of the city's most dangerous project developments. She was in the part of town where even the bravest of hearts were scared to walk through after dark, where the residents killed for anything and nothing.

"Pull ova right here," Virgil demanded.

Before Nita even shifted the gear into park, Virgil was out the car, clutching at his hip and jogging towards a three story apartment building. Nita took this opportunity to look in the mirror and make sure her hair and make-up was still in place. It was. She looked cute today in her tight fitting Akademics jeans suit and stiletto sneaker boots. She was so busy in the mirror applying a second coat of MAC studio fix, she failed to take notice of the junior high school dropouts, who were gathered at the corner of the block, eyeing her vehicle.

Minutes passed and Nita's patience began to diminish. She had been sitting in her car all morning waiting for Virgil as he ran in and out of different apartment complexes. He only stayed in the car long enough to direct her to his next destination. She was fed up and just about to change the music in her CD player when she heard the first shot ring out. She whipped her head around trying to see where it was coming from.

Pop, Pop...

Two more shots. They sounded close. As if it would protect her, Nita rolled up the windows in her car. Still she sat there waiting for Virgil, not wanting to pull off and leave him behind. *I hope he's okay,* she worried and decided to pick up her phone to call him and tell him to hurry. *Come on. Answer the phone. Answer the phone.* Nita was listening to Virgil's answering machine when she saw him limping towards her car.

Pop, Pop, Pop...

Virgil turned around and started running backwards, returning the fire that was being aimed at him.

Pop, Pop...

Virgil's two shots missed their intended target. He was about twenty feet from Nita's car but the bullet in his left calf prevented him from getting there faster. Nita went into a state of shock. The sound of the gun shots and the sight of danger near was more than she could handle. She reached over to open the passenger door for Virgil but he could not make it.

All kinds of shots rang out. There appeared to be two or more gunmen and they all had their weapons aimed at Virgil. When the bullet hit his spinal cord he was so close to his destination, Nita could hear his knees collapse. His forehead met violently with the asphalt. Nita screamed at the top of her lungs and dropped her cellphone.

Pop, Pop...

Now that Virgil's body was no longer blocking the viscous flow of bullets, Nita found herself in the line of fire. The first shot shattered the front passenger side window and ripped through her tender flesh.

"VIRGIL!!!" she shouted. There was no way he could answer her call. Nita didn't feel the bullet, instead she saw her window and was ready to take off. "VIRGIL!!!" Virgil was face down in the street. She didn't want to leave him there for dead.

Pop.

Another shot. *Are they shooting at me?*

"Bitch! You betta pull off!" a woman shouted from a second story window.

SSSCCCUUURRRTTT

She didn't have to be told twice. Virgil's bleeding body lay beside the tread marks Nita made as she pulled off at full speed.

Nita drove a few miles, screaming and crying with no destination. She couldn't believe what she had witnessed before her very eyes in broad daylight. She had sped away from the crime scene making desperate left and right turns and now she was lost and her brain was crowded with fear. She couldn't think straight, much less find her way to a street she recognized. She didn't realize she had been hit until she reached down on the floor to pick up her phone. The red stain on the arm of her denim jacket caused her to feel sick to her stomach. Now that she had seen the blood, she felt an excruciating throbbing pain in her upper arm and shoulder area.

I've been shot. I'm gonna die. The blood had flowed all the way down her sleeve and was now making the steering wheel sticky. *Ohmigod*, Nita thought before fainting behind the wheel.

Chapter 26

By the time Free and B.J. rode into the hospital parking lot, B.J. had explained his current situation to Free as best he could. She now understood that things were hot for him and he could no longer stay in town. Today was turning out to be a terrible day for Free. Could she be losing her boyfriend and her best friend both on the same day?

Just as B.J. was getting into the reason he had to leave his car at the mall, Free's phone rang.

"Calm down. What happened?" Free asked.

"Nita got shot!" Big Nita cried.

Now Free was in the emergency waiting room, hugging her best friend's mom. "What happened?" Free asked again.

"They said she passed out. I'm waiting for the doctor to come back out now. She was in a car accident and somebody called the ambulance. My baby! They said she has a bullet wound. Oh Lord! Please see her through this!" Big Nita was a mess and her words were shooting out of her mouth faster than the bullet that had hit her daughter.

"A bullet wound!" Free screamed then looked over at B.J. as if he had something to offer. His face sported a sympathetic look that said 'your guess is as good as mine.' "Is she okay?" Free shouted.

Big Nita broke from Free and started rushing her words and fighting back tears. "They said the gunshot wound is not life threatening, but she did get scratched up pretty bad after she passed out and ran the car into a tree. My poor baby! I'm waiting for her doctor to come out now."

Free took a seat in one of the few available hard, plastic seats in the gloomy waiting room. For the first time since she rushed into the room, she looked at her surroundings then stared into the ceiling, letting out a silent prayer for her best friend. B.J. sat beside her and gave her lower thigh a firm, supportive squeeze. She had almost forgotten he was there. She introduced him to Big Nita and an older black doctor stepped toward the trio.

"Mrs. Benjamin," Dr. Phillips walked over demanding attention.

"How is she doing, doctor?"

"She's doing a lot better. Your daughter's lost a lot of blood. We're making preparations to operate shortly and remove the bullet from her shoulder. We don't expect any complications there. She suffered a lot of facial cuts from when the windshield broke after she crashed into the tree. We've cleaned and bandaged the cuts caused by the glass but there will be some medium to severe scarring. The important thing is that she is in stable condition and within the hour we will be removing the bullet and you will be allowed to visit with her."

"Oh! Thank you!" Big Nita let out a breath deep enough, you'd think she'd been holding her breath for the past hour.

"Yes Ma'am," Dr. Phillips smiled, happy to be the bearer of good news. The doctor continued in his monotone voice. "One of the sergeants from down at the 32nd Precinct gave us a call not too long ago. Apparently a young man was found slain in the middle of the street not too far from where Tanita was found. A couple of officers should be arriving any minute with a few questions for you. What is your relation to the injured party?" The doctor addressed Free and B.J. for the first time.

"We're her friends," Free answered quickly for both of them.

"I would suggest you stay put and have a word with the officers also. I should be going now." He turned and walked away.

B.J. gave Free an obvious stare that relayed his thoughts. In his present predicament, he was in no position to be conversing with any law enforcement representatives. For all he knew, he could have an unserved warrant or secret indictment hanging over his head.

"Do you have any idea who she was with or what she was doing or who would want to shoot Nita?" Now that Nita was going to be ok, her mother's main concern was finding out who did this.

"I'm in the dark about this whole thing, just like you, Big Nita. She did have a new friend. His name is Virgil. I'm not sure if that's who she was with though."

Big Nita sighed deep, looked at her watch and continued to pace the floor. Free looked at B.J., who was staring at her, waiting for an opportunity to offer his sympathy.

"Boo, I hope your friend's gonna be okay."

"I feel so bad," Free admitted. "We just got into a bad argument."

"Free, listen..." She didn't even give him a chance to finish his sentence. She knew where his head was and therefore she knew what he was about to say. Free reached in her pocketbook for her car keys and passed them over to him.

"Go take care of what you gotta take care of. Just make sure you leave your phone on so that I can get in touch wit' you."

"I got you, boo. Just call me when you're ready," he said standing up. He bent over and planting a kiss on her forehead. B.J. walked over to Big Nita. She had started a conversation with another nervous mother, who was in the waiting room awaiting

information about her injured son. "Excuse me," B.J. approached. "Ms. Benjamin, I want you to know that I'm sorry to hear about your daughter. Your family is in my prayers. I have to get going now but if there is anything I can do to make this time a little easier for you, don't hesitate to let me know. It was nice meeting you. Again, I'm sorry it had to be under these conditions."

"Thank you. Thank you," Big Nita answered then turned to continue her chat.

B.J. turned to look at his new girlfriend on the way out the door. She looked into his eyes and mouthed the words 'be careful'. B.J. nodded his head 'yes' and left. When he got out to the parking lot, he did not locate the Sonata right away. He spent a few minutes looking around for his Cadillac. His mind was so many places.

Focus! he told himself once he eventually got behind the wheel of the Sonata. His first stop was to meet with Randy. He needed to get rid of the $3,500 he had been carrying around in his pocket. He called Randy from a pay phone and arranged to meet with him at their normal spot—the barbershop. As he drove, he allowed his thoughts to gather.

Okay. First things first. I need a one-way rental. Something big, so I can fit a lot of my stuff in it. Dana. I gotta go there. Slim. I gotta buy a calling card so I can give him a call. Taye. I gotta deal wit' his ass, too. Free. I gotta think about what I wanna do wit' her. I know she could use a new car.

B.J. pulled up at the barbershop with his whole future figured out. Relocating to another state was not an option at this point. It was a necessity. If his worst fear came true and the Feds picked him up, he would be looking at a lot of time. That is precisely why he could not afford to waste any now.

"Whassup, playboy? Honey is 'bout her business, huh? Can't be mad at that," Randy greeted B.J. and removed the stack of money from his possession.

"Yeah, you can't say she don't take care of what she gotta take care of."

"Damn, so what you stripped her of her cheese and her wheels, huh?" Randy kidded, referring to the old Sonata his boy had arrived in.

"Yeah, something like that," B.J. smiled, avoiding an explanation. He switched to a more serious note. "Have you heard anything else about the boy Taye, anything at all. Dude actin' kinda strange."

Whenever there was new gossip floating around the town, Randy was usually one of the first people to hear it. It wasn't that he went around inquiring about the affairs of others. He simply knew all of the popular females, who knew all of the hustlers and his women had a way of calling and keeping him informed.

"I been listenin' and dude ain't been up to too much of nuttin' as far as I know. But, you know when a person is too quiet they can't be trusted anyway. I did hear suttin' about da boy G dat was goin' around robbin' dem banks. You know who I'm talkin' about?"

"Yeah, I know exactly who you talkin' about."

"They say he finally got picked up and they caught this ignorant asshole with the same gun he used to shoot one of the security guards at the bank. That boy does everything but think. They tryna throw the book at his ass. It gets worse. They say he singin' like he tryna get a record deal. I don't get it, but these fake gangstas neva cease to amaze me."

"Fo' real?" B.J. replied.

"Fo' real." Randy's words pierced B.J.'s soul all over. He now knew what had caused the temperature to rise on his everyday cool environment. Claustrophobia began to set in.

"That's deep. I'mma get at you, dawg." B.J. clutched at the door handle in a hurry to exit the truck.

"Hol' up. What's this?" Randy stopped him and pointed to the stack on his lap.

"That's 35, twenty-five from shorty and a g from the otha little shorty. You know the otha little shorty got shot tonight."

"Say what?" Randy asked as he pocketed the money he never thought he would see.

"Yeah. She's okay, but they say she fainted and wrecked up her lil' car. They up at the hospital now. I just left there. She was at the wrong place at the wrong time wit' da wrong dude. They say dude ain't make it. Homicide gonna be all ova her wit' all kinda questions."

"You don't say. Damn, I hate dat for her. I'll throw the word out and see what bounce back."

"You do dat. I gotta blow. Holla back," B.J. told him.

"Take ya time."

"Will do."

With that taken care of and a new pertinent piece of information under his belt, B.J. knew his relocation mission was all the more necessary. He made it to his sister's house in record time, while still adhering to the speed limit. Dana was home putting the finishing touches on her catfish dinner.

"Mmm. Smells like I showed up at the right time. You got it smellin' all good in here." B.J. still managed to exude a pleasant disposition to those around him although his world was crumbling all around him.

"Yeah, lil' brother. You just in time. You hungry?"

B.J. spent a few hours over Dana's house eating, gathering his belongings, putting in phone calls and planning his future. His clothes were packed up in several heavy duty garbage bags and his belly was now full. He put in a call to Free, who was at the hospital waiting for him, but in no rush to leave her friend's side. He used Dana's cell phone to call Slim, who was happily awaiting his arrival. After very little urging, Dana agreed to rent B.J. an Expedition instead of an apartment. She tried to convince him to stay in town in hopes that things would cool off, but once B.J.'s mind was made up there was very little that could be done to change it.

Dana was on the phone with a rental car agency at the airport, reserving the truck. B.J. and Mike were seated on the couch arguing over last night's Lakers game.

RRRING...RRRING...

Taye was calling and although B.J. wanted to ignore the call, he knew better than to do that. He had started a game that needed to be finished.

"Yo, WDUP," he answered. It was the first time he had used his cell in hours.

"Yo, where you at dawg? I'm sittin' here waitin'. Did you get in touch wit' anybody yet?" Taye asked.

"Nah, man. I been at the mall ever since I left you. Where you at?"

"Oh, you still at the mall?"

"Yeah, man I'll call you when I get outta here," B.J. lied.

"Alright man. Make sure you do."

"One."

"You ready?" she asked, carrying a yellow piece of paper in her hand.

"Yeah," B.J. answered.

Over at the hospital, Nita was just regaining consciousness.

"How are you feeling, baby?" the young Mexican nurse asked. Nita shook her head up and down slowly. Her neck felt as if her head weighed a ton and her mouth was too dry to form words. "You are one lucky lady," the nurse commented as she poured water from a pitcher for Nita to drink. "It's a miracle you didn't lose the baby." The nurse passed Nita a glass full of water and two Tylenols.

The baby??!! Nita moved as fast as she could to an upright sitting position. "What baby?" she moaned.

"Something told me that maybe you didn't know. You are about eight weeks pregnant, my dear. The baby appears to be doing just fine, but Dr. Phillips wants to run a few more tests. Your mom and your friend are outside waiting to come in. Are you ready to see them?"

"Yeah," she whispered. Nita popped the pills and guzzled the entire glass in one gulp.

"Oh, Nita!" Big Nita rushed into the room seconds later. With all of the bandages, Nita's face was barely visible due to the thin layer of gauze that only exposed her eyes, nostrils, and lips. Big Nita squeezed the back of her daughter's hand and gave it a kiss. "How you feelin', honey?"

"I'm okay, Mom. I'm so happy to see you." Nita cracked a smile for the first time in hours. She was surprised to see Free. She had assumed that Virgil was the friend the nurse had referred to.

"Where is Virgil? Is he okay?" she asked, although speaking was a painful task.

Free, who was standing by the door in tears, answered her question. "He didn't make it. Nita, I'm so sorry." She walked over and took a seat on the edge of the hospital bed.

"No!!!" Nita opened her mouth as wide as the confining gauze would allow. She snatched her hand away from her mother's grasp and fingered her face. She touched her facial area gently then stared at her mom for an explanation.

"Mom, what happened to my face," she cried. She yearned to jump out of the bed and search for a mirror, but her body was weak and still somewhat numb from the anesthesia.

"It's not bad, baby. You just got a coupla scratches from the windshield glass. Don't touch it. It will heal, darling. How are you doing otherwise? The important thing is that you're here and you're doing okay."

"Am I ugly?" Nita's question was directed towards Free. Free wiped the tears from her eyes so that she could get a good look into Nita's.

"Nita you could never be ugly. You'll always be beautiful. The most important thing is that you're doing okay."

Nita was still fingering her face and now began to cry, too. She was so concerned about the damage that was done to her face, she didn't give much thought to the oversized bandage on her shoulder or the fact that she was now with child. Free stayed by Nita's side until nine o'clock that night when B.J. came to pick her up. Much to Free's surprise, he was driving a grey Expedition.

"Where's my car?" she asked after climbing into the rented SUV.

"I got it parked at my sister's house. How are you doing? How is your friend doing?"

B.J. and Free discussed Nita's condition as they drove to Free's apartment. She needed to get a change of clothes before going back to the hotel with B.J. Before long they were pulling up and passing the keys to the Marriott valet guy.

"Who's truck is this?," Free asked.

"I'll talk to you when we get upstairs." When they got to the room, B.J. threw a bag of weed onto the bed. "Roll up."

"Whassup?" Free asked, ready to discuss whatever it was that was disturbing her boyfriend.

"I'm gonna take a shower, baby. I'll talk to you when I get out."

"Well, I need to take a shower, too."

"So join me," B.J. extended an invitation.

"Nah, I betta not. I'm gonna roll dat blunt and wait for you to get out."

"Oh, okay."

B.J. stripped down to his boxer shorts and went into the bathroom. When he came out, Free grabbed her overnight bag and went into the shower. She felt like she needed to cool down, so she showered with lukewarm water, rather than hot. She caressed her body with soapy hands and thought about how good B.J. looked with nothing but his boxers on. She stepped out of the shower, dried off and stepped into a knee length night-gown. When she came out of the bathroom, B.J. had put on a pair of boxers and a wife beater and had already started smoking the blunt she had rolled.

"Boo, can you put some lotion on my back for me?" he asked passing her the blunt. Free adored the curves in his muscular back as she rubbed on the cocoa butter lotion.

"What's on your mind?" she asked, massaging his back. He was seated directly beside her and he turned to face her.

"Man, Free. I gotta be outta here in the mornin'."

Free didn't quite get the jest of what he was saying. When check out time approached the next morning she assumed they would both be getting out of there.

"What you mean?" she asked.

B.J. looked at her, assessing whether or not she could be trusted. He had everything to lose and everything to gain by trusting her. There is a point in every person's life where they feel like they need to trust someone. B.J. had reached that point.

"I gotta blow. I gotta leave town. Baby, I can't live here no more. Ya man is hot. If dem people know my car, then they know me."

"Thanks to ya boy," Free commented. She never met Taye but from what she had heard, she could not stand him.

"Exactly. And I got something for his ass, too."

"So, where you off to?" she asked taking his hand in hers.

This conversation was beginning to be too much for B.J. He wasn't accustomed to putting so much trust into another person. *I only live once,* he reasoned.

"I'm movin' to Atlanta. I was hopin... I was thinkin' maybe it wouldn't be so bad if you were to come wit' me. I could take care of you." He used his free hand to run his fingers through her silky hair. Free was teary-eyed. She just met B.J. and she didn't want to leave him, but she couldn't just pick up and leave town either. What about school? What about her customers?

"I don't doubt it," she answered. "So, just like that, you're leavin' me? There's no other way?"

"Baby, you must not have heard what I was tellin' you earlier. Dem people is on to me. I gotta go somewhere where I can lay low and stay outta dere way. I can't afford to get caught up in nobody else's mess. I gotta go, Babe." A single tear dripped down Free's contoured cheek. She knew she would not be able to go with him.

"I would love to go with you," she said softly. "But you know I'm in school. As much as I want to, I can't just pick up and leave like dat."

"I understand." He rubbed his thumb along the corner of her eyelids. "I understand," he repeated.

He began to kiss on her cheeks and nibble on her earlobes. Chills rushed up and down Free's spine, but the sensation was

bittersweet. She knew she was ready to give herself to him. But then what? She would be all alone and yearning for his touch. B.J. knew exactly how she was feeling because he felt the same way. He wanted all of her, but knew, the more he had the more he would miss.

The tips of her hair were wet and her fresh out of the shower smell had B.J. harder than rocket science. He wanted her so bad he was actually considering ways he could stay in town and be with her longer. That was not going to happen. B.J. was a man of action. He knew what he had to do. He had to create a lifestyle elsewhere, with or without Free. Still, he was willing to do whatever was necessary to ensure this beautiful person before him was a part of his new life.

B.J. wanted to take his time and make the night last as long as he possibly could. He kissed along the straps of her nightgown and played with her long hair. Free tossed her head back and relaxed as she scooted her body back towards the headboard. B.J. followed her lead and found himself on top of her. Free wanted to keep her eyes closed, but she couldn't help but keep her eyes on the noticeable bulge that was making its way up her thigh. He massaged her hips with his fingertips and felt around for a panty line. There was no panty line and Free was dripping wet. B.J. broke away from their extended lip lock long enough to see if she wanted the same thing as bad as he did. She did. She stretched her neck and lifted upward to give him a peck on the lips.

"You feel so good," she breathed. Free was freaky. She hadn't had sex all summer and her resolve was wearing itself thin. That was all B.J. needed to hear. He began to attack her firm titi's with his mouth and hands. For both of them, it was beginning to feel like the start of a beautiful thing. The last thing it felt like was an ending.

B.J. reached his hands under her nightgown to feel what she was working with. Free had her hand inside the opening in the front of his boxers searching for what he had to offer. She was pleasantly impressed, as was he. When she loosened the grip on

his nice sized organ, he buried his head in her belly button. Ticklish, she laughed lightly and brushed her nails through the parts in his corn rows. He kissed and licked all around her waistline.

Please don't do it. Please don't do it, Free thought. She didn't want B.J. to go down on her. She knew that she would enjoy it, but it was too soon. If he went down on her now, what would she have to look forward to? She would also question how many other girls he had put his mouth on. B.J. had no intention of giving Free any head action tonight. He just wanted to tease her until she could take no more. To be honest, B.J. had never even went down on a girl before. He licked from the top of her treasure trail to the warm place in between her breasts. Her night gown was already up above her breast so B.J. helped her out by lifting her up and removing it completely.

Free was boiling hot. She hadn't had sex all summer and she was more than ready to put an end to her drought. She looked at B.J. and knew that it was too soon but something about him made her want to throw in the white flag and surrender. She tugged at the sheets, trying to cover her velvety soft body. "Stand up," she directed. B.J. obeyed and Free joined him, standing next to the bed. They stood inches apart, facing each other. B.J. raised his arms above his head and Free removed his wife beater. She licked around his nipples seductively while she pulled his white and blue Sean John boxers to the floor. They were still standing, inches apart but that did not stop B.J. from poking Free in the stomach. He was so hard, he couldn't hide it if he tried. Now it was B.J.'s turn to give out instructions.

"Lay down."

Free positioned herself comfortably on the bed while B.J. walked over hitting the light switch by the door. It was dark in the room and all was quiet. Free was excited, ready and at the same time sad. She knew he had something good for her. What would she do when he was gone and she wanted more of the good stuff? B.J. laid himself on top of Free, ready to enjoy the ride.

She kissed on his neck, while he handled his business down below, placing his man in her. The pressure of his erect love stick finding it's way into her tight and juicy vagina, was somewhat painful. Free tensed up and wrapped her legs around him, digging her nails into his back to fight back the pain.

"Open up for me, boo."

Free opened her shaky legs even wider and went ahead and wrapped them around his back as well, shutting her eyes and sucking up the pain. B.J. was massaging her with his dick as he made his way into her a couple of inches at a time. Just when Free was feeling like it couldn't get any better, he started to dig deeper with delicate half strokes. *"Damn,"* he thought and then said aloud. He had never been inside anything so tight or wet in his entire life. She began to relax more and more with each stroke and before long her back bone was as flexible as a rubber band. He kissed her poked out lips and started to deepen his stroke. He wasn't even all the way inside of her but he was working on it.

"Ooh," Free let out a sexy moan. B.J. smothered her with his huge body and squeezed her generous butt cheeks with his massive hands. The grip Free had on his stick was just as firm. They were both in a state of pure ecstasy. The couple's orgasms built up to a simultaneous eruption. The sheets were wrinkled and dampened with sweat and semen. B.J. gave Free one last kiss before collapsing on top of her. Moments later Free was calling his name. "B.J." There was no answer. "B.J." Still, no answer. He was sound asleep and still inside her. *Goodnight.*

Chapter 27

B.J. rose with the sun. It was time to roll out. They had checked out of the hotel and were in the rental Expedition and on the way to B.J.'s mother's house. He needed to pick up a few of his belongings and he really wanted to introduce Free to his mom. When B.J. pulled up he didn't see his mom's car parked out front, so he left Free waiting in the truck while he went inside to pick up all of his cash. He wanted to talk to his mom and leave her with a couple thousand dollars, but he would have to call her when he reached his destination and then send her some money through Western Union. B.J. returned to the truck with a small black garbage bag full of money. During the ride to his sister's house he would clear the air.

"Free, last night was so good. I know I gotta break out, but I feel like you're where I need to be. I need you to hear me and listen to what I'm tellin' you. Are you tryna be wit' me, ma?"

"Baby, you know I'm tryna be wit' you."

"Okay, that's what I wanted to hear. I've been giving you a lot of thought. I'm gonna leave you my Caddy to drive. You gotta go and pick it up from the mall. My sister has the keys. Have you been thinkin' about movin' down to Atlanta after you finish the semester? I'll pay for you to go to school down there."

What he was saying sounded like the sweetest song in her ears. After B.J. fell asleep last night, Free gave serious thought to

his invitation to relocate. If she wanted, she could transfer to another community college and she could even think about attending a historically black college or university. That was something she'd always dreamed of. She had enough money to relocate on her own, whether or not B.J. would be taking care of her. She was now beginning to think of all the money she could make while waiting for the semester to end. That would give her over two months of hard hustling and serious studying. Yeah, Free could definitely make a trip to Atlanta work for her.

"That's something to think about," she told him as she stared at him, trying to measure the sincerity in his eyes.

"Come upstairs," B.J. said. "I want you to meet my sister." B.J. made sure he locked the doors on the Expedition and they went upstairs to Dana's apartment.

"How are you?" Dana greeted Free with an oversized smile. She was happy to see her brother with a girl. Not to mention a girl as beautiful and put together as Free.

"I'm doin' okay," Free smiled back. She remembered Dana from T.J.'s funeral. They exchanged names and chatted while B.J. was carrying all of his bags full of clothes and sneakers out from the closet and into the hallway by the front door.

"I think that's everything," B.J. announced, after finishing his task. "I'll be right back. I'm gonna bring these down to the truck. Dana, get my car keys and give them to Free."

"No problem," Dana hopped up.

When Dana finished stuffing all of his belongings in the back of his Expedition, he came back into the apartment to give his big sister a goodbye hug. Free had the key to his Cadillac tucked away safely in her purse.

"Did you go by and see mom?" Dana inquired when they were all standing around in the doorway.

"Yeah. I went by there, but she wasn't home. I'm gonna give her a call a little later on tonight."

"Make sure you do. She would love to hear from you."

"I will. Listen, I just want you to go ahead and keep the money I gave you for the apartment."

"Thank you," Dana replied gently. B.J. dug in his pocket and counted out four fifty dollar bills. He passed them to his sister.

"Hold on to this for the Expedition. I'm probably gonna keep it for a week or two. I'll call you and let you know."

"Oh, no problem," she said, grabbing the money. "Just let me know."

"Be safe," she told him. B.J. gave Dana a big hug. Dana and Free said their goodbyes and expressed how nice it was to have met each other. The couple was now outside and it was time for B.J. to make his power move.

"Get in for a minute," he told Free. He reached into his small garbage bag and pulled out a rubber banded $5,000 stack.

"Listen, Free. I want you to take this home and put it up. This should be more than enough to get you anything you may need to finish the semester. You should be able to take this and get a U-Haul or suttin', hire some movers or suttin', and finish payin' off your half of the bills 'til the lease is up." Free took the big stack into her little hands and hung onto his every word. "Now, I'm depending on you to get my car to Atlanta. Even if you just come to visit for a few weeks in between semesters, but the offer still stands and I'm gonna check around and maybe send you some applications from some good schools down there."

"I can always apply on the internet," Free cracked a smile.

"Okay, Boo. That's what I'm tryna hear. Now, I need you to go home and put this money up before you go and get my car. And watch yourself when you go. If you got any dirt to do today, do it before you go. I already explained to you the situation with that car so be careful when you go. And drive around for a while checkin' your mirrors."

"I can handle it," Free announced with pride.

"I know you can. I'm getting ready to throw my phone away, but keep your phone on and I'm gonna call you tonight and give you a new number you can reach me at."

"Baby, you be safe."

"You too, Baby."

Free and B.J. hugged one last time and gave each other a sentimental goodbye kiss. He had become an important part of her life in record speed and now he was driving out of her life just as fast. Free pulled off first, headed home to handle her business. B.J. sat in the parking lot and made a few important last minute phone calls. Five minutes later, he was on the highway and throwing his cell phone out the window.

Free arrived at her apartment feeling like part of her was still in the Expedition headed south on I-95. She thought about calling B.J. and telling him that she had changed her mind and wanted to ride. B.J. rode down the highway feeling as if he was leaving a part of him behind. As he drove away, his mind was focused on the old life and new love he had left behind.

Epilogue

Nita's shoulder healed and within weeks she regained full use of her right arm, wrist and shoulder. Her face sported noticeable scars and never did return to its original beauty. Her shooter remained unidentified. She made Big Nita a grandmother, giving birth to a healthy baby boy. She named him Virgil Jr., after his deceased father. Nita went on to finish school and is currently living at home with her mom and is still searching for a rich boyfriend.

Before B.J. threw his phone out of the window he made a call and hooked Taye up with his HIV positive hairdresser. Unaware of her condition, Taye had unprotected sex with the girl and became infected. He cooperated with the federal government and gave up the names and whereabouts of almost all of his loyal customers in order to avoid a jail sentence. Many people were sent to prison due to his cooperation. He is still running around Greenview, having unprotected sex with unsuspecting females and desperately trying to get back in the drug game, any way he can.

Free never did make it to Atlanta. She dropped out of school after her first semester, addicted to all of the money she was making. She sold B.J.'s Cadillac and brought the money over to his mother's house. Free is currently single and is the connect responsible for more than half of the marijuana being smoked in the city. She is now purchasing 200 pounds of weed at a time

and she continues to send Ed money and will do so until he is released. She has plans to quit the game and return to school after she reaches her goal of $250,000.

B.J. did well creating a new life for himself in Atlanta. He cut all of his hair off, hooked up with some hustlers in a nearby Alabama town and continues to visit Greenview once a month to see Papi. He and Free got together on several occasions, but they were unable to be together on a permanent basis. The pursuit of money had ruined what could have been a beautiful thing. It wasn't that they weren't in love. They were deeply in love with that cash money. An urban love story.

ORDER FORM

Triple Crown Publications
2959 Stelzer Rd.
Columbus, Oh 43219

Name: ______________________________

Address: ______________________________

City/State: ______________________________

Zip: ______________________________

	TITLES	PRICES
	Dime Piece	$15.00
	Gangsta	$15.00
	Let That Be The Reason	$15.00
	A Hustler's Wife	$15.00
	The Game	$15.00
	Black	$15.00
	Dollar Bill	$15.00
	A Project Chick	$15.00
	Road Dawgz	$15.00
	Blinded	$15.00
	Diva	$15.00
	Sheisty	$15.00
	Grimey	$15.00
	Me & My Boyfriend	$15.00
	Larceny	$15.00
	Rage Times Fury	$15.00
	A Hood Legend	$15.00
	Flipside of The Game	$15.00
	Menage's Way	$15.00

SHIPPING/HANDLING (Via U.S. Media Mail) **$3.95**

TOTAL **$__________**

FORMS OF ACCEPTED PAYMENTS:

Postage Stamps, Institutional Checks & Money Orders, all mail in orders take 5-7 Business days to be delivered.

ORDER FORM

Triple Crown Publications
2959 Stelzer Rd.
Columbus, Oh 43219

Name: ______________________

Address: ______________________

City/State: ______________________

Zip: ______________________

	TITLES	PRICES
	Still Sheisty	$15.00
	Chyna Black	$15.00
	Game Over	$15.00
	Cash Money	$15.00
	Crack Head	$15.00
	For the Strength of You	$15.00
	Down Chick	$15.00
	Dirty South	$15.00
	Cream	$15.00
	Hood Winked	$15.00
	Bitch	$15.00
	Stacy	$15.00
	Life Without Hope	$15.00

SHIPPING/HANDLING (Via U.S. Media Mail) **$3.95**

TOTAL **$**___________

FORMS OF ACCEPTED PAYMENTS:

Postage Stamps, Institutional Checks & Money Orders, all mail in orders take 5-7 Business days to be delivered.